Jeannie's War

Jeannie's War

Carol MacLean

hera

First published in the United Kingdom in 2022 by

Hera Books
Unit 9 (Canelo), 5th Floor
Cargo Works, 1–2 Hatfields
London, SE1 9PG
United Kingdom

A CIP catalogue record for this book is available from the British Library.

Print ISBN 978 1 80032 851 8
Ebook ISBN 978 1 912973 93 4

Look for more great books at www.herabooks.com

Printed and bound in Great Britain by Clays Ltd, Elcograf S.p.A.

1

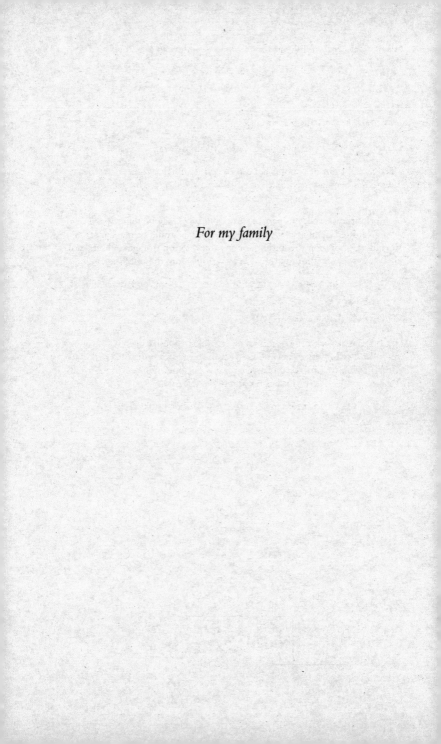

For my family

Chapter One

Glasgow 1939

'…And consequently this country is now at war with Germany.'

The prime minister's voice wavered through the wireless set and Jeannie hardly heard the next words or 'God Save the King' being played through the airwaves as the meaning of it all clutched at her heart. Sunlight was streaming in through the front room window and it seemed odd to hear the birdsong outside and a dog barking as if the world hadn't suddenly shifted horribly.

'That's that, then. Cup of tea?' Mary's voice was brisk but there was a wobble in it. 'Kathy, be a dear and put the kettle on.'

Kathy, only fifteen, burst into tears and ran out of the room. Mary stood up and made a deal of smoothing down her apron. Jeannie stood too and went to her mother and hugged her. She felt soft and comforting and smelt of soap.

'Go after her, will you? You know our Kathy, never one to miss a drama,' Mary said.

'She's upset, Mammy. We all are. What will happen now? Will Jimmy be sent to fight?'

'I suppose he will. I don't know. Let's go outside. I can hear the neighbours.'

I

Jeannie followed her mother out of their tenement home and found their neighbours had spilled out onto the street. Some were talking in groups, Mr Walker was waving his arms and shouting while others were quiet, staring into space. Old Mrs Lennox from the next tenement was being supported by her niece, Judith, who lived with her.

Martin O'Leary came over to them. 'Sure, it's a terrible thing but we knew it was coming. Why's everyone so surprised?'

'Hush now, Martin,' his wife Linda said, resting her arm on her husband's. 'It's the shock, is all. Isn't that right, Mary? What about that boy of yours in the army? Young Jimmy? He'll be all right, my dear, sure he will.'

Mr Walker came over, waving a newspaper above his head. His eyes were bulging with either fear or excitement, it was hard to tell which.

'Eighteen to forty-one call-up in Britain coming, that's what the *Daily Record* says. All our men are needed. If I was ten years younger I'd be marching up right now to enlist. A state of mobilisation in every town and city...'

Linda O'Leary hooked her arms into Mary's, drawing her away from the agitated figure while Martin nodded his head in agreement with Mr Walker and the two men shared the newspaper, stabbing at it with gnarled fingers while they spoke. Jeannie heard Mary speak to Linda. 'How can it happen all over again? They said the Great War was the war to end all wars. We suffered enough then. My Dennis at least came home; there were plenty around here who didn't. Don't they remember that?'

Jeannie let Linda steer her mother away into a group of close neighbours from their tenement. They were a tight-knit community and she was suddenly glad of that.

She glanced around at the familiar street with its row of tenement housing, the brickwork stained black by the soot from the local industries. Kiltie Street was part of the Maryhill area of Glasgow and while there were plenty of similar rows of tenement housing and the familiar sights, sounds and smells of the chemical works, the ironworks, the rubber factory and more, Jeannie loved it because of the nearby river and the busy canal and the open fields and woods.

She'd lived there her whole life. Now this much-loved place was under a terrible threat. It was hard to believe. She had an awful vision of the German army marching its way into Glasgow and right down her street. She blinked and shook her head. That wouldn't do. They had to be brave, all of them. Even if it was difficult with all the shocking news on the wireless and in the papers.

She felt a sudden, intense desire to protect them all. Mammy, Jimmy, Kathy, Isa and Bob, all her lovely family. She had to be strong for them, even if she didn't feel it. If only her dad was there. She still missed him so much, even though it was five years since he'd had a heart attack and passed away. Mammy did too although Jeannie knew she tried hard to hide it from them.

She shook her head to clear it of horrible images of war and tried to blot out Mr Walker's continuing shouts. Now, where was Kathy? She walked along the short length of Kiltie Street, feeling the sun on her arms and hot on the top of her head. She should've been helping Mammy prepare Sunday lunch but now everything was upside-down.

What about Isa and Bob, she thought suddenly. Thank goodness Mammy had agreed to them going. They were safe in the countryside, the schools having left two days ago. If there were bombs... Jeannie glanced up at the blue sky as if expecting to see enemy planes right then and there. She shivered in spite of the warm day.

'Jeannie!' Kathy came running towards her. Her face was blotchy from crying and she wiped her nose with the back of her hand.

Jeannie handed over her hanky and Kathy blew her nose hard. She gave the sodden scrap of cotton back and Jeannie put it in her pocket gingerly.

'What do we do now?' Kathy said, as they walked together.

'Go on as usual,' Jeannie said. 'Until we're told otherwise.'

'You're being daft,' Kathy blew out a breath impatiently. 'Nothing will be as usual now. For one, Jimmy will have to fight the Germans. He's probably on his way to Germany right now. For another, Arthur will probably want to marry you straight away before he's killed in action. How romantic. I'll be your bridesmaid, won't I? Can I choose my dress?'

'Don't be ridiculous,' Jeannie said sharply. 'And don't go upsetting Mammy with your tales about Jimmy.'

'But you believe me about you getting married?' Kathy said slyly.

'No, I don't. Arthur's not even in the army. Besides, he and I have only stepped out together twice. I hardly know him. What's put that notion into your head?'

Kathy snorted. 'Well, if I'm wrong, why is Arthur heading round the corner up there into our street?'

Jeannie looked up and saw that her younger sister was right. Arthur's tall figure was striding towards them. She felt a thrill run through her body. He was broad-shouldered and handsome and he liked her. She still couldn't believe it. She, Jeannie Dougal, was nothing special. But she'd been standing alone at her friend's wedding only a few weeks ago when Arthur had introduced himself and asked her to dance. At the end of the wedding reception he'd asked her if she'd like to go for a walk with him the next Saturday. He hadn't mentioned her birthmark, not once. She was smitten immediately with his blond hair and piercing blue eyes and his polite manners. And it seemed like he was equally smitten with her. He hadn't left her side all evening. Now they were stepping out together. Her first real boyfriend. She felt a flutter of happiness and for the first time she didn't think of herself as ugly, a girl that no one had asked out because she wasn't attractive or chatty enough.

'See you later,' Kathy shouted, 'I'll tell Mammy you'll be late in.'

—

Arthur stopped in front of her and took off his hat. She liked that about him. He had an old-fashioned formality. Not a bit like the boys she knew from Kiltie Street.

'Good morning, Jeannie. You'll have heard the news. I need to talk to you.'

'Yes, of course. Shall we walk?' Her heart fluttered.

'I want you to come and meet Mother. In fact, Jeannie, there's something I want to ask you.'

'What is it?' The fluttering intensified. She thought of Kathy's words.

'We should get married. There's a war on and I'm going to enlist. It's my duty to do so. I want to leave things in order.'

Was that it? Had Arthur just proposed? Jeannie's mind went blank for a moment. Did she want to marry him?

She hardly knew him, as she'd pointed out to Kathy. And yet, he was handsome and a good catch, as her mother would say. She knew from things he'd said and the way he spoke that the Dunns were well-off, compared to her own family. Arthur had a good job in the bank. She'd be secure and Mammy would be pleased. She thought Arthur a very nice young man and suitable for Jeannie. Perhaps she was also relieved that Jeannie finally had a young man at all. And she loved him, Jeannie thought. They might not have been stepping out for long but he was right for her.

'We can arrange the banns quickly. We'll have a small wedding, family only. People won't expect anything splashy in these times.'

Jeannie found herself walking back along Kiltie Street, her arm tucked firmly into Arthur's. She hadn't actually said yes to his proposal, she realised. He had taken it for granted that she agreed with him. Don't be silly, she thought. Of course I'm going to marry him. But I need more time.

'We don't need to get married straight away,' she said. 'A longer engagement will be more acceptable to my mother and I expect, probably yours.'

Arthur stared down at her with those intense blue eyes. She felt that flutter of desire again. Shouldn't she want to get married quickly? She and Arthur could be together properly as man and wife. It made sense but Jeannie's instinct was for a longer engagement. It would give her time to get used to the idea, she argued to herself.

'Very well, as long as we are engaged and I know that you're mine, I don't mind when we get married,' Arthur said. He nodded to himself as if thinking something through. 'Wear your blue cardigan for visiting Mother.

It suits you. I hope we'll be very happy together. I intend to look after you, Jeannie. I want you to know that.'

Chapter Two

The crowd of neighbours had dispersed and Jeannie led Arthur up the solid stone steps of the tenement building and into the close, turning left into their home on the ground floor. The Dougals rented two rooms and a kitchen. They shared a bathroom on the half landing with the O'Learys who lived opposite in the other ground-floor flat.

'Hello Arthur, come away in,' Mary said, smiling at their visitor.

They all went through into the small, neat parlour with its window overlooking the street. The wireless in its walnut cabinet took pride of place next to the fireplace. There were two over-stuffed armchairs and a sofa. Kathy lay on the sofa, reading a book. Arthur remained standing.

'I'll get some tea and biscuits,' Mary said after an awkward pause.

'Thank you, I'm not hungry,' Arthur said stiffly. 'I've asked Jeannie to marry me and she's said yes. We want to go and tell my mother.'

'That's wonderful news. Congratulations to you both. This needs a celebration. Kathy, get the sherry bottle and three glasses.'

'Why am I not allowed any?' Kathy whined. She threw a smug 'told you so' glance at Jeannie as she headed for the kitchen to get the sherry bottle from the press.

'Perhaps just one glass,' Arthur conceded. 'Jeannie, why don't you get dressed properly and then we'll take a drink with your mother.'

Jeannie excused herself and went into the tiny hall to get to the bedroom. Kathy was waiting for her, sherry and Mammy's special glasses in hand.

'I was right, wasn't I? He proposed and you're getting married. I want to wear a green dress for the wedding. It'll go lovely with my red hair.'

'We're not getting married straight away. I want a long engagement. Now hurry up with the sherry glasses.'

'You're mad, waiting to get married,' Kathy retorted. 'If you don't watch out, handsome Arthur will find another girl much prettier than you and marry her instead.'

Kathy's words rang in Jeannie's ears as she went into the bedroom she shared with her sisters and little brother. With Isa gone, the room seemed bigger. She found the blue cardigan that Arthur liked and put it on. Then she hesitated. She went over to the mirror on the night stand. She saw a girl with dark brown, wavy hair and anxious grey eyes. Her fingers strayed to the small strawberry birthmark on her left cheek. She was lucky Arthur liked her. She was engaged now and she wasn't going to be left on the shelf.

Arthur only wanted one small glass of sherry and the atmosphere was rather strained. Mary kept looking at Jeannie and smiling. Kathy's face was sour as she sipped a glass of milk. Jeannie and Arthur left shortly afterwards.

'I hope your mother likes me,' Jeannie said, as she walked quickly to keep up with Arthur's long stride.

'She will,' he said abruptly.

9

'Is everything all right? Have I upset you?' Jeannie asked, dismayed at his tone. Hadn't they just got engaged? Surely, they should both be happy and laughing.

'I'm worried about Mother. How will she cope when I have to leave?'

Of course, he was worried about enlisting in the army and worried about his family. That was natural. Jeannie chided herself for being selfish. She squeezed his arm gently.

'I'll look after your mother while you're gone. That's my job now that I'm engaged to you. Soon, she'll be another mother to me.'

'I expected that of you but I'm glad to hear you say it. You're a kind girl,' Arthur said. 'I have to tell you, Jeannie, that Mother can be difficult. She doesn't keep good health.'

'Oh, I didn't know... I'm sorry to hear that. Can I ask what's wrong?'

It made her realise how little she knew about Arthur. And how little he knew about her. But what he did know was obviously enough for him to fall in love with her and ask her to marry him, she reminded herself. Had their courtship been too swift? There were a couple of girls further up Kiltie Street who had got married recently with boyfriends going into the army. She wasn't the only girl to be moving along fast with her life. Besides, Arthur was everything she wanted in a husband. He was handsome and well-off, able to provide for them both to have a good life together. He was polite and considerate. She found him attractive and wasn't scared of the physical side of marriage with him. What more did she need?

'Mother is an invalid. She doesn't leave the house,' Arthur was saying. 'She's very fussy in her ways so you'll have to do what she wants.'

Jeannie began to dread meeting Mrs Dunn as they walked over from Kiltie Street further up the hilly road to the houses with their leafy surrounds. She didn't know where Arthur lived exactly as he had insisted on coming and picking her up to take her out both evenings. They stopped outside a house with a neat front garden and trees at the back.

'Here we are,' Arthur said. 'Mother doesn't like loud noises, so remember to keep your voice down. But don't whisper, her hearing isn't good.'

Jeannie's head was spinning with his instructions as she went up the path behind him. What had she landed herself in? What kind of monster was waiting to greet her? Arthur opened the front door and she stepped into a cool hallway, smelling of beeswax. It was very still, as if the air hadn't been disturbed for hours. She thought of their home in Kiltie Street full of noise and movement with Isa and Bob tearing about. It was quieter now that they had gone and with Jimmy away but Kathy made enough fuss to fill the gaps, and Jeannie and Mary contributed their fair share of chatter too.

'Mother?' Arthur called. 'I've brought Jeannie to meet you.'

There was no answer and Arthur frowned. He moved from the large hall and pushed open a door. Jeannie followed him into what was a lovely sitting room with a bay window. It could have been bright and airy but the curtains were closed and there was a stale, damp smell. In the dim light she saw a woman with a crocheted shawl around her shoulders slumped asleep in an armchair.

Arthur flicked the light switch and the woman startled, opening blue eyes wide with shock. She clutched at her shawl.

'Are you sleeping again?' Arthur said, sounding concerned. 'The doctor said you mustn't sleep all day.'

'I know, dear. I was just dozing a little.' She turned blue eyes, as beautiful as her son's, in Jeannie's direction. 'You must be Jeannie. I've heard so much about you.'

'Have you?' Jeannie said, flattered that Arthur had talked about her. 'I'm pleased to meet you, Mrs Dunn.'

'Sit down here, Jeannie, opposite Mother so she can see you properly. I'll make tea for all of us. Mother, you'll take a biscuit and build up your strength.'

'I'm not hungry.'

'A biscuit will do you good. I'll bring a plate of them and you should have two,' Arthur smiled.

He left them and Jeannie sat for a moment, unsure what to say. She smiled at Mrs Dunn, eager to make a good impression on the woman who was to be her mother-in-law. She saw traces of Arthur's features but Helen Dunn's face was softer and rounder and her blonde hair had faded to cream. There were lines on her skin, perhaps from her illness, and purple bruises under her eyes as if she didn't sleep well. Maybe that was why she had to rest so much.

'Congratulations on your engagement,' Helen said softly. 'It will be nice to gain a daughter.'

'Thank you,' Jeannie said. 'I'm sorry I haven't met you before now. It was a bit sudden, Arthur's proposal, but we don't want to wait. Not now when there's a war on.'

Helen's eyelids fluttered wearily. 'It's a terrible thing, war. We had enough of it last time round. The war to end all wars, so they said. And now look what they've done.'

'That's enough of that kind of talk,' Arthur said, coming in with a tray of teacups and biscuits. 'We're fighting for king and country now. Jeannie will look after you while I'm gone and I'm sure I'll have leave so I can come home and check up on you.'

Helen nodded weakly. 'Yes, you're right. I mustn't despair.'

Arthur piled a small plate and put it on her knee. 'Eat up, Mother. You need your strength.'

Jeannie felt uncomfortable. Hadn't Helen said she didn't want any biscuits? And yet, here Arthur was practically force-feeding her. But Helen Dunn didn't protest. She looked tired as she picked up an oat biscuit and nibbled on its edge.

'You may pour,' Arthur told Jeannie. 'After all, this will be your home soon. I hope you'll be happy here with Mother and me.'

Jeannie picked up the teapot, praying she wouldn't drop it and managed to fill the three teacups without spilling any. She breathed a tiny sigh of relief and caught Helen's gaze. There was sympathy in the older woman's expression and Jeannie flushed. She didn't need that. She would get used to this. She'd have to. It was just... very different from her own home. It was clear that the Dunns were more than a cut above the Dougals in class. Why had Arthur chosen her and not a girl from a better-off family?

–

Back in Kiltie Street, Mary let the tears roll down her cheeks as she peeled the potatoes for dinner. There was no one there to see. Jeannie was out with her new fiancé and Kathy had slammed into her bedroom in a strop because Mary had asked her to peel the tatties for her. Normally, she'd take issue with the girl but today she hadn't the energy for it. All she could think about was Jimmy, her lovely boy, being sent to Europe to fight the enemy. Jimmy had joined the regular army as soon as he turned eighteen and he was now twenty. He had plenty of army experience so they'd send him for sure.

She put the tatties into the pan to boil and started on the cabbage, pulling the leaves apart to wash them. Jimmy hadn't been home since the summer. He was somewhere at a training camp in England. She didn't know what he was doing, perhaps he was training the new recruits. It didn't matter. She longed to see him. Since Dennis had died five years ago, Jimmy had been the man of the house. She was proud of him. He'd done his best to look after her and to lay down the law to his sisters and small brother.

She sobbed and stuffed her apron into her mouth to stifle the noise. Kathy might be in her bad books but she didn't want her daughter to see her cry.

'For goodness' sake, woman. Dry your eyes. It won't look so bad in the morning,' she said out loud and then managed a shaky laugh.

It sounded like something her Dennis would have said to her. He had a knack of cheering her up. God, but she missed him something dreadful. She had had to be both mother and father to her five children as they grew up and learned right from wrong and how to be kind but not a push-over and all the other things that children had to learn to survive and thrive.

She pushed the cabbage leaves into a pot and set that on the range to cook. There was a scrag end of mutton for dinner and the meaty smell wafted up, making her stomach grumble. She rubbed her eyes dry.

'There, Dennis, my love. All done. It's time to get over myself, as you'd say. We're at war and I can't change that. Our wee family's all torn apart and I can't change that either. And what do I do with our Kathy? That girl's out of control and won't listen to me.'

Dennis didn't answer from his viewing point above and Mary set the table. This was Kathy's task but she didn't have the strength to make her do it tonight. She worried about them all. She worried about Jeannie. She shouldn't. Arthur was a fine young man and he came from a good family. Jeannie would be provided for. The fact was, she was in the way of worrying about Jeannie and it had become a habit. Jeannie's birthmark had faded and reduced over the years but Mary knew her daughter was still conscious of it. She was marked too by the cruel taunts of the other kids in the streets when she was growing up.

It pained Mary to know she couldn't protect Jeannie from that cruelty. Her sweet, shy daughter had had to bear it alone. It was a wonderful miracle that a handsome man like Arthur had fallen in love with her. Mary shouldn't fret any more. She could turn her thoughts and prayers to Isa and Bob instead. She'd made the decision to evacuate her youngest two children. It hadn't been an easy decision and she'd tossed and turned for nights agonising over it. In the end, she'd been persuaded by Miss Tomlinson, their school teacher. Most of the kids attending St Mildred's primary school were going and Isa and Bob would be fine. If they stayed, there was the risk of bombing and in any case, none of their friends were here now. Kiltie Street was strangely quiet with all the children gone.

'Mammy, why are you setting the table? Where's Kathy?' Jeannie burst in, her cheeks pink from the evening breeze.

'Kathy's unhappy with me. Besides, I don't mind setting it out.'

'Give it here. I'll do it. And I'll tell Kathy off later for not doing her chores.'

Jeannie took the cutlery and plates and set them out on the table.

'Mrs Dunn is very nice, Mammy, and Arthur's house is very fine. I felt a bit out of place for a while but then it was all right. She's an invalid but I'm to look after her while Arthur's away.'

'That's taking on a big task,' Mary said. 'It's a lot for Arthur to ask of you.'

'We're getting married. When I'm Mrs Arthur Dunn, I'll have to look after his mam, won't I?'

'All right but don't wear yourself out doing it.'

'I won't.' Jeannie leant over and kissed her mother fondly.

Mary hugged her tightly. 'Tell me, are you happy?'

'I am happy, Mammy,' Jeannie said softly. 'I'm getting married to the man I love.'

Mary nodded. She ladled out the stew and vegetables onto three plates.

'Aye, that's all that matters in the end. He's a fine young man and I hope the two of you will be as happy as your dad and I were.'

'Is that dinner up?' Kathy appeared, her mood seemingly much improved.

'You should've set the table for Mammy,' Jeannie chided.

'Sorry. I'll wash up after to make up for it.'

Jeannie smiled. That was Kathy all over. She was quick to take offence but equally quick to apologise and make up. Since it was usually Jeannie's job to wash up, she was happy at the compromise.

'What's Arthur's house like?' Kathy asked as they sat and ate together.

'It's big. I felt a bit out of place, to be honest, but his mother's nice. I think I'll get along with her just fine.'

'It's funny Arthur chose you and not a girl with money,' Kathy said chattily.

'Kathy!' Mary said. 'He loves Jeannie and that's what matters, not whether she's rich.'

'It's probably 'cos he can boss her about,' Kathy went on. 'Jeannie doesn't say boo to a goose. She'll make a perfect wee wifey for a man like Arthur who has to have his own way.'

Jeannie didn't answer. She ate up the stew and tried not to feel hurt. There was a grain of truth in what Kathy said. Jeannie knew she was too shy and timid but she couldn't help it. Maybe Arthur was a bit bossy but then, husbands were meant to be in charge and the head of the household. It wouldn't do if she tried to make all the decisions, would it? No, she decided, Kathy was just making trouble.

As it got dark that evening, the three of them went round the windows putting up the thick blackout curtains. Mary had got a deal on the material at a market stall and she and Jeannie had sewn them. They were settling down for cocoa when there was a shout and a sudden rapping at the door. Jeannie jumped and Mary clutched at her chest. Kathy tucked up her feet under her backside and grinned.

'You know who that is, Mammy. It's Mr Woodley from up the way. We must be showing a light.'

Mary heard a loud Yorkshire voice calling through the door.

'Mrs Dougal? Mrs Dougal? I have to come in. There's a light on in your house.'

She opened their front door and the bulky figure, complete with ARP warden's tin hat, came in. He thrust out his chest importantly.

'We can't have lights showing, can we now? Don't want Jerry finding his way by them.'

Mary bit her lip as the ARP warden checked their windows and fussily pulled the material across and into place.

He touched his fingers to the brim of his tin hat and bustled out.

'That's the third night in a row,' Jeannie said indignantly. 'I don't believe there's a light showing at all. He just likes to be important.'

'Well, there's no harm in him checking,' Mary said, keeping the peace. 'Sooner or later, he'll get fed up with it and bother someone else.'

It was only when Jeannie brushed her hair that night, sitting up in the bed she shared with Kathy, that she realised that Arthur hadn't said he loved her.

Chapter Three

Isa lay in bed, the blanket tucked up under her chin, afraid to move. She wanted Mammy. She also wanted to cry but didn't dare to make a sound. Outside, something screeched and she whimpered. There were no comforting noises from buses or people shouting. No murmur of voices as Mammy, Jeannie and Kathy talked in the other room. At home, she'd feel her bed bump later in the evenings when Jeannie got into the bed she shared with Kathy because the beds were so close together. She'd feel Bob's warm legs against her and his breathing, deep and even as they lay top to tail. Bob was asleep in a truckle bed on the floor near her in this strange place but he was fast asleep and she didn't like to wake him.

She'd been excited when Mammy told them they were going on a holiday to the countryside. She'd never been before.

'What's it like, Mammy?' she asked. 'Will there be cows?'

Mammy smiled, 'I'm sure there will be cows. And buttercups and fields and fresh air.'

'I don't like cows,' Bob shouted, running around the room with his toy aeroplane, making it swoop and dive.

'You've never seen one, so how do you know?' Isa said.

'Bob, take yourself away outside if you're going to run about,' Mammy said.

'Are you sad?' Isa asked, feeling her tummy go funny. What was there to be sad about if they were going on holiday? But Mammy's eyes weren't smiling, even if her mouth was.

Mammy took her hand and sat her down. Bob ran out onto the street to play with his pals.

'Promise me you'll be a good girl and that you'll look after Bob.'

'But… where will you be? You said we're going on holiday.' Isa's tummy was sore now. She dreaded Mammy's answer because she guessed already what she was going to say.

'I can't come with you, darling. You and Bob have to go to keep you safe. I'm needed here with Jeannie and Kathy. You'll have a lovely time and I'll come and visit.'

'No,' Isa shook her head. 'That's not right. You have to come too.'

She jumped up and pulled her hand from Mammy's grasp and ran outside. She hardly saw the wee boys kicking a ball about, her eyes were that blurry. She ignored Bob's wave and ran along Kiltie Street until she got to the end terrace. Her best friend Jessie lived there. She ran up and in Jessie's open front door.

Jessie was sitting with her arms up as her older sister, Elspeth, wrapped wool around them, unravelling an old jumper to reuse the yarn.

'Want to play?' Isa said.

Jessie nodded in relief and slipped off the wool to Elspeth's indignant cry.

'I've got to go,' Jessie called over her shoulder as the two of them walked quickly out before Elspeth could collar them.

'What's the matter?' she asked Isa once they were safely out of reach of the house. 'You been crying?'

Isa sat on the kerb and kicked at the dust and pebbles. She stared at her scuffed plimsolls.

'Mammy's not coming with us tomorrow. She's sending us on our own on holiday.'

Jessie sighed. She picked up the pebbles and made them into the shape of a heart on the road. Isa decided she'd make one too.

'My mammy's the same,' Jessie said. 'She's got to work, same as Elspeth. I've to go myself. It's in case Hitler throws bombs at us.'

Bombs? Mammy hadn't mentioned that, Isa thought. She probably didn't want to scare Bob. She resolved right then to look after her wee brother and keep him safe. Bob was only five. She, on the other hand, was nearly eleven, which was almost grown up.

'It'll be fun, won't it?' Isa said, gathering pebbles into piles so that she could add more shapes to the hearts.

'Aye, it'll be great,' Jessie agreed. 'We can sit next to each other on the train tomorrow.'

–

In the event, she sat next to Bob on the train because Mammy told her to. The train was full of pupils from St Mildred's primary and Miss Tomlinson was coming with them. She and Bob had a pillowcase each with their clothes and belongings and a jam piece each for the journey. She had a label pinned to her coat with her name on it and she had her gas mask in its box. Jessie was on the seat behind, sitting next to Betty McGaskill who smelt. Jessie kept bobbing her head round to chat to Isa until Miss

Tomlinson told her to stop it. The teacher kept counting them, walking up and down the carriage aisle.

Outside the window, Mammy was waving. She kept pressing her hand to her lips and she didn't smile.

'Is Mammy angry with me?' Bob asked, wriggling on the seat beside her. 'I didn't mean to spill my porridge.'

'She's not angry,' Isa said. But she wasn't sure. Mammy didn't look happy.

'She's gone,' Bob said in surprise.

Isa blinked. He was right. Mammy was walking away down the platform. She hadn't waited to see them go. As Isa watched, Mammy got smaller and then disappeared behind the crowds at the station. They weren't the only school group leaving that day. In fact, she reckoned the whole train was full of children.

'I'm hungry. I'm going to eat my piece,' Bob announced. He delved into his pillowcase.

'No eating and drinking, please,' Miss Tomlinson said sternly. 'We have a long journey ahead, children.'

It turned out she was right. At the beginning it was fun. Everyone cheered when the train started moving and they sang songs like 'Ally Bally' and 'Dance Tae Yer Daddy'. When Miss Tomlinson wasn't watching, Jessie would put her head up round the side of the seat and talk to Isa. After a while it got boring. Bob kicked his feet and managed to kick Isa's ankle. Then she needed the toilet. Just when she thought she had to pee right there on her seat, the train came to a stop at a station. There was a commotion as Miss Tomlinson marched them all out and they queued for ages to use the station toilets.

A group of ladies at the station sent in trays of scones and they munched happily on those. Isa had crumbs on her coat and skirt. Betty McGaskill wolfed hers down in a single gulp and Isa was impressed. Smell oozed from her, and Jessie and Isa screwed up their faces in disgust and made a deal out of wafting the air away with their hands. Betty pretended not to notice.

It was dark by the time the train stopped for good. Bob was asleep, his heavy head on Isa's shoulder. She was tired too and she shook him awake. They stumbled out after the teacher, dragging their pillowcases. The jam pieces were long gone and Isa was thirsty. Her boxy gas mask bumped on her shoulder painfully. Now they had to get on a bus and go on another journey.

Eventually, they disembarked in the middle of nowhere. Isa felt Bob's fingers creep into hers. They were hot and sticky but she held them tightly. Mammy had told her they mustn't be separated at any cost. It was a quiet place and it didn't smell like Glasgow did. They were herded into a hall and had to stand there while grown-ups talked and pointed and wrote on lists.

Most of the children went away then with people. Jessie smiled bravely at Isa as a man and woman took her with them. Then she and Bob were walking with Miss Tomlinson and another woman, who had a brown feather in her felt hat, out into the dark evening. Isa wanted to ask where they were going but didn't dare to. They came to a stop outside a tiny cottage at the edge of the village. The feather hat woman knocked on the door. They all stared at the blue painted door. Finally it opened. An old woman, dressed in black, with white hair, stood there. She was thin and bony with a jutting chin and a great hooked nose. She looks like a witch, Isa thought in panic. Surely Miss Tomlinson wouldn't leave them with a witch?

There was more talk amongst the adults. Isa clutched Bob's hand so hard he protested. She hushed him. There seemed to be a bit of an argument going on. Miss Tomlinson was speaking earnestly. The teacher gave a huge sigh. The witch gave a brief nod and Miss Tomlinson pushed Isa's back gently but firmly until her feet were over the threshold, taking Bob with her.

'I'll come and check on you soon,' Miss Tomlinson said. 'This is Miss Main.'

When the two women had gone, Isa and Bob stood and waited in the tiny hall. Miss Main moved slowly as if her legs were frail and she fetched a candle in a metal holder and lit it. They followed her up a flight of crooked wooden stairs under a ceiling so low that, if she wished to, Isa could have reached up and touched it. At the top there were two rooms. She pointed to one room and then to Isa.

'In there for you.' She gave Isa the candle.

Isa hardly understood her strange accent. She let go of Bob's hand reluctantly and stepped inside. She looked back to see Bob follow her in. The room smelt of wax and old wood. There was a bed with a candlewick coverlet, a desk at the window with a chair and a night stand with mirror and a large jug and dish. A towel was folded on the night stand as if waiting for her. There was also a smaller truckle bed, low to the floor. Isa dropped her pillow case and gas mask on the floor.

'Go to bed and we'll talk in the morning,' Miss Main said, standing in the doorway. 'Don't forget to wash behind your ears.'

When she'd gone, Isa got straight into bed without washing or changing her clothes. She pulled the coverlet up to her chin and fell asleep. She was so weary she didn't even speak to Bob who got into the truckle bed and lay still.

Except that now, in the middle of a pitch-black night, she was wide awake. Something stirred the air and she knew she wasn't alone.

'Who's there?' she whispered, fingers tight on the coverlet.

'I had a nightmare. Can I stay here with you?' Bob said.

He was under the covers before she could answer. He was warm and damp and smelt of pee but she was suddenly comforted. It felt safe with Bob here. They lay like that for a while until she thought he'd fallen asleep. Then came a small voice.

'I wet the bed.'

'Your bed, you mean? Not mine.'

She felt him nodding. She didn't know what to do. What would Miss Main do to them when she found out? Isa thought for a bit until it came to her.

'We'll tell Miss Tomlinson, in the morning. Go to sleep now. It'll be all right.'

Bob snuggled right in to her and soon his breathing was slow and even. Isa shut her own eyes and soon was fast asleep.

—

They were woken by a cockerel crowing. Isa slipped out of bed and pulled the curtain back. It was daylight and a large bird was strutting on the grass in front of the cottage. Nearby, several chickens pecked at the ground. She pushed Bob.

'Get up. There's chickens. Come and see.'

When they had stared at the chickens through the window, Isa decided they should go downstairs. Her tummy rumbled with hunger. They hadn't had any dinner last night and a jam piece and scone only went so far.

The crooked staircase creaked as they tiptoed down. Miss Main stood at the bottom, looking at them.

'Good morning. There's porridge, so come and eat while it's hot.'

They followed her through to a kitchen with an ancient black range and a sturdy wooden table and chairs. The table was set for three with woven mats. At each place was an egg in a blue egg cup and a spoon. Isa went to pull out a chair. Miss Main frowned at her.

'Wash your hands before you eat. Did your mother not teach you that?'

There was a sink with water filled in it. Isa and Bob dutifully washed their hands until Miss Main gave them a towel to dry them. She pointed at the table. Isa and Bob sat down, mouths watering. Miss Main sat at the top end. Isa picked up her spoon and Bob's fingers were on the warm egg when she clapped her hands angrily.

'Little heathens. We say Grace before we eat.'

Who was Grace? Perhaps it was Miss Main's daughter, Isa wondered. Bob kicked her under the table, looking uneasy. Miss Main bent her white-haired head and spoke out loud about God and being thankful for their food. At the end she said 'Amen' and waited until Isa and Bob said it too. Then she picked up her spoon and tapped it on the top of her brown egg. Isa and Bob copied her, too afraid to do otherwise.

The egg was delicious. To follow, there was a bowl of porridge sprinkled with sugar. Isa's tummy was full. Bob winked at her and grinned. Miss Main got up and went to the range.

'There's hot water to wash yourselves. I daresay you forgot last night.' She looked at Isa, who blushed. 'Put on some clean clothes too and then you can gather the eggs in for me.'

They ran upstairs. At their room, Bob paused. 'What does she mean about the eggs? Mammy doesn't gather them. She buys them from Mr Duncan's shop.'

'I don't know. Hurry up and get ready. I want to go outside and see a cow.'

'Isa... my bed...'

Isa had forgotten about that. There was no sign of Miss Tomlinson. What should they do? She went over to inspect the truckle bed. The bedclothes were rumpled and there was a yellow wet circle on the sheet.

Bob lay on the floor and flicked through his *Beano* comic. There was nothing for it. Isa had to go and tell the old lady. She didn't think of her as a witch any more. Not now that she'd had that lovely breakfast. Still, she was scared of how she'd react to the news.

She went back downstairs slowly. Miss Main was carefully putting the clean egg cups on a high shelf. Isa felt ashamed. At home Mammy made her help Kathy with the washing up. She should have offered here.

'You're not changed out of your grubby clothes,' Miss Main said, hardly looking at Isa. 'Go along now.'

'Please, Miss... there's a problem.'

'What sort of problem?' Miss Main sounded like Miss Tomlinson did when the class were being noisy. Her voice went all tight and clipped.

'It's Bob... he's... his bed,' Isa mumbled.

'Speak up, girl. I can hardly hear you. I'm not getting any younger and neither are my ears. What ails him?'

Isa shook her head. She couldn't say it, all of a sudden. Maybe they'd hide the sheet. That way, no one need know. Bob could sleep in with her. Isa brightened for a moment. Miss Main stared at her then went past and Isa heard the creak of the stairs. She ran out and followed the old woman upstairs.

Isa stood outside the room and listened. There was a murmur of voices then silence. Finally, Miss Main and Bob appeared. She was carrying the sheet in a bundle. Bob didn't look too unhappy. Isa breathed out.

Miss Main nodded to a narrow door in the wall next to Isa's bed. 'Fetch a fresh sheet from the airing cupboard and put it on the bed for me. Bob and I are busy.'

Isa struggled with the large sheet but eventually managed to spread it onto the truckle bed and tuck in the edges like she'd seen Mammy do. She strained to hear downstairs, expecting Miss Main to be shouting at Bob. There was nothing. She went down, not sure what was going on. In the kitchen, Bob had his shirt sleeves rolled up and his hands in a bucket of soapy water. He turned gleefully to Isa.

'I've got hot water and bubbles. I'm scrubbing this and then we're to hang it outside to dry in the wind.'

Beyond him, Miss Main put the kettle onto the range for more hot water.

'Get that basket and I'll show you where my ladies like to hide their eggs.'

There was a wicker basket beside the range. Isa picked it up. Its tattered woven side prickled her bare leg. The kitchen door was open. She went outside. The air was cold and breezy. A black hen ran towards her, cackling. Isa screamed and ran into the kitchen.

'Goodness me, you'll give me a heart attack. What's all your nonsense for?'

'That chicken's attacking me,' Isa cried.

Miss Main's face cracked open into a smile and her shoulders trembled. She took Isa by the hand and led her back out into the garden.

'You've a lot to learn, my girl. You can start by being introduced to Penny, my black hen and favourite lady.'

'She's a lady?'

'She's a chicken.'

'But why—'

'Come along, Isa. There'll be no eggs for later if you keep asking me questions.'

—

Jeannie and Kathy worked at Franny's Emporium on the main road. It was a ten-minute walk to get to the shop which sold all manner of things that people wanted and some that they didn't. Franny sat behind the counter each day, rustling in black bombazine, and watched the customers and her two shop girls with beady eyes which missed nothing.

'Get the brush and give the floor a good sweep,' she told Kathy, even as the girls arrived and before they had got their coats off. 'You're late again.'

'And a good morning to you and all,' Kathy retorted.

'None of your cheek,' Franny shot back but her eyes twinkled.

She had a fondness for Kathy which Jeannie didn't understand as her sister gave as good as she got and was often late, despite the short walk from Kiltie Street. She went through to the back room and put the kettle on.

'Black and three sugars,' Franny shouted to her. 'While I can. I've no doubt they'll be rationing that soon enough.'

Jeannie rolled her eyes in the privacy of the room. She made tea for Franny every weekday morning so she knew how the old lady liked it but she always treated Jeannie as if she wasn't very bright and often repeated her instructions. Jeannie reckoned it was because she, unlike Kathy, didn't talk back.

It was a busy morning with all Franny's regulars coming in for a gossip and to discuss the war. Jeannie wrapped up items in brown paper and gave back change from the till. Kathy dusted the shelves of goods and went for Franny's shopping to the grocer and bakery.

Elspeth came in mid-morning. She wandered the narrow aisles, jam-packed with goods, and came to the counter with a tin of Mansion Polish. She placed it in front of Jeannie, who put it in a brown paper bag.

'That'll be sixpence.'

Elspeth looked in her bag and brought out a worn leather purse. She counted out the coins and pushed them across to Jeannie.

'I hear there's jobs going at Fearnmore's factory,' she said.

'Don't they make washers and bolts?'

'My friend told me they're moving over to making things for the war effort.'

'Are you going to apply?' Jeannie asked.

She wasn't that friendly with Elspeth, who was a couple of years older. She knew Elspeth had had a crush on Jimmy a few years before and that Jimmy didn't like her. But Isa was best friends with Jessie and that had to count for something.

Elspeth nodded. 'Aye, too right I am. I can make double what I make as a housemaid at the big house. This is my day off but I work hard for my wage and it's long hours. You should apply too. I've no idea what they're going to be making but I don't care. It's our duty to join up.'

'Don't go putting ideas in her head,' Franny said, from her perch behind the counter. 'She's got a good job here.'

Elspeth shrugged, took her Mansion Polish and left. Jeannie thought about it for the rest of the day. She'd been bored of working in the shop for a good while now but there hadn't appeared to be an alternative – except working in another shop along the main street. Working at Fearnmore would be different and if Elspeth was right, the pay would be better too. She'd give Mammy most of her wages and still be able to save some towards her wedding and life as a married woman.

She broached the idea with Arthur that evening. They were in the Dunns' spacious living room, sitting on the sofa together. Helen Dunn had retired upstairs after greeting Jeannie and having a cup of tea with them. Jeannie had hoped to go dancing or to the cinema but Arthur was against either.

'It's not the weekend,' he said. 'No, we'll stay in and talk to Mother. She'll be glad of the company and we'll save money. You don't mind, do you? I'll take you to the cinema another day.'

Jeannie felt like saying that he didn't need to save money as he had such a good job at the bank but then thought perhaps that was why the Dunns were well-off, if they were thrifty. Besides, she didn't want an argument. Not on their first evening together after getting engaged.

Helen had soon excused herself, pleading exhaustion and indeed, she did look pale with the same violet bruises under her eyes. Arthur looked disappointed but didn't ask her to stay. Jeannie was relieved. She liked Helen but she wanted time with Arthur on his own. They needed to get to know each other better.

'This is nice.' She snuggled into him.

Arthur moved away. 'Jeannie, there'll be none of that. Not before we're married.'

Jeannie flushed. She'd only wanted a cuddle. Or a kiss. He made her feel dirty. 'Sorry. I didn't mean…'

'I like to do things properly,' Arthur said. 'When we're married, it'll be different.' He smiled. 'You'll be the perfect wife for me. I can tell. We'll get along just fine.'

'Of course.' She felt embarrassed and unsure how to go on. She blurted out the first thing that came to mind. 'I'm thinking of applying for a job at Fearnmore factory. It's a short bus ride or a good, long walk. My neighbour says there's places going for war work and the pay is very good.'

His blue eyes bored into her for a long moment. Her stomach flipped. Don't be daft, she thought. It's only Arthur.

'Why would you want to work there when you've got a nice respectable job in a shop?'

'I'm bored at Franny's. I've been wanting a change and this is an opportunity, don't you think?'

Arthur shook his head slowly. 'I would be concerned about you, Jeannie. From what you've said, this Fearnmore factory is farther away from here than the shop. You'd be tired getting there and back – and what if Mother needs you? Besides, when I'm here I want to know that you are too. You're my girl.'

'You'll be in the army and soon enough you'll be away,' she whispered.

'That's not the point. The point is, when I'm back I want you to be there for me. Also, how can you look after

Mother properly when you're commuting backwards and forwards to this factory? No, I don't think it will work. I'll be much happier if you stay at the shop. I don't want my best girl wearing herself out now, do I?'

Chapter Four

Eileen Boyle was nervous. She brushed her thick blonde hair and dabbed her mouth with the tiniest slick of crimson lipstick. She pressed her lips together and smiled at herself in the mirror. That was better. She might have butterflies in her tummy but she looked confident. Buttoning her blue wool jacket, she clattered downstairs to say goodbye to her parents.

Agnes Boyle sniffed when she saw her. 'Let's hope this isn't a mistake.'

'You said I could go.'

'Your father made the decision, not me. If it all goes wrong, it won't be me to blame.'

Behind Agnes, Eileen's father, Robert, packed his pipe with a wad of Sobranie and said nothing. Eileen knew he wouldn't speak up and defend her. He never did.

'You looked so much nicer in your uniform. Smart and neat.'

'I'll earn a lot more at the factory than I did working for Mr and Mrs Scullion,' Eileen reminded her. 'Besides, I told you. They're moving to London for his war work soon so I'd have had to go too.'

Agnes's stony face didn't change. Her mother didn't care whether she was in Glasgow or London. Eileen bit her lip to stop the threatening tears. She had lived in as a parlour maid for three years in a house in Cambuslang on the outskirts of Glasgow. On her Sundays off she had dutifully travelled home to the western edge of the city to see her parents. Sometimes she wondered why she bothered when they never seemed that pleased to see her. Her happiest times had been on her half day mid-week when she went dancing at Green's Playhouse. She forgot all her worries in the freedom of the music and being swept away in the arms of her partner. She hoped she'd meet a fellow and fall in love. But it hadn't happened yet.

'I've got to go. I'll be back for dinner.' She didn't look back as she went out the door to catch the bus.

There were plenty of other people streaming down the street towards the Fearnmore factory. It was situated with the canal to the back of it, near the colour works and on the opposite side of the road from the army barracks. Its smog-blackened stonework and rows of small windows made for an ugly sight but Eileen knew that it was a good place to work, with good employee benefits. Her dad had worked at Fearnmore until he had his heart attack. Now he sat at home smoking his pipe and reading the newspaper. Eileen knew her wages would be useful now she was back living at home.

A horn blew from the factory. People walked faster and when it blew again five minutes later, Eileen was inside the huge iron gates and approaching the area where she'd been told to wait at the main entrance. She stared around. She'd never been in the grounds before. The factory building towered around her. Beyond, she heard the clank and grind of industry up on the canal banks.

A group of girls were already standing at the main entrance, most of them looking nervous.

The girl next to Eileen turned to her. 'I'll never find my way around here. It's so big.'

'They'll give us a tour hopefully,' Eileen smiled.

'I'm Janet Thom.' Janet was small with red hair and grey eyes and freckles all over her pale complexion.

'Eileen Boyle.'

'Pleased to meet you, Eileen. This here is Annie Morris and Jeannie Dougal.'

Eileen smiled at the other two girls. Annie was tall and plump with soft pink cheeks and long black hair. Jeannie was the same height as Eileen and she noticed her thick, dark brown hair and a red mark on her cheek in the shape of a strawberry. Jeannie's gaze flickered when she realised Eileen was looking at her. Eileen looked away quickly. Jeannie was clearly self-conscious about her looks. She didn't need to be. She was very pretty.

A woman walked towards them, her heels clicking. She held a clipboard.

'Good morning. My name is Mrs Glenn. I'm going to check your names on my list and then we'll get you to your department so you can begin your week's training.'

Eileen's heart beat faster as she waited for her name to be read out. It was exciting to be starting something new. She hoped that Janet, Annie and Jeannie would be in the same department. She answered when Mrs Glenn read her name and was rewarded with a small smile. When the list was completed, they were told to follow her. Fearnmore was quite a large factory, and they walked for what seemed like ages while girls filed off into different doorways.

Eventually only the four of them were left. They grinned at each other. It looked like they would be working together.

'This is department number eight; you'll be making bullet casings,' Mrs Glenn said, showing them into a large room and having to raise her voice over the noise of machinery. 'Your supervisor is Miss McGrory.'

A thin woman approached them. Her grey-threaded brown hair was pulled back tightly into a bun and she wore black-rimmed glasses.

'Thank you Mrs Glenn, I'll take over from here. You will need to change into overalls and turbans. Make sure your hair is hidden so it doesn't get into the machinery.'

Eileen followed the others into a side room with lockers. There, Miss McGrory handed out blue overalls in a coarse material and told them to get changed. There were muted giggles as they discovered the overalls didn't fit but after a few minutes of swapping clothes, they were dressed. Janet was so tiny that she had to roll her trousers up, while Annie's ankles were on show.

'I guess we'll all be sewing tonight,' Janet laughed, glancing ruefully at her legs.

'I'll be taking in the waist on these,' Eileen agreed, pinching the baggy material. 'These are not in the least bit flattering.'

'It's not a beauty contest,' Annie said. 'We're here for the war effort.'

Eileen made a face behind her back to Jeannie and was rewarded with a brief smile. Annie was coming across as quite dull. Eileen hoped the other two girls were more fun. It wasn't as if her home life was a bundle of laughs. Therefore, her workplace had to be. They tucked their hair into the white turbans and grinned at each other as they went back onto the factory floor.

The supervisor was tapping her foot impatiently. 'You lot took your time. Tomorrow you'll be quicker about it, do you hear me? You're here to make the bullet casings at these machines. Ruby here will show you what to do.'

A wiry girl with a large turban waved at them from the rows of machines and workers. The noise was unbelievable as the machines, looking like huge mechanical hammers, slammed down rhythmically.

'Some music to work to wouldn't go amiss,' Eileen said in an aside to Jeannie. 'It might make up for the almighty headaches we're going to have tonight from this lot!'

Miss McGrory shot her a black look and stopped in the middle of her speech about safety and shift times.

'And your name is…?'

'Eileen Boyle.'

'Well, Miss Boyle, you're very forward for a girl who hasn't even begun to work,' Miss McGrory said icily. 'Believe it or not, this work is essential to the war effort. Instead of making silly suggestions, I suggest you listen carefully to Ruby's instructions and make very certain you can follow them. A badly made batch of bullets is a disaster, as you can imagine.'

She said no more but her sharp glance made Eileen's heart sink. She had made an enemy on her first day in the job. She saw Jeannie's sympathetic gaze and felt warmed by it but turned away to watch Ruby. She had to do well. She didn't want to lose this job. She had a feeling she was going to enjoy it and working with Jeannie and Janet, if not Annie.

At lunchtime they went to the large canteen with all the other women and girls who worked in department number eight. The sound in here was almost as noisy as the factory floor, with all the chatter and laughter. Eileen felt the tension ease out of her. The work was easy and after Ruby had shown them once, they all went to their allocated machines to push the brass bullet casings into holes set into a plate that went round and round in a swill of soapy water. After a while, the machinery had blurred in front of her.

The four girls took their plates of stew and potatoes over to an empty table.

'Phew, that was hard work,' Janet said, tucking in to her lunch. For a small girl, she ate heartily.

'But rather dull,' Eileen said, 'I wonder if there are other jobs we can do in rotation. I can't imagine spending months pushing bits of brass into holes. I gave up my job as a parlour maid because I heard the wages were double here but I might end up regretting it.'

'According to Ruby, if we do overtime and get any bonuses, we could make as much as six pounds in our weekly pay packet, which is fantastic. That's more than my dad makes and my mam will be glad of those extra wages.' Janet beamed as she shovelled in her stew without stopping.

'I told my parents I'd be bringing in over two pounds a week but now I wish I hadn't promised that, if I decide to go back into service.'

'You don't have a choice,' Annie chipped in. 'You have to do what's best for the factory. I'm happy to be contributing to fighting the war.'

'Fighting the war? We're only making brass cases.' Eileen sighed. It wasn't how she'd imagined it to be. She looked over at Jeannie. What a shy girl she was. She hadn't said anything yet. 'What about you, Jeannie?'

Jeannie looked startled. Her face turned pink as the other three turned to her. 'Oh… I'm just glad to be here. I'm like Annie here, I want to make a difference. I nearly didn't make it at all.'

'Why was that?'

'My fiancé wasn't keen on me working here. I had to persuade him it was a respectable place and that I needed to do something useful for the war.'

Eileen glanced at Jeannie's hand. A diamond ring glittered on her fourth finger. Jeannie's fiancé had been generous or was well-off or both.

'I'll have to take it off before we go back in,' Jeannie said, looking at the ring, 'Miss McGrory has just told me that. No jewellery allowed.'

Janet laughed. 'No persuading for me to work here. My mam practically pushed me into it. With eleven of us under one roof, she needs the wages and the space during the day. I've five brothers and three sisters. We're up in the Holy City.'

The Holy City was an area of Clydebank of close-built white tenements, which was said to resemble Jerusalem, hence its nickname.

'Did you not want to go and work at Singer then?' Annie asked. Singer was the famous factory in Clydebank that made sewing machines and was now turning to war production.

'I wanted something a wee bit different. In Clydebank you're either a Singer family or a shipyard family. I came here because I got told they were sewing parachutes and I'm handy with a needle. Anyway, it doesn't matter, I'm happy to make bullets too,' Janet said cheerfully.

'Singer has its own dance hall. I don't see anything like that here,' Annie said.

'A dance hall full of young lads and old men,' Eileen said scornfully. 'All the available men will be away in the forces.'

'That's true,' Janet agreed. 'My older brothers have all joined up.'

'There's the Locarno or Green's Playhouse up in Glasgow,' Eileen suggested brightly. 'We could all go out one night soon and celebrate our first week at work. How about it?'

'Count me in,' Janet grinned.

Annie looked reluctant and Jeannie didn't answer.

'Jeannie?' Eileen asked. Although the girl was quiet, Eileen liked her and had a feeling they would get on well.

'I don't know if my Arthur would like me dancing while he's away in the army.'

'Surely he wants you to be happy? It's only dancing.'

'I'll think about it.'

Eileen had to be content with that.

'Have you been engaged for long?' she asked, trying not to feel a twinge of jealousy. Wouldn't it be marvellous to be in love and looking forward to getting married?

'It's recent,' Jeannie said. 'Arthur wanted it all settled before he joined the army.'

'Your family must be pleased,' Eileen said.

'My mother's over the moon for me,' Jeannie smiled. 'I know my dad would be thrilled but he passed away a few years ago. I wish he was here so he could know how happy I am.'

'What about you, Annie?' Janet said. 'Have you got lots of brothers and sisters at home?'

'It's just me and my mum,' Annie said, her face flushing. 'Hadn't we better hurry up and take our plates back? The horn's going to go soon.'

—

Very soon the horn did blow again and they trooped after everyone else back into their department for the afternoon. Eileen had a thumping headache by the time they finished. She wondered if she'd be dreaming of brass glinting and soapy water splashing that night. She ran to catch the bus. Janet hurried with her as they were heading in the same direction. It turned out that Annie lived in Clydebank as well so they all sat in the bus together, although Eileen had to remember to get off at an earlier stop before the bus left the city boundary. Eileen wondered why Annie hadn't mentioned where she lived when they'd chatted at lunchtime. She was sorry that Jeannie didn't get the same bus. She wanted to get to know her better.

The smell of cabbage greeted her. Her mother was in the kitchen. Two saucepans steamed up the small room. Agnes glanced round at her, her hair curling in the damp air.

'Put the kettle on. Your dad needs a cup of tea.'

Eileen filled the kettle and set it on the range. She waited to see if her mother would ask about her day. Agnes kept her head down, chopping carrots.

'I made some friends today,' she said. She hadn't had friends at the Cambuslang house. Not really. The other two maids were older and kept to themselves. She'd met people at the dance hall on her half days but no one she cared to get to know properly. She thought of Jeannie, Janet and Annie and brightened.

'Mum, did you hear me?'

Agnes grunted. 'Will you take the tea in to Dad, now? He's waiting for it.'

Eileen poured the tea into a cup, placed it carefully on a saucer and went slowly through to the living room. Her father was asleep in his armchair. She put the cup and saucer down on the table beside him and then went upstairs to her room. The air was undisturbed. She felt a pang of loneliness. If only she was like Janet with eight brothers and sisters, instead of an only child. Would her mother be happier then? She went to her dressing table and picked up the lipstick. She'd wear it on Friday night and go dancing. Eileen smiled at herself in the mirror. Dancing always picked her up. She'd have a good time and forget everything else.

—

Jeannie got home after six. She stumbled along Kiltie Street in the dark, her torch with its paper covering barely casting any light. She nearly hit her head on the baffle wall across the tenement close and then tripped on one of the metal struts inside. They were meant to prevent the building coming down on them in the event of any bombing. She hoped it didn't come to that. She let herself in.

She heard Kathy chatting to Mary and went through to the kitchen.

'Here she is now,' Mary said with a smile. 'Tell us all about it.'

'Let her get her coat off, Mammy,' Kathy protested, and took Jeannie's coat from her. 'I'm glad you're finally home as I'm starving.'

'Sorry, the bus stopped on the main road for a wee while, there was a horse and cart stuck across it and the driver had to help shift it. It's not quite as easy as walking home from Franny's shop.'

'Never mind that. What was it like? Did you meet any nice men?'

'Kathy,' her mother warned.

'It's mostly women,' Jeannie said. 'I'm training to make bullet cases.'

Kathy clattered the plates down on the table and set the cutlery. Mary ladled three bowls of stew and mashed potato and they sat together.

'Bullets?' Kathy pulled a face. 'I thought you were making bombs.'

'Och, you did not. I'm not in a bomb factory. It's Fearnmore, for goodness' sake. It's brass bullets and other parts for the war. I heard a girl telling her friend that they didn't know what the bits were they were making as it's all hush-hush. You do what you're told and keep the machines going.'

'Don't fancy it myself. I'm happy at Franny's. She said to tell you she's missing you. The new girl is clumsy and broke a vase today.'

'Poor Franny. I feel guilty at leaving but, at the same time, I need to do something useful to help end the war.'

'They say it'll be over by Christmas anyway so I don't suppose you'll bring down Hitler all by yourself,' Kathy said cheekily.

Mary shot her a warning look before smiling at Jeannie. 'Well, I think it's wonderful you've stepped up to the mark. I'm sure Arthur is proud of you too.'

Jeannie sighed inwardly. It had been hard work persuading Arthur that she should go. She hated conflict and didn't want an argument. She knew his opinion mattered but a part of her couldn't let it go. In the end, he was distracted by his call-up papers. The matter of Jeannie's employment slid to the back of his mind and when she told him she was going to apply, he hadn't tried to persuade her out of it again. She had waved him off at the station knowing she was going to the labour exchange straight after.

'He doesn't know I've started. I'll tell him this weekend when he's home.' She dreaded it. Arthur was at a training camp not far from Glasgow so often had a weekend pass.

'He's your husband to be,' Mary said. 'You mustn't keep things from him. That's no way for a marriage to be.'

'I know, Mammy. I'll sort it out.'

She wished she had a friend she could ask. She and Arthur were in love so why did it feel awkward between them sometimes? She had gone behind his back to get the job at Fearnmore. Was that right? Should she simply obey him? She thought of Eileen. She was a lovely girl with her blonde hair and chirpy personality. She had confidence, unlike Jeannie. She bet Eileen did what she liked. Or maybe Arthur should be more supportive. Jeannie shied away from that disloyal thought. No, she was at fault. She'd have to make it up to him. Somehow.

'I'm away up to see Mrs Dunn,' she told Mary after she'd washed up the dishes.

'All right, love. Take care in the dark. I'm going to read the letter from Isa and Bob again. They sent drawings too.'

'Will you go and see them?'

'Aye, when I can. They're happy in Perthshire. That Miss Main sounds like a good sort.'

'They'll be missing you, Mammy.'

'I'm missing them too. But we all have to make sacrifices. They're safer where they are.'

Jeannie walked up to where the Dunns lived. The moon had come out and she found her way by its pale light. Arthur had given her a key so that Helen didn't have to answer the door.

'Hello?' Jeannie called softly.

'In here,' Helen's weak voice came from the front room.

'How are you?' Jeannie asked.

Helen was lying on the sofa, covered in a pink blanket. She was pale and her hands were shaky as they readjusted her pillow beneath her head.

'Are you in pain? Can I get you anything?'

'No, dear. Thank you for visiting. Come and sit with me.'

Jeannie sat on the nearest armchair. This was her first visit with Helen since Arthur had gone to his training camp. She wasn't sure what to say.

'How was your first day at the factory?' Helen Dunn asked.

'How did you know?'

Helen's faded blue eyes twinkled. 'Arthur mentioned you were thinking of applying.'

'He wasn't happy about it,' Jeannie said, before she could stop herself.

'I don't suppose he'll be here much though,' Helen said mildly.

Jeannie stared at her. Was Helen on her side?

'Mrs Dunn…'

'Call me Helen, please.' Helen struggled into a sitting position, brushing off Jeannie's offer of help.

'Helen… I didn't want to go against Arthur's wishes but…'

'But you felt he was wrong.'

Jeannie felt wrong-footed once more. She wasn't sure what to make of Arthur's mum.

'Not wrong, maybe. But I feel quite strongly I want to do my bit for the war.'

Helen looked serious. She reached over and took Jeannie's hand. Her hand was cold and Jeannie felt the fragile bones and tissue-paper skin. 'You're quite right, my dear. Arthur will come round to it, I'm sure. He was worried it would be too much for you but I think he's underestimated you. We will all have to do our bit, as you put it. Now, tell me, do you like your engagement ring? It was my mother's and I'm so pleased that now it's yours.'

'It's beautiful,' Jeannie said.

'You wouldn't rather have a new one? Arthur wasn't sure.'

'Oh no. I love that it's been passed down in your family with happy memories. Arthur was pleased too, I could tell.'

Helen smiled and Jean was glad she'd said that. If she was honest, she'd have preferred a ring that she and Arthur chose together. But Arthur had been genuinely delighted when she accepted the ring and she knew it was the right thing to do.

–

Jeannie tidied up, swept the floor and dusted before she left even though she knew Helen had a daily who came in. She offered to help Helen get ready for bed but the older woman refused politely. Jeannie was privately relieved. It was awkward. She didn't know Helen very well. She had made Arthur a promise though and she meant to keep it. She'd keep his mother company while he was gone. After all, one day soon she'd be living here. She couldn't imagine it. The house was so large and draughty. And so quiet. It was very different from home in Kiltie Street. She'd miss Mammy and Kathy so much. Jeannie put her uneasy thoughts aside. They had agreed on a long engagement.

Instead, she thought about her new job at Fearnmore. Her spirits lifted. She really liked Eileen, Janet and Annie. She was looking forward to tomorrow when they'd help the war effort with every brass shape that was made. Miss McGrory didn't appear sympathetic to her workforce. Eileen had already got on the wrong side of her. Jeannie didn't want to be next. She walked home in the dark more by instinct than sight and managed to avoid the brick baffle and the struts inside the close.

An Anderson shelter had been delivered by the Corporation workmen which the Dougals and O'Learys were to share. Martin had complained at how late they were in getting it. Linda and Mary agreed they were glad to get it at all. The problem was Martin's bad back. The shelter was still waiting to be dug in. Jeannie wondered how they'd manage it. She decided to speak to Mammy about it tomorrow.

–

In Perthshire the next day, Miss Main insisted that Isa and Bob write another letter to their mother.

'We just wrote one,' Isa said, looking longingly out at the fields where her favourite cow, Daisy, was grazing.

'I'll draw a bomb killing Hitler,' Bob shouted, running upstairs to get started.

'Or a nice picture of Daisy,' Miss Main suggested. 'Go and get the colouring pencils.'

She hid a smile. She was surprised to find how often she did that these days. The children were funny. They didn't mean to be, but their outlook on life was refreshing. They had been with her over a month now and settled in nicely. Bob's bed-wetting had lessened and Isa's nightmares had stopped.

She hadn't wanted a boy. The beds were made up for the two girl evacuees she'd asked for. The teacher had begged her to take them. A brother and sister who mustn't be parted. She had felt for their mother and given in. Now she couldn't imagine life without them. Isa was full of questions and fascinated by country life and Bob was a dear little boy full of energy and fun.

Agatha Main had been terribly fond of another little boy in the distant past. Her sister's child. That little boy had died when he was five and she could never bear to be near other little boys after that. They reminded her too much of him.

There were painful moments when Bob laughed or ran around like a whirlwind and she remembered her nephew. She had to turn away. But Isa and Bob never let her rest for long. Why did Daisy need milking every day? Why had the chickens stopped laying? What was the smell off the fields? When was dinner? What was for dinner?

She might have been exhausted by it all but instead she felt invigorated.

'Agatha Main, you're a fool,' she told herself at night, getting ready for bed. 'You're nearly seventy and your bones creak. You're too old to play at mammies.'

If that was the case, why did she greet each day now with hope? She didn't quite bound out of bed the way her small visitors did. But she got up sprightly enough. It was better cooking porridge for three and not one. More fun thinking what to cook for an evening meal when there were two appreciative wriggling bodies waiting hungrily. Gone were the long silent evenings. It wasn't that she'd been lonely before. Goodness, no. There was always plenty to do. She wasn't short on activities. Only now she wondered how she'd manage if the children left.

Chapter Five

'Phew, that was a long week,' Eileen said as the girls found a table and sat down with their lemonades.

'It felt twice as long because of Old McGrowly,' Annie moaned.

Janet laughed. 'That's a good name for her. I'm sure she's not so bad. When we get to know her better maybe she'll ease up on us.'

'Ever the optimist,' Annie said.

Eileen smiled and sipped her drink. Janet saw the best in everyone. She was bright and cheerful and when the others grumbled she always kept them going somehow. Eileen hadn't quite fathomed Annie as yet. She could be a stickler for rules and doing 'what was right' and could be downright sour sometimes.

'I wish Jeannie was with us,' Eileen said, looking around at the packed dance hall.

The noise was as thick as the cigarette smoke swirling onto her face. Glasgow's Locarno dance hall was as popular as ever. Khaki and blue uniforms mingled with civilian suits and outnumbered them. There were plenty of young men watching the dance floor from the sides and propping up the bar. Her heart beat faster in excitement. Maybe tonight she'd meet someone special.

'Her fiancé doesn't approve of her going dancing when he's away. I don't blame him,' Janet said, taking a large gulp of her lemonade. 'Fancy another drink? It's on me.'

Eileen was impressed again with how much food and drink Janet could pack away – and how quickly. She was so tiny. Where did it all go?

'What's the point in Jeannie coming?' Annie said, her dark eyes flickering over the dance hall greedily. 'She's got her man. We haven't.'

'It's not all about getting a man,' Eileen protested, half-heartedly. 'Jeannie could have come and danced with us.'

Annie snorted rudely. 'Danced with you, then. I'm here to dance with a gorgeous soldier.'

Eileen knew she was here for the same reason. She didn't agree out loud with Annie, though. It felt too harsh and took the magic out of the evening. She wanted romance and love. She wanted to find that special someone. Jeannie was lucky. She had her fellow and would get married and have her own little house and children. Eileen felt a ripple of envy run through her veins. She desperately wanted children. A boy and a girl. The girl would look like her and the boy like his handsome father.

'Want to dance?' The voice broke into her daydreams. She looked up to see a tall man with dark, slicked-back hair and blue RAF uniform staring down at her.

Annie kicked her under the table.

'Yes,' Eileen said.

As she got up to dance, another blue-uniformed man approached Annie and a soldier arrived at Janet's chair. Soon, all three girls were on the dance floor waltzing in a crowd of hot bodies, with the mingled aromas of white lilac perfume, floor wax and fresh sweat. At first the dance was sedate then, as her partner picked up speed, Eileen began to enjoy herself. It was only on the dance floor that she felt entirely free.

'I'm Eddie,' her partner said, leaning his face in to hers to be heard.

'Eileen,' she replied, turning her cheek from his beery breath.

His hands were hot and damp on her dress. They slid lower to her hips. She moved them up and frowned. Eddie grinned, not in the least put out. He winked at her. Eileen pretended not to notice. Suddenly, she wanted the dance to end. He wasn't even that good-looking. His nose was too big and he had open pores on his cheeks. When the music stopped, she stomped back to the table without saying goodbye.

Janet came back, her face glowing. Her soldier followed her back and pulled up a seat to chat. He was a gangly chap with ears which stuck out but Janet seemed enthralled by him. Annie's dance partner had vanished. Eileen saw him on the floor with another girl. Annie came back to the table, slipping her powder compact into her handbag.

'It might be a dreich night outside but it's hot and steamy in here,' she said. 'I had to blot my face with powder after that dance.'

'Eileen, Annie, this is Alan,' Janet said with a beam. 'Alan, these are my friends. We all work together.'

Alan kindly bought them all more lemonades and a beer for himself. He showed no sign of moving from Janet's side all evening.

Annie sighed as they watched the couple head for the dancing. They looked like an odd match with Alan so tall and Janet so tiny.

'How has she managed it? He has a face only a mother could love but he's attentive, you have to give him that. I've only had one dance and not been asked twice.'

Eileen thought it was because of Annie's sour expression. However, she couldn't say that.

'Never mind, here's a soldier now.'

'He's headed for you, not me.'

She was right. Eileen found herself whirled onto the dance floor for a fast foxtrot. At least this partner kept his hands where they ought to be. She winced as he trod on her feet. He went beetroot red and mumbled an apology. She smiled brightly. He wasn't her special someone. She'd know immediately she met him. But he was a nice young man, if a bit clumsy. She decided to make the most of it. She liked a good foxtrot. Half the battle was avoiding his heavy feet. She was tired when he gallantly returned her to the table where Annie sat glumly.

'Our two love birds have gone out for some fresh air,' Annie said. 'I think I'm off home. You coming?'

Eileen's feet ached. 'What about Janet? We should wait for her and all get the same bus.'

Annie shook her head. 'No need. Alan is seeing her home. I'm going to the powder room. I'll see you at the bus stop.'

Eileen gathered up her handbag and got her coat from the cloakroom. She went outside and was hit by the chilly, damp night air. There were couples kissing and fumbling in the dark. She turned away, embarrassed and fell against a hard chest.

'Sorry,' she said.

'Hey, if it's not the lovely Eileen,' Eddie slurred. His eyes were bleary and struggling to focus. He grabbed her arms and pulled her back in towards him. Before Eileen could move, his mouth was on hers. His lips were hot and slimy. She opened her mouth to cry out and he thrust his tongue into hers. Gagging, she pushed him hard and he stumbled back. She wiped her lips with the back of her hand.

'How dare you!' She was trembling and she tasted beer and something else unpleasant.

He lumbered towards her and Eileen took off. There was no arguing with a drunk. She ran fast towards the bus stop and saw, with relief, Annie's bulky figure waiting.

'There's no rush,' Annie said, as Eileen skidded to a halt. 'Five minutes 'til the bus gets here.'

Eileen couldn't speak for a moment. She tried to control her trembling. She didn't want to have to explain to Annie what had happened. Luckily, the other girl seemed caught up in her own thoughts. Janet and Alan arrived and by then, Eileen had control of her emotions. They chatted in a friendly manner all the way back to Eileen's stop.

She waved goodnight to the others and walked along the street to her home. It was pitch black and her tiny torch gave out a sickly yellow light which failed to illuminate anything. She got home by instinct. She tried the front door. It was locked. She took a few minutes finding her key and letting herself in.

Inside, the lights were off. She made sure the blackout curtains were in place before switching on the kitchen light. She filled the kettle for tea. Her parents hadn't waited up for her. Didn't they care? What if she hadn't come home at all? Eileen wondered if they would even notice. The buzz of dancing faded away. Her mood dipped to its usual level. The back of her hand was covered in smeared crimson lipstick where she had wiped Eddie's disgusting kiss away. Eileen sat down at the scrubbed pine table, lowered her blonde head onto her arms and sobbed.

—

Jeannie trudged up the road towards Kiltie Street in the company of Elspeth. Both girls were exhausted. It was the end of their second week in the factory.

'My head's thumping,' Jeannie said with a yawn.

'Mine too,' Elspeth said. 'I almost wish I was back at the big house being a maid. I thought this would be easier but the hours are just as long. Still, the money's good.'

'I miss the short walk to Franny's,' Jeannie agreed. 'And the chat with the customers while I served them in the shop. I'm glad though to help with the war effort. We're doing something worthwhile.'

Another reason for her thumping head was 'Old McGrowly', as they called the supervisor behind her back. She had called Jeannie over at the end of the morning shift.

'Come and see me in my office.'

Eileen smiled sympathetically as she, Annie and Janet headed for the canteen. Jeannie's stomach grumbled. She was starving. Breakfast, a hurried bowl of porridge, was a distant memory. She followed the supervisor's stiffly held back to the tiny room off the main factory floor. Miss McGrory sat behind her desk. She didn't invite Jeannie to sit.

'Is there something wrong?' Jeannie asked nervously.

The woman stared at her coldly. 'I'll do the speaking, thank you, Dougal.'

Jeannie tried not to be intimidated. She waited.

'You are very slow,' Miss McGrory said finally after a few seconds which seemed to Jeannie to stretch horribly as she waited for her fate.

'Slow?'

'Yes, slow,' the woman said impatiently. 'You were shown last week how to run the machine by Ruby.'

'Am I doing it wrong?' Jeannie asked.

Miss McGrory shook her head. 'We would soon know if you were "doing it wrong", as you put it. You may be working the machine correctly but you're not quick enough. You need to increase your output. There's a war on. We can't carry time-wasters.'

How dare the horrid woman say that! Jeannie thought indignantly. She had taken care to listen to Ruby's instructions and to follow them. It was only her second week in the job. She would get faster. If she was allowed to. Her heart sank. Was she going to lose her job?

'Are you letting me go?' she said.

Miss McGrory's eyebrows rose in surprise before her features hardened again. Jeannie noticed the deep groove on her forehead and the lines dragging at the sides of her mouth. She looked discontented and Jeannie wondered if she ever smiled.

'I'll be watching you next week,' she said. 'You'll have to work harder.'

Jeannie stood there. Miss McGrory made a fuss of looking at her papers on her desk. She looked up, as if irritated by Jeannie's presence, and waved her hands.

'You may go.'

She had found her friends finishing their lunch in the canteen.

'Are you all right?' Eileen asked her.

'I'm too slow, apparently,' Jeannie said lightly. Her eyes filled with tears and she wiped them away before the others saw them.

Janet jumped up and came back a few minutes later with a tray of sandwiches and a mug of strong tea.

'They've only got fish paste left, I'm afraid,' she said cheerfully, pushing the tray in front of Jeannie. 'You can have my biscuits, I'm full up.' She put her plate onto the tray.

Jeannie knew that wasn't true. Janet was never full up. She felt her heart warm at her kindness. It more than made up for the supervisor's nastiness. Even Annie looked sympathetic.

'How can you be too slow?' Eileen was saying. 'We've only just learnt how to run the machines. Don't worry about Old McGrowly. She's not picking on you, she hates all of us for some reason.'

Jeannie did feel picked upon. She had a dreadful feeling that Miss McGrory had it in for her. Even if she didn't understand why.

'We have to run the machines efficiently,' Annie said. 'I suppose if you're not doing that, production slows down and then there aren't enough bullets being produced.'

Eileen shot Annie a look. Jeannie knew Annie was right but she didn't want to hear it. Jeannie worried about it all afternoon. She managed to keep her machine going but found herself fumbling with nerves. She was thankful when it was time to leave for the day.

She and Elspeth were nearly at their respective tene-ment entrances or 'closes' now.

'I'm glad it's the weekend,' Elspeth said, turning the beam of her torch so she could find the stone steps up into the close's dark mouth.

Jeannie was glad, too. A couple of days to herself was appealing. She pushed open the front door and went inside. In the parlour there was a slim, fair-haired man. Mary and Kathy were sitting talking to him.

'Jimmy!' Jeannie cried, and ran to hug him.

'That's a nice greeting,' her brother grinned, and hugged her back.

'When did you get home? How long are you here for?'

Jimmy laughed. 'Hold your fire. Sit yourself down and I'll answer.'

Jeannie plumped down on the sofa beside Kathy. Jimmy took the armchair on one side of the fireplace while Mary had the other. It was lovely to see him, Jeannie thought. She and Jimmy had always been close. She looked at him. He didn't look any different, really. Maybe he was a wee bit thinner.

'Go on then,' she prompted.

They all laughed at her impatience.

'I got home this afternoon. I went by Franny's and found Kathy and was told you'd gone to work at Fearn-more. As for how long, I'm here for a fortnight, if Mammy will have me.'

'It's embarkation leave, Jimmy says,' Mary said.

Jeannie saw the worry in her mother's eyes as she glanced at her eldest child.

'What does that mean?' she asked.

'It's leave so I can see my family before I'm shipped out,' Jimmy explained. 'We've not been told where we're going but it's plain from the supplies coming in. We're off to France, for sure.'

There was a moment's silence while the Dougal family digested this. Jimmy was the first to break it with a merry whistle. He jumped up from the armchair.

'I'm starving, Mammy. What's for dinner?'

Mary got up and bustled through to the kitchen. Kathy followed, complaining about something Franny had done or not done, Jeannie couldn't make it out. Jimmy winked at her.

'Thought that would take Mammy's mind off it. Feeding her family focusses her mightily.'

'Are you scared?' Jeannie blurted out.

Jimmy's jaw tightened then he relaxed and his grey eyes crinkled. 'Naw, I'll be fine. You know me. They don't call me Lucky Jim for nothing.'

'That's right. I'd forgotten your friends' nickname for you. Didn't it begin when you found that sixpence as a wee one at school? And there was the day you fell in the canal and made it out alive. Or the time you drove your bike into a tree and only had a black eye for it.'

Jeannie joined in his cheerfulness. If Jimmy wasn't going to make a big deal out of fighting the enemy in France, then neither would she. He was brave, her brother. She had to be too.

It was after dinner that the peace was broken. They ate a meat pie and peas that Mary had prepared. It was more pastry and carrots than meat but tasty all the same. There was custard and jam for afters. Jimmy stretched and rubbed his stomach.

'That was great, Mammy. It beats the camp grub hands over. Now, if you don't mind, I'm away to see Liz-Anne.'

Liz-Anne was Jimmy's girlfriend. They had been stepping out for more than two years but there was no sign of an engagement despite Mary's hints.

'Oh, Jimmy, you won't like this,' Kathy said, 'but I saw Liz-Anne kissing someone. It was last week in town.'

Jeannie wanted to reach over and slap her sister's face. Jimmy's joy in his dinner had gone. He looked angry and upset. Kathy could be a right wee cow.

'Kathy,' Mary said. 'Why can't you keep your mouth shut? It doesn't concern you.'

'He'd rather know, Mammy. Wouldn't you, Jimmy? If I had a boyfriend who was carrying on with another lassie, I'd want to know about it,' Kathy defended herself.

Jimmy didn't answer. He got his jacket and went out, slamming the door behind him.

'Now you've done it,' Jeannie said. 'You shouldn't upset him when he's about to go overseas to fight.'

'You upset Arthur by working at Fearnmore.'

'That's different.'

'It is not. You're just saying that to make yourself high and mighty.'

'Och, there's no talking to you,' Jeannie said, annoyed.

She got up and began to do the washing up. Kathy was meant to dry the dishes. Instead, she went into the bedroom and shut the door loudly. Mary sighed.

'I don't know what to do with her these days,' she said, taking the tea towel and beginning to dry the dishes as Jeannie rinsed them.

'She's fifteen. It's a difficult age,' Jeannie said.

'You weren't difficult.'

'I was too shy to be so.'

'That's true. I was more concerned about you being quiet,' Mary smiled. 'Wait 'til you have children. You never stop with the worrying.'

–

Jimmy didn't return until late. Jeannie heard him shutting the door as she lay in bed. Kathy was snoring gently beside her. Her feet were cold and she thought about putting them on Kathy's warm legs but didn't want to wake her. It struck her that they could have a bed each while Isa and Bob were away but it didn't seem right somehow. As if by doing so, they might never come home again. She wondered what had happened between Jimmy and Liz-Anne. She thought about Arthur. He was coming home tomorrow on leave. She ought to feel excited about seeing him but she didn't. She drifted off to sleep, confused about her feelings.

–

There was a clattering and hammering in the tenement's back court which, instead of the more usual concrete, was made up of a large grass area. Mary was pleased. The Anderson shelter was going up. She went outside to see. Jimmy was digging furiously. He had come back late and this morning he hadn't mentioned Liz-Anne at all. Mary knew he'd tell her in his own time. She suspected it was over between the two young people. Now, he was taking it out on the soil.

'Good morning Mrs Dougal. A fine day.'

'Mr Woodley,' Mary said in surprise.

The air raid warden was dressed in old trousers and a checked shirt and had a spade over his shoulder. Without his familiar tin hat, his fair hair was thick and tufted.

'I've come to lend a hand. We must all help each other in these difficult days.'

He went past her and stood to watch Jimmy for a moment. Before long, he was shouting instructions. Jimmy, good-natured, was obliging him. Mary thought how annoying Mr Woodley was. He was loud and blustering and just couldn't help interfering. What her mother would've called 'a right wee busybody'. Then she felt guilty. He had come to help. She should be glad. Jimmy couldn't sort the shelter by himself.

'What's he doing here?' Jeannie asked, coming to stand by her.

'Helping.'

'I don't like him. He's always complaining about the lights and our blackout.'

'Not for a while now,' Mary said, trying to be fair. 'And it is his duty as air raid warden.'

'He thinks he's the bee's knees. Poor Jimmy.'

'Aye, well, Jimmy can stick up for himself,' Mary sighed, thinking of her son going over to France.

'Did he and Liz-Anne break up?' Jeannie said, hugging her arms in the chilly autumn air.

'He didn't say but from the look on his face, I'd guess so. It's a pity. I was hearing wedding bells for the two of them.'

'Well, I'm glad,' Jeannie said. 'She wasn't good enough for him. She was always a flirt.'

'It can't be good just before going overseas,' Mary frowned.

'He's a lovely lad, he'll find someone else,' Jeannie said.

'Is Arthur coming over today?' Mary changed the subject. She liked Arthur. Jeannie had done well for herself and when she was Mrs Dunn, she'd be comfortably off.

There was a pause. Mary looked at her elder daughter. She couldn't read her expression.

'Is everything all right, love?'

Jeannie gave a little start as if she'd been miles away. 'Oh, yes, Mammy. Whyever not? Arthur is coming over. He can help with digging the shelter in.'

'He'd better hurry, then,' Mary said wryly, 'because if he doesn't, Mr Woodley will have dug the whole thing single-handedly. Poor Martin. I hope he doesn't feel badly about it.'

'I think he'd be very happy not to have to break a sweat. It's heavy work. I hope Mr Woodley doesn't put *his* back out. He's quite old,' Jeannie remarked.

'He's not that old,' Mary said. 'He's probably about my age.'

'There you are then, just what I said,' Jeannie replied cheekily, kissing her on the cheek.

Mary swatted her and they both laughed.

Kathy came out and made a deal out of shivering. 'What are you doing? Arthur's at the door.'

'Didn't you let him in?' Jeannie said, sounding exasperated.

Kathy shrugged sullenly. She clearly hadn't forgiven Jeannie for yesterday's argument. Mary missed Dennis suddenly. He had been good with his children. He had a knack of cheering Kathy up and of boosting Jeannie's confidence. He and Jimmy were good pals. It was a terrible shame he had never met Bob who was born just after Dennis had his fatal heart attack. On her own, Mary had to swim along and through her troubles. Sometimes she floated, sometimes she felt she was sinking. Especially when it came to Kathy.

Jeannie disappeared and arrived back with Arthur.

'Hello, Arthur,' Mary said warmly. 'How's your mother?'

'She's much the same, thank you, Mrs Dougal. We have a daily who goes in to keep her comfortable and she enjoys Jeannie's visits.'

63

'Are you going to help dig in the shelter?' Kathy said with a sly smile.

Arthur glanced at Jeannie and then at the toiling figures in the garden.

'That's kind of you,' Mary said. 'You must've put in your own already?'

Arthur's polite smile was strained. 'I paid a man to do it.'

'Oh, of course.' She must remember the Dunns were not like them. Which was why it was good for Jeannie to marry Arthur. Mary was concerned about the invalid mother and the burden that would fall to Jeannie, but money went a long way to helping with that.

'But surely you'll help Jimmy?' Jeannie asked.

Arthur looked at them. Mary was sure he was going to refuse but he took his jacket off and folded it neatly before handing it to Jeannie. He rolled up the sleeves of his immaculate white shirt and went slowly across the muddy lawn to the men.

'Let's leave them to it,' Mary suggested.

If she had to listen to Mr Woodley's booming voice for another minute she might scream. Dennis had been a gentle, quiet man, never one for raising his voice. She didn't know what he'd have made of their bossy neighbour.

By the end of Saturday, the Anderson shelter had been dug in and earth mounded up against its sides and across its top. The men had built in a couple of benches. Jimmy had insisted on putting in two oil lamps and Mary had found blankets. It smelt unpleasantly of damp earth. She prayed they'd never have to use it. Harry Woodley had gone home but returned with packets of seeds.

'Broad beans and beets. People are growing them on top of their shelters. I'll pop these in for you.'

'Thank you.'

It was a kind gesture and she felt slightly guilty for thinking badly of him. She left him to it. He was whistling 'Pack Up Your Troubles', a tune she normally liked but which now grated on her nerves. She went inside and took up her knitting. She was making socks for the Women's Voluntary Service and had promised to help in their canteen too. She soon forgot about him.

Jimmy took Jeannie aside that evening.

'Fancy a walk?'

'It's awful cold,' she said reluctantly but he seemed keen so she nodded.

He lit up a cigarette once they had turned the corner of Kiltie Street.

'When did you start smoking? Mammy won't like that.'

'That's why I waited 'til we were out of sight,' Jimmy said with a laugh. 'All the lads smoke. One of the few joys left to us.'

'Oh, Jimmy. Is it that bad?'

'Not at all. I've made some good friends over the last couple of years. Remember; I chose this, I haven't been called up.'

'True, but there wasn't a war on when you joined the army. It's different now.'

'Aye, well.'

There was nothing more to say to that so Jeannie kept quiet. She was going to miss Jimmy when he left. They had thirteen more lovely days until then but when would she see him after that? She was tired of the war already and it had only just begun.

'Jeannie…'

'Hmm?' She was miles away in her thoughts.

'This Arthur… do you really love him?'

'Of course I do. Why are you asking?' She was unsettled. She turned the engagement ring on her finger, feeling the cold metal slip on her skin.

He hesitated. She saw the red glowing end of the cigarette in the darkness. She imagined Mr Woodley running up the road after them, shouting at Jimmy to stub it out and almost let out a hysterical giggle.

'He's an odd sort,' Jimmy said finally.

'Mammy doesn't think so. She thinks Arthur's a fine catch. He's good-looking and wealthy and—'

'But what do *you* think?' Jimmy cut across her gabbling.

'I love him,' Jeannie said. 'I love him and I'm going to marry him.'

She did love him, of course she did. He wasn't an easygoing sort of man but they rubbed along all right. He might be stiff and proper on the outside but inside, she knew there was a different Arthur who loved and cared for her even if he found it difficult to show that. It was too late for nerves anyhow. She'd made her promise and she intended to keep it.

Jimmy flicked the stub away and its glow died, leaving them in the dark. He began to hum 'When I'm Cleaning Windows' and Jeannie joined in, finding the words until they were both singing and chuckling as they wandered the familiar streets, circling round before the canal and reaching Kiltie Street once more.

Chapter Six

Before Christmas, Jeannie made the journey to Perthshire. Mary had a head cold and was too ill to go. She sent Jeannie away with a bag of gifts and a fruit cake.

'Made with apples and raisins while we can still get them,' she said. 'They're talking of food rationing in January. Tell Isa and Bob I love them and I'm that sorry not to be seeing them.' Mary coughed and held her hand to her mouth until the spasm passed.

'I will, Mammy. You take care of yourself and make sure to let Kathy help out.'

Kathy scowled. 'I don't see why you get to go on holiday and I'm left here.'

'It's hardly a holiday,' Jeannie said. 'Besides, you're only fifteen and Mammy needs you here.'

'You get all the fun. It's not fair.' Kathy ran back inside without saying goodbye.

'Don't mind her, love. I'm very glad you got time off work to go.'

Miss McGrory had made it plain she wasn't happy at Jeannie's request but as Jeannie was entitled to take holiday leave, there wasn't much the supervisor could do about it. Muttering about lack of duty, she had signed her off in the book. Eileen had hugged her and wished her a good trip.

'It must be lovely having a wee sister and brother. I'm an only child,' she said wistfully.

'You can share my eight,' Janet offered with a grin. 'You're so lucky, I can't imagine how peaceful it must be at your house. I can hardly hear myself think at home.'

Annie didn't offer any comment but wished Jeannie a pleasant journey. She never mentioned her home life and the others didn't like to pry.

Jeannie hugged Mary and at the end of Kiltie Street she turned back. Mary was standing there still. She waved and Jeannie waved back. Then she was round the corner and at the bus stop waiting for the bus into the city centre to catch the train to Perth. Poor Mammy, Jeannie thought. She missed her wee ones. Jeannie missed them too. It wasn't the same at home without them. But they are safer where they are, she reminded herself.

This time of year, in normal times, they would all have played board games or cards at home. There was nothing nicer, Jeannie felt, than sitting in the parlour with a roaring fire, kneeling on the floor, ready to move your token along the board with Jimmy teasing Isa and Bob, and Kathy having a fit when she lost the game. Mammy would sit, smiling at the lot of them from her cosy seat in the armchair, her knitting on her lap and a pot of tea beside her. Jeannie was caught between laughing and crying as she remembered those happy occasions. The bus arrived before she could dwell on it too much.

She had started early in the day but it was long after midday by the time she reached the village. The train was packed with servicemen and there had been long delays. At one point it had been shunted into a siding for hours. With dismay, she realised she wouldn't have much time to spend with Isa and Bob at all. She had intended to stay until before dinner, not wanting to invite herself to eat at their host's expense. Now, she would need to find a place to stay overnight.

She stood in the village as the bus drove off. Where was she to find her brother and sister?

The air smelt fresh and sweet. It was quite different to the city. The lane she found herself in was lined with small cottages and the autumn leaves underfoot carpeted the village in pretty shades of yellow, orange and brown. Not far away, Jeannie saw a patchwork of fields with grazing cows and beyond, there were woodlands. A flock of crows flew up in the nearest field and she felt strange, as if she'd entered a foreign country.

'Can I help you?' A woman pushing a pram stopped near her. She looked at Jeannie with suspicion as if she might be a German spy.

Perhaps they weren't used to strangers, Jeannie thought. It was such a tiny place. She imagined everybody must know each other. She must stick out like a sore thumb.

'I'm looking for Miss Main's house,' she said.

'It's the last cottage along the lane,' the woman pointed.

'Thank you,' Jeannie said, but the woman was already pushing her pram away.

It didn't take long to walk the lane, to the accompaniment of the birds chirping and the occasional deep 'moo' from the cows. She tried to imagine Isa and Bob here and failed. They were city children. Mammy shooed them out in the mornings to school or play and out they stayed until dinner. What kind of life had they here? It was a far cry from Kiltie Street.

The cottage was like a picture postcard. It had a blue painted door and whitewashed walls. Plants grew around it. It was too late in the year for flowers but Jeannie thought it would be lovely in the summer. She used the door knocker and waited nervously.

An old woman with white hair and a beaky nose opened it. She had surprisingly bright blue eyes, not faded by age. She was dressed in black as if in mourning.

'Mrs Dougal?' she said. 'I got your letter saying you were coming.'

'I'm Jeannie. My mother, Mary, couldn't come as she's got a terrible head cold.'

'I'm Agatha Main. Come away in. I'll call the children.'

Jeannie stepped into a neat, clean home full of colourful cushions and ornaments and vases of dried flowers. Within minutes there was the loud clatter of feet and Bob stormed into her, almost knocking her over. She hugged him tightly and kissed the top of his head. She felt unshed tears fill her eyes. She had missed him so much. Bob hugged her back fiercely for a few seconds then wriggled free.

'Where's Mammy?' he said, looking past her hopefully.

'She's not well, got a feverish cold but she sends her love.'

Bob's face fell. Then he grinned up at Jeannie. 'Do you want to see my comic collection? Miss Main gets me a *Beano* or a *Dandy* when she goes to the town.'

'Why don't you bring them down from your bedroom for your sister to see?' Miss Main suggested from the kitchen doorway where she had appeared.

Bob ran off and Jeannie followed her hostess, wondering where Isa was. The kitchen was a warm, homely space with a large, black range taking up much of the area and blasting out a welcome heat. Isa was standing on a low stool at the sink, her hands covered in soapy bubbles. She didn't look at Jeannie. She had a pottery teapot and cups and was pouring water from one to the other with great concentration.

Miss Main smiled. 'Isa's a great help in the kitchen. Aren't you, dear? Come and say hello to your sister. She's had a long journey to see you.'

Jeannie watched her. Isa was taller and she was wearing a new dress that she didn't recognise. Her hair was longer too. She was growing up. A wave of sadness hit her. Isa and Bob were changing and she and Mammy and Kathy were missing out on that. Something caught in her throat and she cleared it.

Isa reluctantly dried her hands and came to greet her. Jeannie hugged her but Isa didn't return it, her body soft and unresisting.

'Are you here to take us away?' she asked.

'No. Not at all. It isn't safe yet. I'm here to see you and just for today.'

Isa nodded and a slow smile crept across her face. 'Do you want to meet Daisy?'

'Daisy?'

Miss Main smiled, too. 'Why don't you introduce Daisy while I put the kettle on for tea?'

'Oh, my mother sent this,' Jeannie said, delving into her bag for the fruit cake.

Jeannie watched Isa as she chattered away, leaning against the fence outside where Daisy placidly chewed the cud in the field. She was happy here and Jeannie knew that would make Mammy glad. She ought to be glad too but instead she felt uneasy.

'Don't you want to come home to Kiltie Street?' she asked, when Isa finally drew breath and stopped speaking.

Isa shrugged and kicked her feet against the fence. Miss Main called them in for tea and they went inside. Jeannie took off her coat and felt the warmth of the kitchen sink into her skin. Bob arrived with a pile of comics to show her. They drank tea and ate slices of Mary's rich fruit cake and scones which Miss Main had baked. There was butter and jam with the scones which Jeannie savoured. Food wasn't so easy to get now at home.

She picked up her bag and took out the small gifts. There was a small set of lead soldiers for Bob and a wooden puppet for Isa. Mary had sent a box of embroidered handkerchiefs for Miss Main. The two children took their gifts eagerly. Miss Main thanked her kindly.

'We've got something for you as well,' Isa said.

She went upstairs and came down with a notebook. Jeannie opened it up. It was full of drawings of the village, Daisy, black chickens and of the family.

'This is lovely,' she said, 'Mammy will love this, and so do I.'

–

She lay in bed that night, staring up at the ancient wooden beams above her. Miss Main had kindly invited her to stay after hearing of her long journey. There was a bus in the morning to the station in the nearby town. She couldn't sleep. It was so quiet outside with none of the city sounds. An owl hooted mournfully. The bedroom smelt of old wood and beeswax and of the dried lavender bunches which adorned the window sill, in front of the thick curtains. She was sharing the narrow bed with Isa and heard her soft breathing and Bob's light snores from the truckle bed nearby.

Everything had changed. Her wee sister and brother were growing. They had new clothes and they didn't smell of home any more. She noticed they looked to Miss Main for their instructions and hadn't taken notice of Jeannie in that way. At dinner, they had said Grace and frowned when Jeannie had picked up her knife and fork to eat.

The war wasn't going to be over by Christmas, whatever people said. Jeannie had an awful feeling it wasn't going to be over any time soon. It was horrible and it hung over them all, spoiling everything. How could she be happy when Jimmy and Arthur were going away to fight? When Isa and Bob were away from home and seemed to be slipping further away in spirit?

She fell asleep only hours before she had to get up to catch the bus. She kissed the children and they waved as she got a seat and the bus pulled away. Miss Main had her arms around them and they both leaned in to the old woman as if she were family.

–

Christmas Day wasn't a public holiday in Scotland and the girls were at work. In the canteen at lunch break, they huddled together with bowls of soup and slices of bread and butter.

'I was hoping for mince and tatties the day,' Janet said, ruefully stirring her soup. 'I doubt this will fill me up.'

Eileen and Jeannie shared a grin. Nothing filled Janet's stomach for long. Annie took delicate sips of her soup.

'Anyone celebrating Christmas, then?' Eileen said. 'I see they've put a Christmas tree up in the city centre. Lovely, it is. There's glass baubles all glittery. Cheers me up no end.'

'Why do you need cheered up?' Annie said, raising her dark eyebrows.

'I don't know. It's the winter and always so dark and cold.' Eileen shuddered.

'The dancing warms you up,' Janet said. 'Me and Alan have had some great dances.'

'I'll bet Alan warms you up,' Eileen teased and was rewarded by Janet's blush.

Annie made a face. 'Don't be disgusting, Eileen.'

'I didn't mean…' Eileen gave up. She hadn't meant anything rude by it but Annie could be a right prude. She turned to Jeannie. 'So, will you be celebrating this evening?'

Jeannie shook her head. 'Mammy doesn't do Christmas. We'll have our nice meal and gifts on New Year same as always. There's a party and the neighbours all come.'

'It sounds nice,' Eileen said.

She thought of her own home. It felt like the Boyles didn't celebrate either Christmas or Hogmanay and New Year. Tonight, her mother would put a good meal on the table but there wouldn't be any singing or gifts. Hogmanay would be quiet, too. Her parents didn't talk much to their neighbours and never invited them into the house. They kept themselves to themselves, as Agnes Boyle was fond of putting it, as if it were a virtue.

'It will be nice but it won't feel the same this year with Jimmy and the wee ones away,' Jeannie said. 'Why don't you come? You can stay over if you don't mind sharing a bedroom with me and our Kathy.'

'Do you mean it?' Eileen asked.

'If your parents won't mind.'

'They won't even notice I've gone.'

The girls laughed as if she'd made a joke but Eileen was telling the truth. She'd hardly be missed. How kind of Jeannie to invite her. She wanted to give back as well. She knew that Arthur was home on leave.

'How about coming to a dance at the Locarno?' she said. 'You and Arthur. We've got a good crowd going this Friday: me, Janet and Alan, and Annie. Say you'll come.'

Instead of looking pleased, Jeannie looked downright awkward and Eileen wished she hadn't offered.

'Thanks, Eileen. I'll ask Arthur but he's not that keen on the dancing.'

Eileen wondered just what Arthur was keen on. From things she'd let slip, it seemed like Jeannie never went anywhere with him when he was home on leave. Arthur apparently didn't like going to the cinema either. He and Jeannie spent their time together at his house, keeping his mother company. Jeannie said Arthur's mother was lovely. But still, Eileen mused. When you were young and in love, surely you needed to be together without anyone else at times? If she was in love... she sighed inwardly. When was that likely to be? She might be in demand as a dance partner and boys might like her looks but she still hadn't met anyone who made her heart sing.

After work, Jeannie caught up with Eileen to walk out of the room. The machines were thankfully silent after the day's work.

'You didn't say if you were celebrating this evening?' Jeannie asked.

'There will be a good dinner, at any rate,' Eileen said, determined to stay cheerful.

Jeannie was silent. She looked distracted.

'What's up?' Eileen said.

'Nothing.'

Eileen didn't like to pry. She made to turn down onto the street and in the direction of her bus when Jeannie pulled her arm to stop her.

'Actually, it's… Arthur. He's on extended leave. He'll be home until New Year.'

'That's good, isn't it?'

'He's only got more days because they're moving his unit down south somewhere. It means he won't be coming home so much next year.'

'I'm sorry, Jeannie. That's a pity and you'll miss him. At least he's not being sent overseas yet.'

'Yes, you're right. I mustn't grumble. Other people have it a lot worse than me. See you tomorrow.'

Eileen waved. She watched her friend walk in the other direction, her back slumped. Another, taller girl joined her and Jeannie's figure straightened as they walked briskly away, talking. Eileen didn't know her companion very well, only that she was Jeannie's neighbour, Elspeth. What was bothering Jeannie? It felt as if she had been going to confide in Eileen but in the end, had decided not to. Janet and Annie caught her up right then and she forgot about it.

The days rolled past quickly and the weather got steadily colder. It began to snow in between Christmas and Hogmanay and there were icicles hanging from window sills and door frames. Eileen was desperate for her two days off work. It was exhausting at the factory with the long hours and the noise of the machines, not to mention Miss McGrory's beady gaze on them and her acerbic comments.

She let herself into the house. It should have been warm, if not welcoming, but the air was just as cold as outside. Eileen shivered and kept her coat on. There was no smell of dinner cooking either.

She went through to the living room. Her father was there, sitting in front of a small fire which was more damp smoke than flame. His mouth was clamped around his pipe. He barely looked at Eileen but at least he lowered his newspaper.

'Where's Mum?' she asked, rubbing her fingers together to try to get the circulation back into them.

'She's gone upstairs with one of her headaches. You'll have to make the dinner.'

Eileen knelt in front of the fire and put on another scoop of coal and wafted it with an old newspaper from the pile they kept for making tapers. Soon she had a few flames licking up.

'There we are, Dad. That'll be a bit warmer.'

'Thank you, dear.' He was hidden behind the news-paper again.

Eileen took off her coat and hung it up in the hall. She put on her mother's kitchen apron and settled in to peeling potatoes and carrots. There was a piece of pork, ready, trussed in string and buttered, and she put that into the oven. Dinner would be late. She went out into the hall and stared up the stairs. Should she go and see how her mother was? She put one foot on the bottom stair. Then, she stepped back off it. She went back into the kitchen and put the vegetables into a pan to boil.

At dinner, no one spoke. It was an unwritten rule that they were quiet while eating. She waited until they had all finished their sponge pudding before speaking.

'I'm invited over to Jeannie's for a New Year's party. I don't have to go if you'd rather I stayed in?'

'What do you think, Dad?' her mother said.

Her father grunted as he packed his pipe ready for an after-meal smoke.

'I'll have to stay over,' Eileen said.

'As long as you're back at a reasonable hour the next day,' Mr Boyle said. 'You don't want to wear out your welcome.'

It made her feel small and sad inside. Her parents thought she was a nuisance to Jeannie's family. She nodded and stood up to collect the dirty dishes. The room was silent except for the soft popping sound of her father taking in pipe smoke and letting it out again.

–

There was a festive air at the end of the working day before Hogmanay celebrations, even though the factory was staying open during the holiday and not everyone had time off. Those that did were determined to make the most of it. Workers poured out of the Fearnmore factory gates, shouting to each other. Eileen had lost her friends in the rush out the door and hung back in the streaming crowd to try to find them. Someone brushed past her. It was Miss McGrory, wrapped in a large grey coat and a matching woollen hat with a diamanté brooch on it.

'Have a nice Hogmanay,' Eileen called.

Miss McGrory looked straight through her and kept on walking. Eileen made a face to her vanishing back. What a horrid woman! What did she have against them?

–

Jeannie hurried home on Hogmanay, glad to be finished with work. When she woke the next morning and looked outside, the snow was falling heavily. Mammy liked every room scrubbed, dusted and polished on New Year before the party. She nudged Kathy's sleeping body. Her sister grunted but didn't move. Jeannie left her. Downstairs, Mary was already up and making porridge.

'I'm looking forward to the party,' Jeannie said, slipping into her seat at the kitchen table.

Mary pushed a bowl of hot porridge across to her.

'It'll be fun. It always is. But dear God, I miss Jimmy. He's never been away from home on Hogmanay before. And Isa and Bob. Have I done the right thing, leaving them away up in Perthshire?'

'Of course you have,' Jeannie soothed. 'Sit yourself down and eat your breakfast. I'll fill the teapot.'

'We'll keep busy with the cleaning today,' Mary said. 'That will take our minds off those that are missing.'

The house shone when the first guests arrived. Mary, Jeannie and Kathy had spent the day with polishing rags and their efforts showed. Not a speck of dust nor a floor unscrubbed was to be seen.

'What will the New Year 1940 bring?' Mary asked. 'I pray that this war will end and that my children come back to me.'

Jeannie didn't have an answer to that. She kissed her mother and went to answer the door. She was wearing her new dress, a present from Mary and Kathy. It was blue with white polka dots and she felt very smart in it. She had curled her dark hair and used her coral lipstick. She wanted to look pretty for Arthur.

Martin O'Leary was the 'first foot' through the door, and as tradition in Scotland demanded, he brought coal wrapped in newspaper, a paper twist of salt and a small, traditional, black bun to bring them luck for the New Year. Linda followed him in the door.

'The black bun hasn't as much fruit in it as last year and I couldn't get ground ginger but I hope it's tasty and that you never go hungry,' she puffed.

'Come away in and thanks for the luck you've brought,' Mary smiled. 'May 1940 be better than 1939 has been.'

'Aye, well, there's no sign of that,' Martin began, until Linda dug him in the ribs with her elbow and he was quiet.

'Aren't you a pretty picture,' Martin said to Kathy, who was in the parlour, pacing about excitedly.

Jeannie had to admit that Kathy looked good. Her younger sister was wearing an olive-green dress with a white Peter Pan collar. She wore a silver necklace, a present from Mary and Jeannie. She had complained earlier to Mary that the outfit was too young for her. She wanted a dress like Jeannie's. To please her, Jeannie had curled her red hair and let her use her lipstick. But Mary had made her rub the lipstick off, saying she was too young for all that. Kathy had pouted but Mary was adamant.

Eileen arrived next. Jeannie welcomed her in and introduced her to the others.

'It's nice to meet you, dear,' Mary said. 'Jeannie talks about you a lot.'

'Does she?' Eileen flushed prettily. 'That's nice.'

Kathy gave her a sideways look. Eileen was beautiful, Jeannie decided. Her blonde hair was perfectly glossy, her green eyes accentuated by black eyeliner and her lips were a deep, ruby red. Kathy couldn't take her gaze off the older girl; she seemed smitten. Eileen chatted to her while Jeannie helped her mother bring in the sherry glasses on a tray. But where was Arthur? Jeannie fretted. He was late. Mary had invited Helen Dunn, too. Had they decided not to come? Perhaps the Dougal festivities were beneath them.

There was a knock at the door. Jeannie flew to it and opened it. Arthur and Helen stood in the doorway, their coats covered in snowflakes.

'Come away in, please. Let me take your coats. What a night!' Jeannie said, talking too much in relief.

'We drove down,' Arthur said. 'It's too far for Mother to walk.'

'Of course,' Jeannie said, as if people in Kiltie Street had cars and drove all over the place, when in fact she had never been inside a motor car. 'Well, I'm glad you made it. Everyone is here. Please come through.'

'You're looking lovely tonight,' Arthur said, leaning in and giving her an unexpected kiss on her cheek.

Jeannie hugged him impulsively. His arms wrapped around her and he returned her embrace before setting her back on her feet and giving a little awkward cough. Beside him, Helen smiled at them both and it warmed Jeannie's heart. They were going to be her family. She was so very lucky.

She felt awkward and very aware of how small their home was compared to the Dunns'. Helen didn't appear to notice however and allowed Arthur to guide her through to the parlour. Introductions were made and the comfortable armchair given to Helen. Mary brought her a soft blanket for her knees.

Jeannie and Kathy laid out the food in the kitchen for their guests to help themselves. Eileen came through to help and Kathy dashed back through to the parlour, keen to be in the thick of the chat.

'That's a nice dress,' Eileen said to Jeannie.

'It was my present from Mammy and Kathy. What did you get from your parents?'

'A pair of socks and a sewing kit. Very practical. Mum and Dad always give me something to improve me.'

Jeannie didn't know what to say. There was an unhappiness about Eileen despite her gaiety at the factory and her stories of the dance halls. All she could do was offer her friendship. She wasn't sure it was enough.

'It was so nice of you to invite me tonight,' Eileen said.

'I'm so glad you came. It's lovely to have a friend to stay.'

'It's lovely to have a best friend to share things with,' Eileen smiled at her. 'In fact, I was going to ask you about last week… it felt like you were going to tell me something but then you didn't?'

'Oh… it was about Arthur but I didn't want to burden you.'

'It's not a burden if we're friends, is it? A problem shared is a problem halved, or so my granny would say.'

'It's silly but I was wondering if I'd made a mistake getting engaged. Arthur can be… distant sometimes. But then tonight he's hugged and kissed me and I know he loves me. He just finds it hard to show it.'

Eileen hooked her arm into Jeannie's and pulled her in tight. 'You're very lucky, you've found your man. Hang on to him, that's my advice. I wish I could find a special chap.'

'You're so beautiful, of course you'll meet someone,' Jeannie said. 'And, in the meantime, you've got me as your best friend for company.'

'That's the nicest thing anyone's ever said to me,' Eileen said. 'Best friends forever, Jeannie Dougal. That's a promise.'

The party grew noisier as the evening progressed. Martin's cheeks were red with the heat of the fire and more than a couple of glasses of whiskey. Even Helen had colour in her face after accepting one of Mary's generous glasses of sherry. The plates of food were eaten with great enjoyment and then they sang old favourites such as 'We Three Kings' and 'Auld Lang Syne'. They wished each other a Happy New Year and raised a toast to absent friends. Despite the jollity, they were all too conscious of the events happening in Europe and Jeannie felt Jimmy's absence keenly. Whenever she looked at Mary, there was a sadness in her mother's eyes although she was a good hostess, singing along with the rest of them and keeping the conversation going.

After that, Martin and Linda said their goodnights and went across the corridor to their own home. A short while later, Arthur said it was time he and his mother went. Jeannie put her coat on to see them to their car. Arthur fussed over Helen, telling her how to get into the car. Jeannie wondered that she didn't snap at him, he was so bossy. He shut the passenger door and turned to Jeannie.

She knew better than to expect a passionate kiss from him. Especially outside and with Helen in the car nearby. The snowflakes swirled around them. It could have been a romantic moment, she thought.

'I won't see you for ages,' she said.

He leaned in and kissed her cheek. His fingers touched her face and Jeannie shivered with pleasure.

'Just remember you're mine,' Arthur said. 'No one else will want you with that birthmark disfiguring your face. But I want you, Jeannie. I will be back for you.'

She was stunned at his cruel remark. It was as if he'd landed a blow on her cheek. Hurt and upset, she could hardly look at him as he slid behind the steering wheel and the car drove off.

Chapter Seven

The wintry weather continued into January. Everyone agreed it was the worst winter for a long while. The pipes froze in Kiltie Street and for a few days the Dougals and their neighbours had to trudge along to the last tenement in the row, where Harry Woodley's tap was thankfully working. Martin and Harry fixed up a hosepipe and this was used to fill kettles and pans. Mary kept a kettle on the range so that the family had warm water to wash their hands.

Despite the days when there were storms and flurries of snow and a few mornings when they stepped off the doorstep and sank up and over their ankles into the drifts, Mary was able to travel to Perthshire and bring Isa and Bob back home.

Most of the children in Kiltie Street had come back by now, since there was no sign of invasion or bombing. The schools were still shut and the street rang with the sound of children's shrieks as they hurled snowballs at each other and built snowmen with increasingly dirty snow.

There had been no warning of Mary Dougal's visit and Agatha Main had to school her features when she opened the door to Isa and Bob's mother.

'I've come to take them home,' the woman standing on her doorstep told her.

Agatha saw the swirling snowflakes drift onto Mrs Dougal's wool coat and melt like tears.

'Come in, please. Where are my manners? You must be freezing. How was your journey?'

She kept the conversation going as she led the way into her warm kitchen. Isa was mixing dough in a large, brown ceramic bowl while Bob was intent on his beloved comics, sitting at the table and kicking the chair legs as he'd been told not to do a hundred times.

'Mammy!' Isa dropped the wooden spoon and ran to her mother, pressing her head to her mother's chest with a wide smile as her arms went round Mary's middle.

'How did you get here?' Bob said in surprise. He leapt up too and hugged her other side so that Mary Dougal looked as if she'd sprouted extra arms and legs.

Agatha calmly filled the kettle and put it on the range to heat. Inside, her heart was pounding and every beat told her that she was going to lose the children. Of course, she knew that it had to happen. But so soon? They'd hardly been with her but for a few months. She had thought… hoped… they might have stayed until the war was won. And anyone sensible had known it wasn't going to be over by the Christmas just gone, and possibly not by the next one either.

'You'll take a cup of tea?' she asked.

'Thank you,' Mary said.

'Isa, help me set the table. Show your mother what a big help you've been to me.'

Isa obediently set out the table mats and brought cups and saucers. She carefully sliced a fruit cake that Agatha brought down from the shelf and Bob gave each of them a small plate to put it on.

'There's no bombing in Glasgow. All the children are coming back. I've come to bring you home. To Kiltie Street,' Mary said.

'I don't want to go,' Isa said. 'I want to stay here. You take Bob and I'll stay.'

Agatha looked at the girl she'd come to love as her own. 'You'll do what your mother says, Isa.' Oh Lord, but it hurt.

'I'll come home with you, Mammy,' Bob said. 'But, I'll miss Isa if she's not coming and I don't want to go without Miss Main and Daisy and Penny. Can they come too?'

For a moment, the two women stared at each other in perfect understanding. Despite the awful burning in her chest, Agatha knew that between them, they had to make it right for the children. That was all that mattered.

'Daisy and Penny wouldn't like the big city,' she said gently. 'So, I'll have to stay here and look after them while you help your mother by going home. Can you do that for me?'

Isa looked miserable but the children both nodded, glancing between Agatha and their mother as if unsure who to please and what to do.

'There's an early bus and train tomorrow,' Mary said. 'We'll be home before you know it. Jeannie and Kathy are looking forward to seeing you.'

'I'll make you up a bed in the parlour for tonight,' Agatha said.

The mention of Mary Dougal's other children reminded her that she had no claim on Isa and Bob. Not really. She had cared for them as if they were her own but they had their own family. It would be so very quiet when they left but she'd spent many years alone and she'd cope.

Chin up, Agatha! She'd been through worse and survived. She'd manage but she would never forget them.

–

It hadn't been an altogether smooth return to home life.

'We can't eat. We haven't said Grace,' Isa said, as they sat down to dinner.

Mary put her fork and knife down and said a private prayer. She asked God to give her patience with her youngest daughter. She glanced across at Jeannie who had put her own cutlery down patiently. Kathy's lip curled but she said nothing. Bob steepled his small hands earnestly while Isa said the words, 'For what we are about to eat, may the Lord make us truly thankful'.

She stumbled through the rest and looked relieved as she finished with a loud 'Amen.'

They all began to eat. Mary had fried rissoles without onions as there weren't any to be had but the rissoles were bulked with breadcrumbs and quite tasty. Then there were boiled carrots and potatoes, with custard and jam for dessert. Rationing had begun with bacon, butter and sugar and she was certain it wouldn't end there. Jeannie got up and brought the teapot to the table. Surely, they wouldn't ration tea, Mary thought. Where would they be without a strong, hot cuppa?

'Thank goodness the water's on again,' Jeannie said. 'I got fed up lugging the kettle down the road every wee while.' She poured the tea for each of them and for a moment there was peace.

'I'm going to be a farmer when I grow up,' Isa announced.

'Don't be daft, you can't be a farmer,' Kathy said scornfully. 'You'll have to marry a farmer and be the farmer's wife.'

'I can so,' Isa argued. 'I know how to milk Daisy and how to gather the hens' eggs every morning. Miss Main said I was a very clever girl and that I might have been country born.'

Kathy made a face as if to say, 'what nonsense'.

'Let's eat without arguing,' Mary said, trying to keep the peace.

'Miss Main said that an argument is simply a strong discussion,' Isa informed her.

'Is that so?' Mary felt if she heard one more of Miss Main's opinions, she might scream.

She looked at her youngest children. Bob was tucking in vigorously to his dessert and had a smear of jam on his chin. He seemed happy to be home, playing with his friends. When asked about Perthshire, he said he'd had a great time. A happy-go-lucky boy, he was cheerful wherever he was. What a pity that Dennis had never got to meet his younger son. Bob was the image of his father and their personalities were so similar, she knew they'd have got along just fine. It was hard for boys when they had no father figure to look up to. Jimmy did his best but still…

Isa was a different matter. She had made it quite clear she was cross at being brought back to Glasgow. She wanted to stay in the country with Miss Main and the cottage and the animals. She'd changed in looks too, Mary thought with a pang. She had grown while she was away. Now she was all gangly legs and thin arms. She dressed in clothes Miss Main had acquired for her since she had outgrown those she had taken to Perthshire. Today, it was a navy blue skirt and grey cardigan with a darned elbow. Good quality clothes, cared for lovingly and handed down from a local family that Miss Main knew in the village.

Mary was grateful to Miss Main for the excellent care and affection she'd shown her children. But something had vanished, some closeness between her and Isa and she despaired of ever getting it back. She had confessed as much to Harry Woodley, of all people. She had been down to the bottom of the street to fetch more water, a saucepan in each hand, the week before when the pipes were still frozen. He had ushered her in to his ground-floor home. The hosepipe was hanging out of the window but not in use.

She took the opportunity to glance at his home and was surprised to find it was neat and tidy despite the lack of a woman's touch.

'And how are you today, Mrs Dougal?' Harry asked. 'Your fingers are white, not a good sign. You need your gloves on.'

Honestly, who did the man think he was! She had never met such a bossy know-it-all. Still, he was right; her fingers were sore with the cold weather and from holding the metal handles. She handed him the pans and hid her hands in her coat pockets.

'You haven't said,' he prompted, his cheeks bright red with the breeze and his fair hair sticking up in clumps.

'Said what?'

'I asked how you are today.' He whistled as he filled the two pans from his tap.

And for some reason, instead of giving a standard response or telling him to mind his own business, she had told him.

'I've got my children home but I don't think Isa wants to be here and it's hurtful. She wants to be back in the country with Miss Main and Daisy and Penny the hen and all manner of other creatures she's given names to.' Mary sighed and then winced as the blood came back into her fingertips from the warm kitchen.

'Ah, well, give her space. I'm sure she'll adjust. Young 'uns are adaptable, aren't they,' he said in his Yorkshire accent which she still found difficult to understand sometimes.

'You don't have children,' Mary stated. By which she meant that he couldn't possibly understand what she was going through. Even as she said it, she knew it was not a kind thing to say.

'No. My wife and I were not blessed in that way.'

There was an awkward pause, then she took the full pans with a small nod of thanks and hurried away. She couldn't help it. He put her back up, like an angry cat, hackles raised.

Jeannie's voice broke into her uneasy thoughts and brought her back to the present.

'What's that, love?' she asked.

'I was saying that I'm going out dancing this evening as it's Friday. Eileen's coming by and we'll get the bus into town together.'

'That's nice.' Mary approved of Eileen, having met her at New Year. Besides, it would do Jeannie good to go out and have fun. She was too pale and had been quiet since the New Year party. Mary put it down to her missing Arthur, who hadn't yet written.

'Can I go, Mammy?' Kathy pleaded.

'You know the answer to that,' Mary said. 'Now, help me clear up the dinner dishes. Isa can wash up and you

91

can dry them. Afterwards, we can put the wireless on and listen to some music with cocoa. That sounds like a lovely Friday evening to me. Bob, wipe the jam off your face and get your pyjamas on.'

–

Jeannie went into the back room, leaving a commotion behind. Isa was singing and crashing plates, Kathy was complaining to Mammy and Bob was doing a good job of not going into the back room to get ready for bed. She slipped on her blue dress with the white polka dots and rolled her stockings up her legs. Her old shoes would have to do. She rubbed in black boot polish on the heels where they were scuffed, careful not to get it on her dress. Her hair was freshly washed and dried before the fire and needed only a brush to bring out its shine. A little dab behind the ears with Mammy's precious White Lilac perfume and she was ready.

She took her engagement ring off and laid it on the dressing table. It glinted as if in reproach. She hesitated, then slowly took it up again and slid it onto her ring finger. Normally, she would never have said yes to Eileen's wheedling about going dancing. Even if saying no would have meant Eileen might have to go on her own. Janet and Alan were having another evening to themselves at the cinema and Annie, for some reason, couldn't go.

Arthur didn't like her going dancing. Jeannie knew it and that's why she always said no when invited to go. He hadn't outright told her he didn't like it but whenever she suggested going, he always found an excuse not to go and there was an assumption that she wouldn't go on her own.

But Arthur had hurt her badly with his last remark before he left. Her self-confidence, always low, had dipped even further. Never a rebel and shy by nature, Jeannie nevertheless had her pride. Arthur may have dented it badly but she wasn't completely beaten down. Going to the dancing was a way of getting back at him, she admitted to herself. Besides, he didn't have to know she'd gone. It would be her little secret. She applied her coral lipstick and smiled at her reflection.

Eileen arrived in a puff of freezing air. She pulled her woollen beret off, revealing perfectly curled blonde hair and laughed. 'I feel like a snowman in this weather. We're lucky the buses are running.'

She didn't look like a snowman. Her lipstick was crimson and matched her dress. Jeannie had seen it before; it was Eileen's favourite. It wasn't as if either girl had a large selection of dresses to choose from. But it didn't matter what Eileen wore, she always looked gorgeous. Jeannie wasn't envious. She couldn't compete and didn't want to. She was content to be her plainer friend.

'You look lovely,' Mary said, giving Eileen a warm hug.

Eileen looked momentarily surprised before hugging Jeannie's mother back.

'Thank you. Jeannie does too, don't you think? The blue dress suits your colouring, Jeannie.'

Jeannie smiled, pleased at the compliment. 'Let's go before the snow starts again, shall we? Night, Mammy. Don't wait up.'

'I will wait up and expect you home at a reasonable hour,' Mary said sternly but she was smiling too and Jeannie kissed her soft cheek.

'I love you, Mammy.'

'Och, away with you and enjoy yourselves. You're only young once.'

'You could come too, Mrs Dougal,' Eileen suggested. 'Have a twirl on the dance floor?'

They all laughed and the two young women buttoned their coats, wrapped their scarves around their necks and pulled their woollen berets down over their ears before venturing out to the bus stop.

Locarno's was hot and busy, the air thick with grey cigarette smoke. They left their coats in the cloakroom and weaved their way to an empty table. Soon, they were sipping lemonade and watching the dance floor. As yet, the young men in their khaki and blue were lounging at the sides of the room and propping up the bar, watching the girls. A few brave souls were already dancing in the public eye and gradually more couples drifted onto the dance floor.

'It's a shame Janet and Annie aren't here,' Jeannie leaned across to speak to Eileen. It was hard to hear with the loud music from the live band blasting out.

'Janet and Alan are going to the cinema to see Betty Grable in *Million Dollar Legs*,' Eileen said, shaking her head. 'Honestly, those two are inseparable these days. I can hear wedding bells. Which Janet deserves. She's the most cheerful person I know in spite of the long hours at the factory and this horrid war.'

'I'm glad she's got Alan,' Jeannie agreed. 'What about Annie, why's she not out tonight?'

'You know Annie,' Eileen shrugged. 'Ever mysterious. It doesn't matter how long we've been friends now, I can't place her somehow. Anyway, she wouldn't say why she can't come tonight.'

Jeannie was actually a bit relieved. Although they were all friends, she didn't click with Annie like she did with Eileen and Janet, and dreaded her occasional sharp retorts.

Whereas they were like water off a duck's back to Eileen. She never let Annie's little comments affect her.

'What made you change your mind?' Eileen asked. 'I thought Arthur didn't like you coming dancing?'

'He doesn't but… well, he doesn't need to know everything.' Jeannie felt bold saying it and when Eileen threw back her head and laughed, she felt strong and independent. It was heady, like a sip of Mammy's New Year sherry.

There was a prickle between her shoulder blades as if someone was watching her and she turned and glanced around.

'When are we going to get asked to dance?' Eileen said, tapping her fingernails impatiently on the table. Then her smile widened as her gaze fixed beyond Jeannie. 'Hello, who's this?'

'Care to dance?' Two soldiers arrived at their table.

The taller one had his gaze firmly fixed on Eileen. He was handsome, with slicked-back black hair and even features to go with broad shoulders and long, muscular legs.

'I'm Jonny and this is my pal, Bill.' His accent was not local.

The other soldier was shorter with brown hair a shade lighter than Jeannie's and hazel eyes.

'Are you American?' Eileen fluttered her eyelashes and pushed a blonde curl behind her ear. Jonny seemed mesmerised.

'Canadian,' Bill said.

Jonny gallantly offered his arm to Eileen and they went off to the dance floor without another word. Jeannie's heart pounded nervously. She hadn't expected to be left with a strange man. But then, what had she expected? Of course Eileen would dance and not be short of partners. The question was, what should Jeannie do now?

'Would you like to dance?' Bill asked.

She shook her head. He sat opposite her and she wished he'd go away. She took a sip of her lemonade.

'Can I get you another of those?' he said.

'No, thanks. I'm only halfway through this.'

He took a swig of his beer. Jeannie took another sip of her drink. This is ridiculous, she thought. I'm not even thirsty. It's just something to do with my hands. Maybe I'll sit on them instead!

'So, you don't like dancing?'

Jeannie, having avoided his gaze so far, looked up to find him smiling and his eyes creased in a friendly manner.

'I'm engaged.' She splayed her fingers so he couldn't miss the ring with its lovely chip of diamond.

'Nice,' he commented.

There was another silence. The back of Jeannie's neck was hot and she lifted her hair from it. Couldn't he take a heavy hint? She wasn't interested. The music stretched on as if the dance would never end.

'Look,' Bill said, finally. 'It's only a dance. I like dancing and I'd be glad to partner you, no strings attached. Honest.'

The music changed for the next dance and Eileen and Jonny didn't reappear.

'Very well,' she said stiffly. 'I'd like to dance.'

'That's good, because you're at a dance hall.'

Again, she wasn't sure if he was teasing her. His accent was a rich, lazy drawl that was attractive. It should have sounded out of place in a Glasgow dance hall but these days, Jeannie heard all sorts of voices as she went about town. People were mixing and travelling through as the armed forces moved strategically around Britain.

It was strange to be held by a man that wasn't Arthur. Bill was a good dancer, she realised. He kept time to the music and moved her expertly and soon she was enjoying herself immensely. She glimpsed Eileen's blonde hair in the crowd and Jonny was a head taller than most of the other men in the room. They danced three in succession before Jeannie asked for a break.

Bill disappeared to get more drinks and Eileen and Jonny arrived back at the table, laughing with heads together. So that's the way it goes, Jeannie thought. She hoped Eileen wouldn't abandon her to get home alone in the freezing dark.

'Gee, you girls know how to show a guy a good time,' Jonny said, sitting next to Eileen. He couldn't take his eyes off her. 'How about another dance once we've sat for five minutes?'

'I'm up for that, if you are,' Eileen said, fanning herself from the heat. 'The next is a slow waltz.'

Jonny's eyebrows rose and his smile widened. He winked at Jeannie and she looked away, embarrassed. She pretended to search for Bill and actually felt relieved to see his stocky figure calmly walking back from the bar between the crush of bodies. Soon, Eileen and Jonny were lost in the dancing again while she and Bill sat and drank. Now she was glad of the lemonade.

'Did you want something stronger?' Bill asked, pointing at her drink.

She frowned. 'No, thank you.' What kind of girl did he think she was?

They sat for a while longer.

'You don't have to sit here with me, you know,' she said. 'Your friend Jonny is quite taken with my friend Eileen but that doesn't mean we have to keep company. You can ask another girl to dance.'

Bill nodded. When Jeannie stubbornly stared in front of her, he finally got up and left. She didn't see him for a few minutes then spotted him on the dance floor with a slender girl in a yellow dress. There was a brief burning sensation in her chest. Jeannie turned away. She was not humiliated. She had told him to go. She rubbed her diamond. She was going to be Mrs Arthur Dunn one day soon. Suddenly, she wanted to go home.

'Please, Eileen,' she hissed, when she caught hold of her friend.

Jonny had gone to the bar.

'Right now?' Eileen asked, reluctantly. She looked at Jeannie and relented. 'All right, let me say goodnight to Jonny. You get the coats. Where's Bill?'

'Never mind Bill,' Jeannie said. 'Just hurry up!'

The frozen air sharpened her mind and brought her senses back as they hurried along to catch the bus. They gripped each other's hand and giggled as they tried not to slip on the icy pavements in the pitch dark. Jeannie's torch gave out its usual feeble yellow light that showed very little. Eileen's wasn't much better.

They sat on the bus, shivering. There was no heating and it rattled along through the night.

'Jonny wants to see me again,' Eileen said happily.

'He's very good-looking,' Jeannie offered.

'Mmm, isn't he, though?' Eileen agreed dreamily. 'Like a film star with that handsome face and American drawl.'

'He's not American. Bill said they were Canadians.'

'American, Canadian, it's all the same to me. Quite exotic and different from this old dump.'

'I didn't realise you hated Glasgow.'

Eileen sighed and leaned her head against the bus window. 'I don't really. Forget what I said. I'm being silly. Sometimes, I… I'd like to get away from here. That's all.'

'Will you see him again?' Jeannie changed the subject.

'Yes, I will. What about Bill?'

'Oh, no. He was only there because Jonny likes you. I've got Arthur, of course. I can't go around with other men.'

'Why not? Arthur won't know. You might like someone else better in the end.'

Jeannie was scandalised. 'I'm engaged to Arthur. I'd never break that. Mammy would never forgive me for the shame.'

'Sorry,' Eileen yawned. 'I didn't mean to upset you. Here's your stop. See you Monday.'

Jeannie waved goodbye and stepped off the bus into mushy snow which sank into her stockings over her shoes. Her feet were soaked and frozen. It must have snowed again while they were at Locarno's.

'Uggh,' she said out loud.

Another bus went by, sending up a spray of dirty water and she shrieked. Head down, she began to walk in the direction of Kiltie Street.

Gradually, she became aware of footsteps behind her. She hurried on, her feet slipping on the wet, snowy pavement. She thought whoever was behind her speeded up too. Jeannie gripped her torch. She glanced back over her shoulder but it was so dark she saw nothing. Or was that a darker shadow? Convinced someone was following her,

Jeannie's heart started pumping far too fast. Her palms were clammy despite the cold.

She was nearly home. As she turned the corner into Kiltie Street, a figure loomed out of the black. With a scream, Jeannie fell off the kerb. She landed heavily on her knees and cried out with the pain.

'Get away from me,' she yelled, as the man approached. 'I've got a weapon.' Her torch had flickered and died but it was heavy. It could land a good blow.

'Jeannie? Are you all right? It's me, Bill.'

Her fear subsided and anger took its place. What on earth was Bill doing here? Had he followed her from the dance hall? The cheek of him!

'Why are you here?' she snapped.

She struggled up from the slush, her dress and stockings drenched and her knees stinging. He offered his hand but she brushed it away.

'I got on the bus after yours,' Bill said, 'I'm trying to get to my barracks but I'm lost. I followed you, thinking this was the way.' He scratched his head. 'But it's not.'

'Oh.' She felt foolish.

She took a step onto the pavement and winced. Her knees really were sore.

'Here, let me take you home first,' Bill said. 'Then I'll find my barracks. It's the least I can do.'

She was going to argue but a wave of faintness washed over her. She was tired and in pain. She leaned right in to him, linking her arm with his. She was aware of his warmth and an aroma of cigarettes, beer and some kind of plain soap. Together, they hobbled the short distance down Kiltie Street to number four.

'Where's your friend Jonny?' Jeannie asked.

'He missed the bus. Is this your house?'

He held her carefully as they went up the stone steps and Jeannie fumbled for her key. She needn't have bothered. The door swung open and there was Mary. She had stayed up, waiting.

'What's happened to you? Heavens, your knees are bleeding. Come away in.'

Soon, Jeannie was sitting in the warm kitchen while Mary dabbed at her knees with cotton and Dettol. It stung horribly. She bit her lip to prevent a cry. Bill sat, looking relaxed. He had politely turned away while Jeannie took off her stockings.

'Thank you for bringing her home,' Mary said to him.

'It's no trouble, ma'am.'

'I'd like to thank you properly. Will you come for your lunch tomorrow? We're not far from the barracks and it'll be Sunday. Surely, they'll let you come?'

'That's very kind. I'd like to.'

Jeannie was aghast. What was Mammy doing? She didn't want Bill to spend a lunch with them. She'd spent the latter part of the evening getting rid of him. But it was no use. Once Mary got an idea, she saw it through. Jeannie could argue all she liked; it was too late to change her mother's mind.

They watched him merge with the darkness outside once Mary had given him instructions for how to find his barracks.

'What a nice young man. Thank goodness he found you.'

'I'd have been fine.' She sounded grumpy and she knew it.

'You go on through. You look exhausted,' Mary said, firmly.

And that was the end of the matter.

On Sunday morning, Mary was making fish paste sandwiches for lunch. There was a small sponge cake, made with margarine and not butter. She hoped it was enough for them plus Bill. There was a hard knock at the door. It was too early for their visitor. She wiped her hand on her apron and went to see. Harry Woodley stood there, beaming.

'Where's your Isa?'

'Pardon?' she said.

Isa ran through from the sitting room where she was playing with her paper dolls and stood beside her, curious. Mary wasn't going to admit she was curious too.

'Come on, then. Come and see what I've got,' Harry said.

He set off towards number eight without looking back. Mary and Isa stared at each other, then Mary shrugged. They put on their coats and went after him. He didn't go into his home but went through the close and out into the back court.

'What is that?' Mary asked.

Besides the Anderson shelter, the back garden of the tenement was simply grass. But now, a makeshift fence of corrugated metal making a square had been set up. Harry lifted Isa and she peered in.

'Come and see, Mammy!' she cried.

Mary went over, gingerly. She looked in to see a piglet snuffling in the grass. It had dug up little brown patches. There was a wooden box for it to shelter and straw to curl up in.

'You want to be a farmer, don't you?' Harry said to Isa. She nodded, excitedly.

'Well, here's your chance. You can help look after piggy here by collecting scraps from the neighbours to feed him.'

'Can I, Mammy? Please, please…'

Mary hadn't seen Isa grin since she came home. Her little face was lit up with anticipation.

'What is all this?' she said to Harry.

'We're starting a pig club. Lots of people are doing it. We'll be properly registered, don't you worry about that. The government will get their share, sadly. What do you say? Are you in?'

Isa was jumping up and down with joy. Harry's big red face was grinning. Mary threw up her hands. She knew when she was beaten. She watched the big man and the little girl as they talked about the piglet. There was a kindness to him, she realised, beneath all his bluster. He'd listened to her worries about Isa. And he'd found an answer that even she had been helpless to find.

Chapter Eight

Bill arrived for lunch, bringing chocolates. Jeannie knew he'd appeared in Kiltie Street because she heard the local children shouting. When she leaned out the window it was to see him with a band of them following. She noticed a few of the younger women leaning out of their windows to watch him, too. It wasn't every day that a uniformed male walked along and up the close to number four. She could just imagine the gossip.

His hair was neatly brushed and he took off his cap politely as he was invited in. Jeannie had set the table with Mary's good tablecloth and placed the plate of sandwiches on it and the sponge cake in the centre. Mary had insisted on using her best china tea set despite Jeannie's protests.

'He's not the king coming to visit,' she said to her mother.

Mary raised her eyebrows. 'He's a young man far from home, fighting for our country. I like to think that wherever Jimmy is, someone might do the same for him. Besides, didn't he rescue you last night and all?'

Jeannie put out the cups and saucers without further argument. Mammy had made a good point. Kathy laid out the napkins.

'Is he handsome?' she asked, flicking back her red hair.

'No, he's not,' Jeannie said shortly.

Kathy stuck out her tongue at Jeannie. 'What's got into you? A barrel of laughs today.'

'I don't see why Mammy invited him, that's all. I've got other things to do with my day off.'

'Like what?' Kathy said. 'Arthur's away. If your Bill wasn't visiting, Mammy would have us clean the brasses. So I, for one, am grateful he's here for lunch.'

'He's not my Bill,' Jeannie said.

Kathy looked at her slyly. 'If he's not yours, can I have him?'

'Don't be ridiculous. He's not a toy to be handed about.'

The knock on the door halted further bickering. Isa, who'd been listening avidly to her older sisters, ran to open it. Bob left his jigsaw and stared in interest at their visitor. Bill, quite at ease, took the offered chair and smiled at them all. Jeannie was annoyed to find that in the daylight he was not bad-looking at all. Kathy nudged her but she ignored her.

'Hello, Bill,' Kathy said, stepping forward and holding out her hand. 'Thank you for saving our Jeannie last night.'

Jeannie rolled her eyes. She caught Bill glancing at her with his warm smile, and blushed.

'Let's sit up and eat,' Mary said, bringing the teapot to the table. 'Bill, I do hope this is enough. I'm sure you're used to better, coming from Canada.'

'Mammy, what do you know about Canada?' Kathy asked. 'Why are they better than us?'

Bob sidled up to Bill, leaning onto his arm, and pushed his toy aeroplane under his nose. 'Do you know what this is?'

Bill took it and studied it seriously. Bob rubbed his nose with the back of his sleeve until Mary swatted him.

'I'd say that's a fine Spitfire you have there,' Bill said easily.

Bob nodded and insisted he sit right at Bill's side. Kathy swiftly took the seat on his other side and smiled prettily. That meant Jeannie was sitting opposite him so when he looked up, he was gazing right into her eyes. Blast the man. She kept her own gaze on her plate as if the fish paste sandwich was fascinating. Mammy was chatting politely, asking Bill about his family.

'My father's an engineer. He works on roads and bridges mainly. My mom is a home-maker and I have one sister, Amy, who's a kindergarten teacher.'

'Kindergarten?'

'She teaches the little kids not yet ready for school.'

'I go to school,' Bob piped up. 'But school's shut now so I play with my friends instead,' he finished gleefully.

'Don't get too used to it,' Mary warned. 'Miss Tomlinson told me they'll be open again on half days soon.'

Bob pulled a face and they all laughed.

'I didn't much like school myself,' Bill told Bob, 'but if you stick with it and get your grades, you can get a job you enjoy afterwards.'

'Did you have a job in Canada?' Kathy asked.

She propped her chin on her hands and fluttered her eyelashes. If Jeannie could have reached, she'd have given her sister a kick under the table. Bill answered as if he hadn't noticed Kathy's flirting.

'I was studying to be a mechanic. I guess I'll go back to it when this is all over.'

There was a brief silence as they were reminded as ever of the war and its impacts.

'We've got a pig,' Isa said, breaking the pause. 'I call her Patty but Harry says we shouldn't name her 'cause one day we're going to eat her. Do you want to see her?'

'Perhaps later, love,' Mary said. 'Bill hasn't had any sponge cake yet. Jeannie, cut some slices. More tea, Bill?'

Jeannie cut generous slices of cake, and handed one on a plate to Bill. He smiled as he took it but Jeannie didn't smile back.

'Thanks, this looks great, Mrs Dougal. So, Isa, tell me about Patty. Where do you keep your pig? Did you know there are lots of farms in Canada? In fact, there's a pig farm not far from where I live.'

Isa regaled him with Patty's good points – of which there were many – and told him about how they gathered up the swill and how Patty loved cabbage leaves.

'Is Canada like Glasgow?' Bob interrupted.

Bill grinned. 'It's like Glasgow in that the people are friendly. There are lots of Scottish folk or people who can trace their ancestors back here. But it's a big place, you know. Wide open grasslands and big forests that stretch for miles. Lots of fresh air. At least, where I come from. There are cities too but I'm a country boy.'

'Did you want to come and fight?'

'Bob,' Mary warned.

Bill shook his head. 'It's all right, Mrs Dougal. It's a good question, Bob. When the call came to defend the motherland, I took it. It's the right thing to do. No one wants a war but we can't let Hitler win. There are plenty of Canadians who feel the same way. I came over on a ship with a lot of them.'

'Is there really a farm full of pigs near your home? Don't they have cows and chickens like the village we lived in?' Isa said, turning the subject back to what she was interested in.

Jeannie watched as he chatted with Isa, and Bob chipped in too. He was very relaxed around the children and patiently answered all their questions. She could see that Mammy liked him. Kathy seemed infatuated. Only Jeannie wished him gone. She knew she was being unfair. He had kind hazel eyes and the creases around them suggested he laughed a lot. His smile was endearing and he had a crooked front tooth.

After lunch, Jessie called for Isa, and Bob went with them. There was a game of hopscotch outside on the street for the girls and marbles for the boys. Jeannie took the plates through to the kitchen to wash up. Bill came through and offered to dry.

'You're the guest, you don't have to do that,' Mary told him.

Kathy called for her and Mary excused herself. While she was gone, Jeannie turned to Bill.

'Mammy's right. You shouldn't be doing the washing up. Go back to the living room.'

'Is that a direct order?' Bill asked.

Jeannie frowned at him but he simply took a tea towel, picked up the first plate and began to dry it.

'And don't mention that we met at that dance,' she hissed, keeping an eye out for Mammy's return.

'My lips are sealed.'

She sloshed a plate, giving an involuntary cry as hot, soapy water splashed onto her dress.

'Does it matter if we met at a dance?' Bill said.

Jeannie mopped her damp dress with the hand towel and glared at him. 'Of course it does. I'm engaged to

Arthur. I shouldn't have been dancing with someone else. Mammy might wonder at you following me home.'

'I wasn't following you home,' Bill reminded her. 'I was trying to find my barracks.'

'It doesn't matter,' she said, flinging the towel down. 'Just don't mention anything. Please.'

'As you like. It was only a dance, you know. Nothing else.'

Why did her stomach flip when he said that? Of course it was only a dance but he didn't have to make it so plain that he wasn't interested in her. She knew that her birthmark put men off. He didn't have to spell it out. She touched a finger to her cheek, unconsciously tracing its faintly raised border.

Mary bustled in. 'That girl will be the death of me. She's only gone and snagged her cuff on the door handle and wants me to sew it right there and then. As she's fifteen, she can sew it herself. Now, Bill, another cup of tea?'

'Bill has to go back to his barracks, Mammy,' Jeannie cut in. 'We can't be greedy and take up all his free time.'

'Well, we've enjoyed your company,' Mary said. 'Thank you for the chocolates.'

'Thank you for lunch,' Bill replied. 'I've enjoyed myself too. You have a lovely family, Mrs Dougal.'

He collected his cap and put it on as he left. Jeannie and Kathy stood behind Mary at the door as she saw him out.

'Come and see us again,' Mary called. 'Don't be a stranger.'

Bill waved and then he was walking smartly along Kiltie Street with Bob and his friends running alongside.

'Why did you invite him to visit again?' Jeannie cried.

'What's got into you, love?' Mary said. 'It's unlike you to be so unkind. He's a young man, far from home. It's not much, sharing a meal and a conversation but it's the least we can do.'

Jeannie flushed at Mammy's gentle reproof. She knew she was acting strangely but she couldn't help it. Bill unsettled her but she didn't know why.

–

'I don't know what got into her. It was rude, the way she said he had to go,' Mary told Helen Dunn later that afternoon, as she delved into her knitting bag for a partly done army sock.

'It doesn't sound like Jeannie,' Helen agreed. 'She's such a lovely young woman. She's a credit to you, Mary.'

Mary had taken to visiting Helen instead of Jeannie whose hours at the factory were longer these days, leaving her less time to check in on Arthur's mother. At first, Mary had been daunted by the size of the house and the signs of wealth but Helen's friendliness had put her at ease. She had been prepared to find Helen as stiff and proper as Arthur but had gone to the house feeling it her duty to look after Jeannie's soon-to-be mother-in-law. She was pleasantly surprised to find that Helen had a quiet sense of humour and didn't seem to mind the difference in their stations in life.

Perhaps she should've expected that. After all, Helen had been to their small home for New Year and appeared to enjoy herself. It was a far cry from this large, silent house. Given the choice though, Mary would always take her own wee flat for its warmth and company. There wasn't a chance to be lonely there.

Anticipating the wedding had given them something in common to discuss. They soon realised how easy it was to chat with one another.

'Hmm, that's nice of you to say, but she wasn't at her best today and I've no idea why,' Mary sighed. 'Perhaps it's this awful war. It's changing people. They said it would be over by Christmas and now here we are at the end of January and it's only going to get worse.'

'It's a terrible time,' Helen agreed. 'Especially when we both have sons in the army. But we must make it through each day and keep our chins up.'

'I feel ashamed being so negative. You're absolutely right.'

'Don't be ashamed. We all have our moments. I certainly do. I have too much time to think, sitting here looking out the window all day.'

'How are your joints today? Can I get you anything?'

'I have a little more energy today.'

Mary noticed that Helen looked brighter, with more colour in her usually pale cheeks. She was sitting upright instead of lying down, and her blanket had been put aside.

'Have you got another pair of knitting needles?' Helen asked.

'Indeed I do. Will you knit with me?' Mary said, pleased. 'I've to finish this pair of socks and another dozen intended.'

'I haven't knitted in ages so I'll be rusty but I'd like to give it a go.'

Mary handed Helen the needles and a ball of green wool along with the pattern. She didn't need to see the pattern herself; it was imprinted on her mind now that she'd made so many socks. She planned to make scarves and vests too for the services. Maybe one would reach

Jimmy. They had had a letter from him recently but no mention of where he was, just that he was fine and they weren't to worry.

'Have you heard from Arthur?' she asked Helen.

'I've had two letters since he was home at New Year. He's in England though he can't say where. He doesn't tell me much about himself. Mostly, he sends instructions of what I've to do.'

Mary didn't know what to make of that. She looked up from her row of plain and purl to see Helen's mischievous smile.

'Arthur cares for you so well,' she said.

Helen sighed and set her knitting aside. Mary noticed she had only knitted a row. At this rate, her army sock wasn't going to appear for a few weeks, let alone its matching pair.

'The trouble with Arthur is that he cares too much.'

'What does that mean? If you don't mind my asking.'

'It means… well, you're right, Arthur does care for me in his own way and I shouldn't mind. You see, he's a chip off the old block. The very image of his father. Sandy died two years ago and Arthur has taken on his role as man of the house.'

'I'm sorry for your loss,' Mary said, sympathetically. 'You must be very glad you have Arthur to look after you.'

Helen picked up the knitting and slowly began to purl. She spoke again, addressing herself to the wool rather than to Mary.

'Sandy was a difficult man to live with. When I married him, I vowed to love, honour and obey, of course. I didn't realise that the third was to be the most important part of our marriage. He couldn't abide disagreement. Everything had to be done his way.'

She finished a row and turned it. Mary's own knitting had slowed as Helen told her story. It felt almost too intimate. She didn't know the other woman very well and yet she seemed to need to let it all out.

'He was a domineering bully,' Helen went on plainly. 'It became easier not to argue, not to put my point of view across. Not to have opinions. In the end, I took to my bed and slept more and more. I had terrible headaches and started to have joint pains. I became an invalid so that he'd leave me alone.'

'I don't know what to say. I had no idea…'

'I'm embarrassing you,' Helen said, not sounding at all apologetic. 'I feel that we've become friends and I want you to know the real me.'

'I'm so sorry you've had such a terrible time.'

'Thank you, dear. When Sandy passed away, I thought I'd feel better. That sounds awful but it was hard to grieve for my husband, being the man he was. Yet my fatigue continued, along with my pain. Arthur took Sandy's death very hard. He worshipped his father. He treated me in much the same manner only after I was widowed, he took it upon himself to make sure I took my medicine, took my rest and ate well. I think he means well… he doesn't want to lose another parent.'

'Arthur is a fine young man,' Mary said stoutly. 'I hope that he and Jeannie make a good marriage between them.'

Helen's knitting needles clicked furiously and the wool tugged and jumped from the ball.

'I do hope so,' she said finally. 'Do you know, I think I'm quite tired. I might go and lie down. Will you let yourself out, dear?'

As Mary walked down the hill towards home, her thoughts were troubled. Was Jeannie making a mistake, marrying Arthur? If he was really like Helen's husband, would he be a bully to her lovely, shy daughter? But then, Helen had said he meant well and it sounded as if he was being over-protective towards his mother. That was all.

She took in a deep breath of the evening air. Och, she was worrying about nothing. Jeannie would be fine. Imagine her getting to live in that beautiful, big house, probably with a housekeeper to help her cook and clean. It was worlds apart from their flat in Kiltie Street and Jeannie would want for nothing. Arthur had been polite and well-mannered the times Mary had met him. Maybe she'd misunderstood Helen.

–

'You are beautiful, did you know that?' Jonny lay, propped up on one elbow in Eileen's bed, looking down at her.

Shyly, she pulled the sheet up over her bare breasts. Jonny pulled it down again.

'It's too late to be modest.' He stroked his hand over her nipples and she felt them rise with his touch.

They were upstairs in Eileen's bedroom. Her parents were out for the evening. Mr Boyle was at a council meeting as he was now involved in organising the air raid precautions for the local area. Eileen's mother was visiting a friend from the church to discuss the flower arrangements for the following week. Eileen and Jonny had sneaked in the back door after a walk in the nearby fields. She hoped none of the neighbours had seen them. She doubted her parents would care enough to ask questions but if they did, she'd say Jonny came in for one cup of tea before leaving.

He had kissed her as soon as they were in the hallway.

'Jonny!' she whispered. 'What if my parents came back early?'

He ignored that, kissing her more urgently, slipping his hot tongue into her mouth until she gave in and kissed him back. His hands slid up inside her blouse and vest. She felt his fingers curl to the sensitive skin on the curves of her breasts and pushed him away.

'What?' Jonny played the innocent but there was that wicked smile that had charmed her the first time they met.

She felt as if she was burning up with her need for him. 'Wait here,' she said. 'I'll go and check.'

She hurriedly peeked into the kitchen and living room but they were empty. With relief, she realised that both her parents had gone out just as they said they would.

'Wanna check upstairs?' Jonny asked cheekily. 'Are they in the bedrooms, waiting to jump out at us?'

'Don't be daft.' Eileen shoved him with a giggle.

'That's more like it,' Jonny murmured, holding her closely and kissing her again.

Eileen let herself be drawn into it. Her passion was rising, like a wave coming up in stormy weather. Before she knew it, they were lying on her bed and Jonny was tugging at her knickers. She wriggled out of them, desperate for his touch. He fumbled with his own clothes, cursing in his hurry to get out of them. She giggled, feeling the headiness of her own emotions. She was sure she was in love with him.

She felt his hardness poking at her inner thighs, then a moment of pain before he thrust inside her. She gasped. He didn't look at her; his eyes were shut as he moved rhythmically above her. Eileen gripped his shoulders as she moved too. She was beginning to crescendo when he groaned and lay on top of her. For a moment she couldn't get her breath.

He stared down at her and she saw how handsome he was. His fingers stroked her leg. She felt him shift and he turned and slid into her. It was better the second time.

'I love you,' she whispered as they lay back, panting.

Jonny lit a cigarette and she watched the grey smoke rising to her bedroom ceiling. She'd have to open the window when he'd gone otherwise her parents would be suspicious. At least it would get a reaction from them, she thought almost angrily. Sometimes, it felt as if she didn't exist at all.

A tiny part of her wondered if this was why she'd let Jonny make love to her. What if they were discovered? Her mother and father had to react to that. There'd be no avoiding a conversation and a spilling of emotions then. She imagined crying out how much she loved Jonny and that they were getting married whatever her parents thought. She pictured her mother's horrified face and her father's concern that they were doing the right thing.

She saw her father patting Jonny's muscular shoulder and congratulating them both while Agnes Boyle wept tears of happiness, once she had come round to the idea.

'We could get married,' she whispered, rolling onto her side to look at him. 'We love each other, don't we?'

Jonny sucked on his cigarette, making the ash glow. He swung himself out of bed and she saw the muscles ripple in his smooth back. She stroked the bumps of his spine idly, caught up in her own dreams.

'Gotta go, kid,' he said lightly. 'It's been good. See you soon.'

She lay in bed and listened to him patter down the stairs. There was the sound of the back door opening and closing. Eileen snuggled down under her sheet and blanket. Just a moment to savour what they had done and then she'd get up and peel the potatoes for dinner.

Chapter Nine

In February, Arthur came home on a forty-eight-hour pass. Jeannie was desperate to see him but she was due in for her shift at the factory so she had to wait. She met up with Elspeth at the end of the street and they ran along to the bus stop. The bus went ever so slowly as there was a freezing fog covering the streets and making it difficult to see the buildings and other traffic as they trundled along.

She got changed quickly, shrugging on her overalls and pushing her hair up under its turban. The others had already gone through to the factory floor, including Elspeth. She hurried, almost tripping on her own feet, to get to her place but Miss McGrory, stony-faced, beckoned with a commanding finger. Jeannie followed her into the supervisor's office with a sinking feeling.

'You're late, Dougal.'

'I'm sorry, the bus—'

'I don't want excuses. There's a war on, in case you've forgotten. It's not good enough and it's not the first time. I'm putting you on a warning.' Miss McGrory's flinty stare made Jeannie's stomach lurch.

'It won't happen again,' she said.

The supervisor was right; she had been late before but that had been a slow bus too. It had stopped to let on a group of soldiers who had been a merry lot for such an early morning bus ride. There had been a sing-along which had entertained Jeannie and Elspeth and cheered them up before work. Somehow, Elspeth had been spared Miss McGrory's wrath on that occasion too. Jeannie couldn't puzzle out why she was being picked on.

'You're right, it won't happen again,' the supervisor was saying severely, 'because if it does, I'll be docking your wages. Another warning and you're out.'

Jeannie hung her head. Could Miss McGrory actually sack her? Surely they needed all the workers they could get. It wasn't fair. She didn't dare ask why the woman had it in for her. Was she imagining it? But when she braved a glance, Miss McGrory's expression was almost spiteful. Jeannie was shocked.

'Now, get out there and do your job,' she spat.

Jeannie fled. Her hands were trembling as she fed the machine with parts. Eileen threw her a sympathetic look but Jeannie knew she'd burst into tears if her friends were nice to her right then. She concentrated on her task and comforted herself with thoughts of Arthur. It would be lovely to see him after all these weeks.

'Old McGrowly was on the war path today, was she not?' Annie said as they put their trays down at a table in the canteen at dinner time.

'Yes, and I was in the firing line,' Jeannie said, glumly.

'What happened?' Eileen squeezed her arm comfort-ingly. 'I knew something had when you were late in and then Miss McGrory appeared after you. She reminds me of a teacher I had at primary school who terrified me. She had a face like that, too.'

Jeannie took a forkful of vegetable pie but found it hard to swallow. She coughed and Janet had to thump her back for her.

'She's put me on a warning because I've been late twice even though it was because the bus was slow.'

'That's not fair,' Janet cried. 'How can you help it if the bus is delayed?'

Jeannie shrugged helplessly.

'We'd better all watch out if she's in a bad mood,' Annie said. 'I can't be late home from my shift.'

'Why's that, then?' Janet asked, putting her vegetable pie and mash away at a record speed.

Annie mumbled under her breath and went a beetroot red.

'I don't want to be late tonight either,' Janet said quickly, as they all felt awkward for Annie.

'Meeting your lovely Alan?' Eileen teased.

It was Janet's turn to flush. 'How did you know?'

'Oh, just a lucky guess, I suppose,' Eileen laughed.

'You're always together. It wasn't hard to guess,' Annie said, her colour back to normal and clearly keen to focus the attention away from herself.

Janet sighed. 'I'm in love with him and I think he feels the same way about me.' She turned to Jeannie. 'How's your Arthur?'

'I'm seeing him this evening.'

'We have to grab our happiness, these days, don't we?' Janet scraped the last of her custard from her bowl and beamed at them all.

–

Jeannie was exhausted by the end of the day. Elspeth yawned endlessly as the bus home juddered and creaked in the dark evening.

'I'm away to my bed after dinner, I'm that tired. I feel I could sleep for a hundred years,' Elspeth said. 'What about you?'

'Arthur's home on leave so I'm seeing him.'

'Lucky you. Going to the cinema, are you?' Elspeth's head drooped as another yawn hit her.

'Probably we'll stay in with Arthur's mum.' Jeannie knew it sounded dull. Most couples made the most of any leave and went dancing or to see the latest film. She was very fond of Helen but she really wanted some time with Arthur alone. Maybe she was being selfish.

'Make the most of it.' Elspeth waved goodbye as they arrived at Kiltie Street and she headed up the stone steps to her home. 'You're very lucky to be engaged, and to such a handsome fellow as Arthur Dunn.'

Yes, she was lucky. Jeannie smiled as she headed for her own home. Despite her tiredness and the nastiness of her supervisor, she had a warm glow right there in the middle of her chest. She was in love and she was loved in return. There was nothing to beat that. She was lucky to have a loving family too, she thought, as she arrived home and smelled stew and cabbage simmering on the range.

Her family were sitting at the kitchen table and Mammy was about to serve up.

'There you are,' Mary said. 'You're late.'

Jeannie burst out laughing and the tension of her day evaporated with each convulsion. She wiped her eyes and saw them all staring at her, open-mouthed, which set her off again.

'Oh, I needed that,' she hiccupped and sat down.

'What's that all about?' Mary asked, pushing a plate of hot stew with cabbage and tatties towards her.

'Nothing, just a hard day at work,' she mumbled, shovelling down the stew and savouring its salty taste.

'Mammy, Jeannie's got bad manners,' Isa complained, pointing at her older sister.

'Can I eat like that?' Bob said, eagerly gobbling his own food faster.

'Hold your horses. Jeannie, will you put your fork down for a wee moment, for God's sake. It's not a running race.'

'Sorry, Mammy. Arthur's home and I'm that desperate to see him.'

'Aye, well, I can understand that but you're meant to set an example to the wee ones. So, slow it down, please.'

Kathy nibbled her dinner delicately. She put down her fork and knife in between bites and smiled triumphantly at Jeannie.

'I'm eating nicely, Mammy. Aren't I?'

Mary had a rule that she wouldn't roll her eyes at her offspring but she was hard put on this occasion.

'Yes, love. Very nice. But you, on the other hand, need to eat faster otherwise we'll all be here for a month of Sundays.'

'Don't eat everything,' Isa cried as the family tucked in to their dinner.

'Why ever not?' Mary said.

'It's a crime to waste food,' Kathy chipped in. 'You're meant to scrape your plate clean.'

'Patty needs to eat, too. I'm collecting the scraps and there's not going to be any if you lot keep eating like that,' Isa wailed.

Jeannie and Mary shared a glance. Isa had stopped insisting on saying Grace before meals and references to Miss Main's opinions had waned. Instead, Isa had taken on her role as farmer seriously. She was often to be seen, bucket in hand, pestering the neighbours for their food waste. Patty had to be the most pampered pig this side of the Clyde.

'It's the vegetable peelings that go in the scraps bucket,' Jeannie said gently. 'Not our dinner. I bet Mammy's kept all the tattie skins for Patty, haven't you, Mammy?'

'Of course,' Mary said. 'There's even an outer leaf of cabbage which a beastie had eaten holes in. Patty's favourite veg, isn't it, love?'

Isa sniffed and wiped her nose on her sleeve. She seemed mollified.

'Is Bill coming tonight?' Bob asked, clearing his own plate without a thought for the pig.

'Not this evening. He'll be over in a couple of days. I expect he's kept very busy at the barracks, being in charge of the stores.'

Bill had become part of the family, Jeannie thought sourly. He was liked by everyone and Mary encouraged him to visit when he was able. Only Jeannie had misgivings. He made her feel uncomfortable and on edge. She had to admit he was a kind, generous man and yes, he was good-looking. His quiet ways were attractive, if you liked that sort of thing. Which she didn't.

She put thoughts of Bill MacKenzie firmly out of her mind. Arthur was home. That was all that mattered.

'Can I go now?' Jeannie leapt up.

'What about your custard?' There was a pan of it on the range, keeping warm. The sweet scent hung over the warm kitchen, mingling with the aroma of stew and cabbage.

'Och, I'll have it later. Bye.'

Jeannie sped away into the back bedroom to change into her blue dress, the one Arthur liked. She brushed her hair until it shone and pushed it back from her face with two clasps. She stopped. She took the clasps out again and let her hair hang down in a curtain which covered her cheeks. She hadn't forgotten Arthur's parting remark but she had forgiven him. She was sure he hadn't meant it the way it came out. Still, there was no reason to make her birthmark more visible.

She put on her woollen coat and stuck her beret on her head before walking along Kiltie Street and up the steep slope to where the Dunns lived. She saw her breath, white and misty in the black night and shivered. She was looking forward to getting indoors. Arthur opened the door and she ran into his arms. She pressed herself against him, glad of his solid warmth, and raised up on tiptoe to kiss him. For a moment, he returned the pressure of her lips before pushing her away.

'Mother will see us,' he said. 'Let us not be unseemly.'

Jeannie was deflated. They hadn't seen each other since New Year. Surely, they were allowed a kiss? 'Helen won't mind. She knows we love each other.'

Arthur turned back in to the house and Jeannie had to follow. Helen was sitting in the front room, her knees wrapped in their usual blanket. She smiled apologetically at Jeannie.

'Hello, dear. I'm sure you two young people would like some time on your own.'

'Not at all, Mother,' Arthur said. 'Jeannie will make you a cup of cocoa and I'll bring you a sandwich. You must eat. You're too thin.'

Privately, Jeannie wished Helen would go upstairs. She looked perfectly healthy and not too thin at all. In fact, she looked better than Jeannie had seen her before. Guiltily, she realised she hadn't visited much over the last few weeks. Mammy had gone instead. The gap in visiting allowed her to see Helen's progress. Arthur's mother's skin had good colour, her blue eyes were vibrant and her posture sprightly.

'I insisted Mother put a blanket round her,' Arthur said, as they went into the large kitchen to make the cocoa. 'She must keep warm.'

The Dunns' home was very warm. There was a good fire in the front room and a fire in the kitchen grate, too. What luxury.

'Perhaps you worry too much about her,' Jeannie said, heating the milk in a pan on the range. 'Your mother and mine have been knitting socks for the army and I know Mrs Dunn has been to the WVS centre with my mother to help sort out the piles of donated clothes.'

A flush rose on Arthur's face. 'I know what's good for my mother, and I'll thank you to keep your opinions to yourself.'

Jeannie stirred the cocoa in dismay. The evening was going all wrong. Arthur was angry with her already.

'I'm sorry,' she said. 'Let's make the most of the evening. I've missed you dreadfully.'

Arthur's tight expression relaxed. 'I've missed you, too.'

'Have you?' Jeannie brightened. 'Come on, I'll bring the cocoa and we can have a lovely chat with your mother. I want to hear all about what you've been doing.'

They sat in the front room with the cocoa and some sliced beef sandwiches. Arthur fussed round his mother, insisting she eat a sandwich although she protested she wasn't hungry, having had dinner barely an hour before.

Arthur stood over her until she took the first bite. Jeannie felt quite uncomfortable.

She was relieved when he sat beside her on the couch and took up his own cup of cocoa. For a moment there were no sounds except the crackling fire and the chink of good china as they put their cups down.

'Jeannie tells me you were at the WVS centre with Mrs Dougal,' Arthur said.

Jeannie's heart sank. She looked at Helen and tried to convey her apology.

'How did you get there?' Arthur asked. 'Don't tell me you walked because I know that can't be true.'

'I took the car, dear,' Helen said mildly, although Jeannie noticed her hands were trembling as they held the half-eaten sandwich.

'You drove Daddy's car?'

'I can drive, you know. Your father taught me how. There was enough petrol for a short journey.'

'But Mother—'

'I won't drive again,' Helen interrupted him. 'I don't want the bother of getting the petrol coupon and filling it up.'

'Very well, we won't speak about it again.' Arthur shot her a black look.

'Tell us what you've been up to,' Jeannie said, desperate to lighten the mood. 'Have they kept you busy training?'

'You know I can't say much. Loose lips and all that,' Arthur said.

He did tell them a few stories about the food at camp and some of the men he was training with. Shortly after that, Helen told them she was going upstairs to bed.

'I'm tired and need a good night's sleep,' she said firmly.

This time, Arthur didn't argue. He took her arm and guided her out of the room. She managed a brief wave to Jeannie before she was out the door. When Arthur came back, his mood was gloomy. Jeannie searched her brain for a distraction.

'Shall we put the wireless on? We can try and get some music,' she suggested.

'Do what you want,' came the reply, as Arthur slumped on the couch.

Jeannie tuned in and found big band music.

'Have you a pack of cards?' she asked, determined to make the most of the evening.

They played Old Maid and Gin Rummy while the fire glowed beside them and the music swirled in their ears. Arthur's mood picked up as he won more games than Jeannie. She was careful to lose more than she won. Arthur's lean features were accentuated by the firelight and she thought again how handsome he was. She could hardly believe he had chosen her to be his wife. Plain Jeannie Dougal was to become Mrs Arthur Dunn.

She snuggled in to him on the couch. For once, he didn't push her away. His arm went round her and he kissed her. All her nerve endings tingled. He didn't try anything further and Jeannie was grateful. He was a gentleman and like her, he wanted to wait and do things properly. She wanted to be married before they slept together.

She knew if she wanted to get married quickly, Arthur would agree. But something held her back. I want to do it properly, she thought. I don't want it to be a hurried affair because the war is on.

'Will I see you tomorrow?' she asked, stroking the back of his hand and feeling the fine hairs on his wrist.

'We'll have a walk in the morning but I have to travel back in the afternoon. It's a long way south, made longer by slow trains.'

He walked her home and Jeannie thought what a lovely evening they'd had. She was looking forward to the morning and she knew she'd made the right decision getting engaged to Arthur. Nothing was going to change that.

Saturday morning was cold and bright. Jeannie lay motionless, wrapped up in the blankets as Kathy got out of bed. She made a face. Jeannie didn't have to get up but she did as she worked in Franny's shop six days a week. It was closed on Sundays. Her breath was white in front of her face and she shivered. There was ice on the inside of the window sill. It was sunny but there was no heat in it. She tugged the blankets over to her side of the bed spitefully. Jeannie mumbled in her sleep but didn't wake up.

Kathy blew out an angry puff of air. It wasn't fair. Jeannie had everything she wanted, while she, Kathy, had nothing. Jeannie didn't have to work every weekend. She had a gorgeous fiancé and Mammy let her wear lovely dresses, perfume and make-up. Meanwhile, Kathy had to work six days a week with a measly Sunday off when no one was doing much anyway. She wasn't allowed to have boyfriends. Mammy said she was too young. As for her clothes… they were fit for Isa and not for her. Peter Pan collars and dull colours and shapes. She longed for a pinched-in waist and a jaunty hat instead of last year's second-hand skirts and a shapeless beret she'd had for ages.

Still, she perked up, Franny's shop had become much more interesting of late. The servicemen from the nearby barracks had discovered they sold cigarettes and tobacco.

Franny, with her keen nose for business, had also branched out into biscuits, chocolates and sweets when she could get them. There was often a trail of soldiers to flirt with as Kathy took their orders. There was one fellow, in particular, who piqued her interest.

She ate her porridge and downed a cup of tea. Isa was hovering as usual to see if she left a bit. She took delight in scraping her bowl and licking her spoon before shoving them across to her little sister to wash up. Isa's turned-down mouth made her smile. She put on her coat, jammed her beret over her bright red hair and set off jauntily down Kiltie Street to get to the main road where Franny's Emporium stood amongst a row with the butcher's, greengrocer's, baker and the tobacconist who was furious that Franny was selling cigarettes and had threatened her that he was going to put a stop to it.

'Good morning, Franny,' she called, putting her coat on the hook in the back room.

'Someone's very chirpy this morning,' Franny grumbled but her smile said she was only pretending. 'Get along with you now and get my cuppa. I'll have it—'

'—Black with one sugar,' Kathy finished for her, putting the kettle on in the usual morning ritual.

'I'd have it black with three sugars if it wasn't for the bloomin' rationing,' Franny sighed. 'What's it coming to when an old woman like myself can't have her morning tea the way she likes it?'

Looking at Franny's large, round body, encased in the black bombazine she always wore, Kathy thought that sugar rationing might not be a bad idea. Doris, Jeannie's replacement, was sweeping the floor. She was a mousy little girl with thin hair and looked as if a puff of wind would blow her away. She wore thick glasses and was incredibly clumsy. On her first day at work she'd broken a vase. Since then she'd cracked glasses, dropped plates and dented the kettle.

Kathy, however, was glad of Doris. All her old jobs – sweeping the floor, dusting the shelves of goods and going to get Franny's messages – had all passed to the other girl. Since Jeannie had left, Kathy had been promoted to serving customers. Which meant she was able to have a gossip with Franny's women customers and to flirt with all the men.

She looked up hopefully as the bell went to see who was coming into the shop. There were three soldiers but he wasn't there. She wondered what his name was. He'd been in the shop three times by now and she was certain he liked her. His gaze followed her when she picked out the Woodbine cigarettes he asked for. He was tall and fair-haired, with a wicked grin.

Never mind. She'd wait. He was bound to come back. And when he did, she'd be ready. Kathy leaned on the counter, making sure the soldiers got a good eyeful of her chest. She'd deliberately opened the top button of her blouse as she'd taken her coat off at work. Mammy would have had a fit but Franny never noticed much.

Her red hair swung glossily and she tucked a curl behind her ear, drinking in the soldiers' admiration. Mammy was wrong. Kathy was fifteen, practically a grown-up. She was old enough to work for a living and to bring a wage into the household. Therefore, she was old enough for a boyfriend. Whatever Mammy said.

–

Eileen threw up twice in the night. She had felt unwell Friday afternoon and Old McGrowly had begrudgingly let her knock off early. Once home, she had gone straight to bed, her stomach churning. Agnes had shouted up to tell her dinner was ready. Eileen had groaned at the thought of food but stayed in bed. Before long, her bedroom door opened.

'What's the matter with you?' her mother asked.

'My tummy's sore and I feel really sick,' Eileen murmured.

Agnes came over to the bed and laid a cool hand on Eileen's forehead.

'No fever. It must be a stomach bug. You won't be wanting your dinner.'

Eileen longed for a cuddle and for her mother to soothe her and tell her all would be well and she mustn't worry because Mum would look after her. Instead, she heard Agnes harrumph, making it clear that Eileen was a nuisance for wasting food.

'I'll put yours in the oven to keep warm. You can have it later,' she said.

'Thanks, Mum,' she replied weakly.

Jonny called to take her out and Agnes insisted she come downstairs to speak to him. Clearly, she thought Eileen was exaggerating her symptoms. They stood in the hall, Eileen conscious that her parents were in the living room and could hear them.

'You look rough,' he said, sympathetically.

He looked handsome, as usual. His hair was slicked back and his even teeth gleamed in the lamp light. His uniform was crisp and his shoes shone. She felt a flicker of desire over the waves of nausea which threatened to swamp her.

'I'm feeling sick,' she said. 'I can't go dancing tonight.'

She waited for him to offer to sit in with her but he didn't. He beat a hasty retreat to the front door.

'That's too bad, kiddo. Another time, yeah?' He slipped away as Eileen stood there, stunned.

'For goodness' sake, Eileen. Don't just stand there, fix the blackout curtain,' Agnes said, impatiently, brushing past her to adjust the front door and its heavy, black material. 'We don't want the warden round here, giving us a fine.'

In the middle of the night, shivering with the after effects of throwing up, Eileen listened for her parents' door. It had a distinctive creak and they kept it shut at night and when they weren't using it. She wasn't allowed in their bedroom, ever. She heard nothing. Neither her mother nor her father cared enough to check she was okay. Her mouth wobbled in self-pity. She shuffled back to bed.

In the morning she felt much better but weak from her empty stomach. She put on her dressing gown and padded downstairs. There was no sign of her mother but her father was sitting in the living room, reading the newspapers. He was smoking his pipe, and a cup and saucer were balanced on the arm of the chair precariously.

'Good morning, Dad. Do you want another cup of tea?'

'Yes, please. Are you feeling better? You had your mother worried.' He stared at her over the rim of his reading glasses and flicked the newspapers into order.

Worried? Her mother? Not likely, Eileen thought. Her father's tone was almost accusing as if it was Eileen's fault that her mother was worried about her.

She made herself a slice of toast and spread it thinly with jam. There was no butter and she hated the taste of margarine. She'd rather do without. She drank a cup of tea and took one through to her father. He was deep in the papers and didn't look up or acknowledge the fresh brew.

She was bored. She had planned to spend the day with Jonny and now he wouldn't come. She knew he had other girls. She'd been a fool to think he loved her and that he'd marry her. She saw the way women looked at him. She saw the way Jonny looked at them, too. He had even told her that he wasn't into commitment. That was a few days after she'd given herself to him, body and heart. She cringed, remembering how she'd said she loved him and talked about their wedding.

Even knowing he was a cheat, she couldn't give him up. She was very attracted to him. He was a great dancer and they had a good time together. More than that, she didn't want to feel lonely all over again if he left her. So, she pretended to be as free and easy as he was. She didn't care if they were exclusive, right? She was sophisticated, like him. They went dancing a lot. She hardly saw the others – Jeannie, Janet and Annie – except at work and in the canteen. Jonny's pal, Bill, didn't come dancing either. Jeannie's Arthur didn't like her going dancing, Janet and Alan mooned over each other at the cinema or on long walks and Annie went about with a face like a wet Sunday and wouldn't tell anyone why.

'Can I borrow a book from Mum's bookcase?' she asked her father.

He grunted from behind the newspapers and she took that as a yes. Her parents had a small bookcase in their bedroom. Very occasionally, Eileen was allowed to borrow a book. She had to ask her mother and Agnes would bring the book to her. She wasn't to go into their bedroom.

But Agnes was out. Her father hadn't said where but Eileen guessed she was at the nearby WVS centre. She was doing her bit for the war effort by serving in the canteen. She wasn't going to be home any time soon.

With an air of excitement, she pushed open the bedroom door. The room was sparse. A double bed with a faded blue coverlet and green blankets took up most of the space. There was a small bedside cabinet to either side and a dark wood wardrobe filled the rest of the room. She could smell her father's aftershave and a faint trace of the carbolic soap that Agnes used. She had once, as a small child, sneaked in to see her parents' room. Agnes had found her and given her such a scolding, she'd been terrified and never done it again.

Where was the bookcase? She went round to the right hand side of the bed and there it was, low down next to the wall. It hardly deserved the grand title of 'bookcase'. It was a single shelf propped on bricks which held ten books. She ran her finger along the spines and read the titles. There were adventure stories, thrillers and romances. Her parents liked to read but they weren't intellectuals.

She picked a book at random, unsure whether she'd read it or not. She took it through to her own bedroom and lay on the bed, idly flicking through it. As she did so, a photograph fluttered out. Eileen picked it up. It was a studio shot of a small boy, perhaps two or three years old. He was wearing a sailor suit and looked solemnly at the camera with big, dark eyes. He clutched a toy yacht in one pudgy hand.

She turned it over, looking for a clue as to who it was. The back of the photo was blank. She went back downstairs.

'Dad, who is this?' she asked.

She had to repeat her question. Robert Boyle put his head above the paper, looking annoyed at being disturbed. When he saw what she was holding, his face blanched.

'Where did you get that?'

'In a book I borrowed from your bedroom. You said I could borrow one,' Eileen said, puzzled and alarmed by his expression.

'You take that photograph and you put it right back where you found it. Do you hear me?' Her father's voice was expressionless but somehow it frightened her.

'All right, Dad, I will. I'm sorry...'

She stumbled as she spun on her heel.

'And, Eileen—'

'Yes, Dad?'

'Never, ever, mention this to your mother. Do you understand me?'

Chapter Ten

'What do you mean, you're not coming?' Jeannie cried in dismay one evening in May.

Kathy shrugged, not meeting her sister's accusing stare. 'Judith asked me to sit with her tonight.'

'Mrs Lennox's niece, Judith? Since when were you two best friends?'

'Since a while. You don't know everything about me, Jeannie Dougal. In fact, there's lots you don't know.'

'What's that supposed to mean?' Jeannie said.

Kathy stuck her tongue out at her. 'It means, keep your big nose out of my business. I'm not a child any more.'

'Well don't act like one then,' Jeannie snapped.

She stared at herself in the bedroom mirror. She had her blue dress on and she'd styled her hair into a victory roll especially.

'You're leaving me to go to the cinema with Bill on my own,' she grumbled.

'I daresay you and Bill will manage,' Kathy replied airily, putting on her own dress, a yellow cotton print and tying a yellow ribbon in her hair. 'Can I borrow your white sandals?'

'Why are you getting all dressed up to go next door to Judith?'

'Because I like to look nice, that's why. The sandals?'

'Oh, very well. Help yourself. Maybe Bill won't turn up,' Jeannie said hopefully.

There was a knock on the front door. Kathy ran through to answer it and Jeannie, sitting on the edge of the bed, heard her sister's high-pitched laughter and Bill's deep tones, though she couldn't make out what he was saying. Then Mammy was calling her impatiently and reluctantly, she pushed herself up. Why did no one think that her going out to the cinema on her own with Bill was a bad idea? What would Arthur think? The problem was that Mammy thought of Bill as part of the family, almost. She would think it kind of Jeannie to go with him. She put on her jacket and went out into the hallway.

Bill looked as well turned out as ever, although the creases in his trousers were at risk as he was kneeling on the floor showing Bob how his toy aeroplane would take off from a runway. Bob provided the sound of the aeroplane's engines as Bill made it soar into the air.

'Bombs ahoy!' Bob shouted, jumping up and down.

Jeannie muffled a giggle as Bill followed the small boy's commands. Bill swooped round with the toy, looking almost as absorbed in the game as his companion. He stopped when he saw her.

His hazel eyes lit up and she smiled politely. She had tried not smiling when he came to visit but it had been hard to keep the habit up. Eventually she'd given in to the fact that he was a nice man. Arthur couldn't object to her being polite to a fellow soldier, could he?

'You look pretty this evening,' Bill said.

'Thank you. Are you ready to go?' Jeannie's voice sounded nervous to her own ears. This was ridiculous. It was only Bill. What did she have to be nervous about? It wasn't a date. She looked at Mammy, hoping she'd somehow prevent Jeannie going out. But Mammy was smiling at them both.

'Have a nice evening out,' she said.

'Sorry, I can't come, Bill,' Kathy said sweetly. 'Maybe next time. I've got to keep my friend company. She looks after her old auntie next door.'

Like butter wouldn't melt in her mouth, Jeannie thought, annoyed. Kathy practically skipped out in front of them and up the steps of next door's close. Jeannie and Bill walked on out of Kiltie Street and didn't see Kathy's head poke out of the close to check they had gone. When she was certain they had, she walked quickly out of the street in the direction of Franny's shop where she had arranged to meet her soldier on the pavement outside the shop door.

At first, Jeannie didn't know what to say to Bill. She kept quiet as they caught the bus. He didn't seem to mind the silence. The bus was busy and other people's chatter filled the air as they went along the main road, under the canal and then past the park where the railings had been removed and rows of allotments had replaced the flower beds. The Astoria, on Possil Road, was a grand building, able to seat three thousand people. They joined a long queue waiting to see Irene Dunne and Charles Boyer star in *When Tomorrow Comes*.

It was a romance and a heartbreaker. At the end of the film, Jeannie cried. Bill gave her his handkerchief. They shared the last of the chocolate mints he'd bought in the foyer and walked to the bus stop.

'That was lovely,' Jeannie sighed.

Bill raised his eyebrows. 'You cried.'

'Yes, it was so sad when they parted.'

'Gee, it's a strange entertainment when you cry but say you had a good time.'

Jeannie laughed and Bill grinned at her. She realised she had enjoyed herself. Bill was good company. When she glanced at him, she saw his hazel gaze was intense.

'Listen, Jeannie—'

'No. Don't say it. Please don't spoil it,' she said quickly.

Bill's jaw tightened. 'I'm sorry but I have to. I like you, Jeannie. I know nothing can come of it but there you have it. I'm falling in love with you.'

'I'm in love with Arthur,' she said.

Her heart was fluttering in her ribcage and the whole world had shifted strangely off its axis. The pretence that Bill was simply 'family' had shattered. What would Mammy think if she knew how Bill felt? Never mind Mammy, what did she think herself?

'I know,' Bill said. He said it quietly and she felt she might cry all over again.

'Why did you have to say it?' she cried. 'Why did you have to change everything?'

'It doesn't change anything. We can go on the same way, being friends.'

'It doesn't feel like that.'

The bus arrived and other couples joined them and there was no space for a private conversation. Jeannie was glad. At the stop near Kiltie Street, she didn't wait for him but jumped off and almost ran the short distance home. Bill didn't follow her.

—

The wireless broadcast right at the end of May was disturbing. Mary clutched Jeannie and Kathy's hands as they listened at nine p.m. that evening to the plummy tones of the presenter telling them that 'all night and all day men of the undefeated British Expeditionary Force have been coming home...' They heard that the soldiers were eager to get back across to 'fight Jerry' and at that, Mammy's grip tightened further until Jeannie's fingers hurt.

'Is our Jimmy there?' Kathy asked fearfully.

Mary shook her head. 'I don't know but I pray to God he's not.'

Jeannie thought that he must be. Where else were they fighting but in France? She almost couldn't breathe with the terror she felt for him. *Please, please let Jimmy be all right*, she prayed.

The newspaper headlines in early June screamed '*Nazis Circle Dunkirk with Big Guns*'. Jeannie bought a paper in her lunch break and then wished she hadn't. She read about how embarkation of troops continued despite the German air force and heavy artillery, and that British soldiers were besieged in Calais but were holding out. She peered at the photographs, looking for Jimmy but didn't find him. What a fool she was! If he was there, he was one of hundreds of thousands of young men caught up in the drama. Nausea flooded through her in waves.

'Are you all right?' Eileen asked, catching her up on the way back into the factory. 'You're quite pale.'

Jeannie pushed the newspaper at her. Eileen read it with a creased brow before handing it back.

'Is it your brother?'

Jeannie nodded, unable to speak for a moment. Eileen put an arm around her and squeezed.

'He'll be safe, I'm sure of it. Look how many men they're getting off the beaches. Besides, you don't know if he's there, do you?'

'Where else?'

'Look, we can't speak now, Old McGrowly's bound to tell us off. Shall I come and visit soon? We can have a good chat over a cup of tea.'

Eileen had visited the Dougals a few times since New Year, since Jeannie's mother had invited her and told her to come when she liked. And she did like it. There was a lovely, warm atmosphere in Jeannie's home. It was a small flat and somewhat shabby but clean and full of love. She could feel that. It made a contrast to her own chilly home. Jeannie's friendship meant a lot to her and they were becoming closer. She had even told her friend about Jonny cheating on her and was glad of Jeannie's sympathetic ear.

One Saturday, soon after the news from Dunkirk, Jeannie was returning home with groceries. She'd queued for hours to buy onions which were in short supply and managed to get two mean-looking specimens. Picking up their week's meat ration she walked home, enjoying the sunshine. As she turned the corner into Kiltie Street, she saw a tramp limping along. With shock, she saw him turn up the steps to number four. There was something familiar about him. Even as she heard Mammy's cry, she began to run, the bag of food hitting her legs unheeded.

She ran through the open door and straight into the parlour. Mary stood there, her hand to her mouth, eyes shining with tears of happiness or disbelief. Jeannie pushed past her and stared. Jimmy lay on the couch, fast asleep.

'Is it really him?' she whispered.

Mary grabbed her. 'It's him. My poor darling boy. Look at the state of him. Boil up some water now and get a cloth.'

A horrible stench rose from Jimmy's sleeping body. Jeannie's glance took in his rumpled uniform, dark and crusted as if seeped in water and then dried repeatedly. One of his trouser legs was torn off to the knee and there was a filthy bandage on his shin. She hardly recognised him with his thick, auburn beard.

'Get the water, Jeannie,' Mary urged. 'Let's get him clean and proper before Kathy gets back from work. Isa and Bob are at Jessie's birthday party so they won't be home for a while. Hurry now.'

Jeannie filled the kettle. Jimmy was safe. But what a state he was in. She wasn't sure if she should be happy or sad at the sight of him. She stoked the range and got the heat up. When she went back through, Mary had a pair of scissors and was cutting Jimmy's uniform off.

They removed his boots, Jeannie gagging at the stench that arose from his socks. They had to soak his socks to get them off. His feet were cut to ribbons and they both stifled cries at the sight. The dirty bandage on his lower leg revealed a deep gash, not yet healed. Between them, they managed to get his clothes off. Even as they turned him on his side to help the process, Jimmy didn't wake up.

'Is he sick?' Jeannie whispered.

Mary shook her head. 'He's exhausted. What have they done to my wee boy?' Then, she stiffened her shoulders in resolve. 'Come along, let's get him clean and dry.'

They gently sponged his body and dried it. Jeannie wrapped another, clean bandage around his leg and more bandages on his feet.

'If that leg wound doesn't mend soon, we'll need to have Doctor Graham look at it,' Mary frowned.

'We can't dress him, what'll we do?'

'Get blankets from the cupboard to cover him.'

They laid blankets over his prone body and Jimmy snored on. When Isa and Bob came home, full of stories about Jessie's party and the biscuits they had eaten and how they both ate two fish paste sandwiches and Jessie's mammy let them have more, Mary hushed them and let them tiptoe in to stare at their big brother. Kathy arrived home later, her face flushed with the sun.

'Why won't he wake up?' she said.

Jimmy slept for two whole days. When Jeannie got home from her shift, he was sitting up on the couch with a bowl and his shaving stick and a razor in front of him on the low table. His beard was gone and he looked like Jimmy again. Except for his eyes. There was a look in them that made Jeannie shiver. He had a hollowed-out gaze and there was no special Jimmy grin for her.

'Was it very bad?' she asked softly.

He looked right through her, then focussed as if seeing her for the first time. He rubbed his face and with shock, Jeannie saw he was trying not to cry.

'Oh, Jimmy.' She ran to him, sat beside him and put her arms around him.

He turned his head to her shoulder and wept. She felt the hot tears soak into her cardigan.

'Sorry,' he mumbled.

'Will you tell me about it?' Not that she wanted to hear but she knew he had to spill it out, like lancing a wound.

'We queued for days on the beach, waiting to be rescued. When the boats came, we had to swim out. Men were clinging to the sides... I saw pals drowning.' He swallowed convulsively. 'I didn't make it onto the first boat. I had to wait…' He turned to her, red-eyed. 'Still believe I'm Lucky Jim?'

Jeannie didn't know what to say. She simply hugged him.

'I'm going to lie down for a while,' he said quietly.

She let him go and stood watching until his breathing was deep and steady.

'I'm that worried about him,' Mary said later, as the two women stood in the kitchen chopping the vegetables for tea.

'What can we do?' Jeannie asked.

Mary shook her head and sighed. 'Nothing but wait. Time's the healer.'

'He only has a week's leave.'

'Aye, and that'll have to be enough. We're lucky he came home at all. Mrs Shaw along the road got a telegram. Her oldest boy's dead. One of women at the WVS her husband's missing in action. She keeps coming to work at the canteen anyway. Says it keeps her mind off it all. Can you imagine?' Mary pushed the carrots into the pan and made an effort to smile. 'Now, tell me, is Eileen coming for her tea tonight?'

Jeannie knew the effort Mammy made in changing the subject. She played along, concern for Jimmy in the back of her mind all the while. 'Yes, she is. We're going for a walk after.'

'She's a lovely girl. I hope her mother doesn't mind her coming so often.'

'From what Eileen says, her mother doesn't notice. You don't mind her here, do you?'

'Not at all. I feel a wee bit sorry for the lass. There's something lonely about her.'

Jeannie looked at Mammy in surprise. Eileen was bright and beautiful and always up for dancing and fun. She'd never thought of her as lonely. When Eileen arrived, Jeannie thought Mammy was surely wrong. Her friend's blonde curls bounced as she related a funny story about a man on the bus with a dog that howled.

'By the end of the journey, everyone was singing along with the dog,' Eileen giggled. 'You should've seen it.'

Before Jeannie could warn her, Eileen had walked into the small parlour. She came to an abrupt stop at the sight of Jimmy stretched out on the sofa.

'Oh,' she exclaimed.

At the sound, Jimmy awoke. He rubbed his face and sat up. His fair hair stuck up from sleep and his shirt was creased. He stared at Eileen. When Jeannie glanced at her friend, she saw Eileen staring back.

'This is my brother, Jimmy,' she said, but Eileen didn't seem to hear her.

'Hello, I'm Eileen.' She moved to the sofa and stuck out her hand.

Jimmy grasped it like a lifeline. Neither seemed to notice Jeannie.

'I'll put the kettle on, shall I?' With no answer from either, she went through to the kitchen to see Mammy.

'They're acting a bit odd,' she frowned. 'I really want them to get along.'

'You can't force it,' Mary said. 'Either they will or they won't. Pour me a cup too, love.'

They were deep in conversation when Jeannie took the tea tray in.

'Will we walk along the canal after our meal?' she asked Eileen.

'Aye, that'll be nice,' Eileen agreed, accepting her cup of tea.

'I might join you,' Jimmy said, still looking at Eileen as if he couldn't tear his gaze away. 'If you don't mind going slow for my feet.'

'The more the merrier,' Jeannie replied, pleased and surprised that Jimmy was going to leave the sofa he'd been on since he got home.

Mary approved, too. 'Fresh air's good for you. Put a bloom in your cheeks, so it will.'

Eileen's pretty face was already flushed. Later, the three of them went up on the canal towpath and strolled along. They went slowly, with Jimmy's limp and healing feet. There was a fine view of Glasgow and the hills beyond. The canal was full of vessels and cargo and there was a stink of diesel and wood and coal smoke. It was early summer and the day was light until nine. The birds were singing in the sooty-leaved trees. There were a couple of men welding iron bolts onto a heavy metal gate soon to cross the canal for defence in case of Hitler's bombs.

Unbidden, Bill's words came into Jeannie's mind. *I'm falling in love with you.* She was fooling herself if she claimed it had come as a surprise. She'd seen the way he looked at her. And what did she feel? There, her mind refused to go. He was kind, generous, good-looking and her family loved him. He was a catch for any girl. But not her. She was promised to Arthur.

She tried to ignore the conflicting emotions evoked by thinking of Bill. She watched her feet instead. Her clumpy, black shoes treading steadily along the dusty towpath. Her childish ankle socks white against her tanned legs. No stockings to be had these days. She heard Jimmy's breathing and Eileen's tuneful humming. There was the comforting solid feel of them beside her as the path was too narrow really for three to walk abreast.

'Are we going to the barracks dance, then?' Eileen asked, linking arms with Jeannie on one side of her and Jimmy on the other.

Jeannie groaned. 'I've not told Bill either way.'

Bill had visited less since the evening he and Jeannie had gone to the cinema, but he still came to the house and played with Isa and Bob and chatted with Mary and Kathy and Jeannie. He said no more about being in love with Jeannie and she was glad. She pretended it hadn't happened and tried to avoid him. Earlier in the week, before Jimmy had arrived home he'd told her about a dance at the local barracks and asked if she and her friends wanted to come.

'Tell him we'll come,' Eileen said. 'You know I love to dance. Annie will too and we'll persuade the love birds, Janet and Alan, to tear themselves away from cosy nights in.'

'All right, if you insist.' Jeannie wondered if Bill would ask her to dance.

'Arthur won't mind, will he?'

'I had a letter from him. He's busy but can't say much about what he's doing or where he is. He doesn't ask what I'm doing either, so I don't have to tell him about the dance.'

Jeannie had discovered that it was easier not to say. If she did, Arthur would instruct her on how to go about it, or forbid her outright. If he didn't know, life was easier for both of them, she argued to herself.

'What about you, Jimmy? Do you fancy a night out dancing?' Eileen said gaily.

Jeannie froze. Her brother had been through hell. He hadn't left the house until this evening. A dance was frivolous after what he'd experienced.

'Aye, why not,' came the easy reply. 'I can't dance on these sore feet but I'd like the company.'

She bit her lip to stop her cry of surprise. Eileen pulled them both in to her with their linked arms and laughed. Above them, two seagulls called soulfully. Jeannie shivered.

—

'Bloody hell, what's that stink?'

'I'll thank you to mind your language,' Mary said, reprovingly. Her eyes watered with the smell and she was regretting her kind, neighbourly offer of help.

Isa ran into the hall. 'Have you come to help? Mr Woodley's boiling up the pig swill in Mammy's big, black soup pot. It's smelly, smelly, smelly,' she sang.

Jimmy grinned and ruffled her hair. 'No thanks, I'm off for a walk.'

'You've only just been out. Have you the energy?' Mary asked, concerned he was overdoing it.

'I'll find it rather than stay in this smog.'

Mary suspected he was out for a cigarette and wisely didn't say more. She was glad he was up and about. She knew he wasn't healed. She saw a darkness in him that surfaced now and then. His leave was almost up and he was heading back to his regiment the next day. She hoped the barracks dance this evening would buoy him up.

'Come on, Mammy. Mr Woodley's asking for you.' Isa tugged at her apron.

'Why does he need me? There's no complexity to boiling up pig food.'

Isa skipped away without answering. Mary raised her eyes to the heavens. Harry Woodley had taken over her kitchen. It was only fair to take it in turns to boil the swill for the pig and he had taken the brunt of it in his small, sparse kitchen. She wondered if the smell would linger for long afterwards.

'Ah, Mrs Dougal, there you are. Come and tell me what you think.'

Mary's kitchen seemed smaller with the large man taking up room. For a moment, she was back in the past when Dennis would stand at the sink after a day's work, his big body hunched over as he scrubbed the coal dust away. It was a long while since a male apart from her sons had been in the kitchen. As soon as Harry opened his mouth, the resemblance to Dennis shattered. His loud voice and accent were quite different.

'Isa, get up here, young lady, and give this a stir. This is what farmers have to do.'

Isa gleefully took the wooden spoon and stood at the range on tiptoe so she could see into the pot with its foul contents.

'I'll have to get you a low stool or you'll have to eat your greens and grow,' Harry remarked.

'I have grown. Mammy says I'm like a sapling since I came home from Miss Main's,' Isa said indignantly.

'What kind of a sapling? A dandelion?'

'A tree, of course, silly.'

Mary listened to their easy banter as Harry teased her daughter gently. What a pity he hadn't been blessed with children, she thought. He'd have made a wonderful father. As this idle thought went through her mind, she realised she was staring at him. Harry caught her gaze and winked. Mary grabbed a cloth and made a good job of wiping the table top. Really! He had no business winking. She ought to throw him out right now.

She didn't, of course. They needed the swill to fatten the pig and Isa was enjoying the activity. Besides, when she risked a glance at him again, Harry was grinning as he tested the mix to see if it was cooked. There was no real harm in him, she decided. As long as he didn't think he could become too familiar with her. If he did, he had another think coming.

The barracks dance was held in a large bare hall with a wooden floor and draughty, ill-fitting windows. There was a makeshift bar at one end and tables and chairs around the sides. A live band was set up in one corner. The air was stuffy and grey with cigarette smoke when they arrived and they heard the music and laughter before they entered.

Eileen was wearing her red dress and had painted her lips to match. She knew she looked good and there'd be plenty of offers for dancing. But she was interested in only one man and that was Jimmy Dougal. She'd always believed in love at first sight but it had never happened to her. Until now. The moment she saw Jimmy sitting dishevelled on that sofa, she'd fallen for him. And she was certain he felt the same way about her.

She looked at her friends and felt a warm glow of love for them all. Janet and Alan were a sweet couple. They were holding hands and Janet was on tiptoe whispering into his ear. Alan had to bend down, he was so tall. They shared a grin. Whatever Janet had said, they were happy with each other.

Jeannie was pretty in a yellow summer dress Eileen hadn't seen before. Matched with white sandals, the outfit enhanced her dark brown hair which curled to her shoulders this evening as she hadn't swept it up. Annie's lumpy figure couldn't be disguised but she had a clear complexion and long, thick hair. No sullen expression either. They were all out for a good time. She was all too conscious of Jimmy next to her. They weren't touching, yet she felt a tingling down that side of her body. He was smart in a civilian suit, as his uniform had been damaged beyond repair.

Bill met them at the door with a wide smile. 'Hey folks, welcome. I've got us a table at the back not too close to the band. Boy, those guys can play but it's loud.'

Eileen noticed Jeannie stiffen. What was going on between those two? Anyone could see they were a good match and it was obvious that Bill adored Jeannie. Privately, Eileen thought Jeannie should dump Arthur and step out with Bill. She hadn't said that to Jeannie. Bill MacKenzie was a touchy subject.

The hall was full of men in khaki and Annie's face lit up. It was a pity she had a sharp tongue. It put men off. She'd complained to the others that she never got a second date. Eileen could have explained why, but was too kind. Annie would have to figure it out for herself.

Beers and lemonades were bought and they crowded round the table that Bill had bagged. The band was excellent and Eileen's foot tapped along with the music.

'Want to dance?' Jimmy asked her.

'Yes, please.' She thought he'd never ask! She couldn't wait to feel his arms around her on the dance floor.

They joined other couples, swaying to the tunes that the band blasted out with vigour. Jimmy shuffled, because of his sore feet, but she didn't care. His touch set her nerves on fire.

'Will you write to me?' he said. 'I'm off to join my regiment tomorrow.'

'Yes, I'll write. As often as you like.'

She felt his breath tickle the top of her head and saw the strong line of his jaw as he swallowed.

'I'd like it if you were my girl,' Jimmy said, his Adam's apple bobbing in his neck.

She realised with a sweet pang that he was nervous. She loved him more by the minute.

'I'd like that too,' she said and tilted her face up.

His mouth closed gently on hers and Eileen gave herself up to his kiss. She didn't care if anyone noticed but most couples were too wrapped up in themselves. There was an intensity to the dancing, everyone conscious of the war and that time for enjoyment was fleeting.

'I love you, Jimmy Dougal,' she said silently. It was too soon to say it out loud. They hardly knew each other. Maybe once they'd written a few letters, she'd tell him. Eileen's heart soared. That lonely core inside her had dissolved. She wasn't alone any more.

Janet and Alan were dancing, too. Janet waved to her excitedly. Eileen waved back with a smile. Annie was dancing with a soldier shorter than her. Where was Jeannie? Eileen glanced around. She caught a flash of yellow dress as the dancing couples moved. There she was. She was in Bill's arms. He was a good dancer, spinning her round. She was glad. Her friend deserved some fun.

As the evening wore on, Jimmy stopped dancing and began drinking. Along with the beer, he got whisky after whisky. Eileen sat with him, trying to chat but he became morose. Staring into his glass, he hardly spoke.

'Haven't you had enough to drink?' she said, as he threw the contents of the glass down his throat.

'Not yet,' he said bleakly. 'I'm going to get another. Do you… do you want a lemonade?' He staggered as he got up and steadied himself. Without waiting for her reply, he pushed through the crowds to the bar.

Worried, Eileen tried to find Bill. Jimmy was bent on self-destruction tonight. She hoped Bill could stop him. She squeezed through the bodies, looking for Bill's light brown hair and broad shoulders and Jeannie's pretty yellow dress. Soldiers grasped at her, or called out. She shook her head. No, she didn't want to dance. No, she didn't want a drink. No, she didn't want to sit on the soldier's knee while he sang to her.

With a gasp, she almost fell outside into the cool, summer evening air. Where was Bill? She couldn't handle Jimmy alone. There were some couples outside in the shadows or leaning up against the walls of the building. Low murmurs of conversation rose in snatches. She tried to see faces but it was difficult in the dusk.

And then there they were. Bill and Jeannie kissing under a tree. Eileen stood stock still. They hadn't seen her. Their embrace was tight.

'Who'd believe it? Little Miss butter-wouldn't-melt-in-her-mouth Dougal kissing a man who isn't her fiancé.' Annie's snide voice came from behind her.

'Hush,' Eileen whispered harshly. 'They mustn't know we've seen them. Come on, Annie. Come away.'

She pulled at Annie's arm. An almighty crash sounded from within the hall. The couples outside looked up, startled. Eileen saw Jeannie's white face staring at them in horror. She turned and ran back inside, knowing in her gut what was happening. She was right. The dance floor had emptied. Beside their table, Jimmy stood over a prostrate figure, his face bloodied and his fists raised.

'Jimmy!' Jeannie cried, rushing past her.

Bill was close behind. Even as the other man rose from the floor, swinging his arm at Jimmy, Bill and others were holding both men back. The fight was over.

'What's going on?' Eileen said, reaching them.

'He called me a coward,' Jimmy slurred. 'Asked why I wasn't in the forces.' He slumped back into the chair behind him.

Jeannie looked as if she was going to cry. Bill put his strong arm under Jimmy's shoulder and dragged him up. 'Come along, buddy. That's enough for tonight. Let's get you home.'

Walking behind with Jeannie as they made their slow way back to Kiltie Street, Eileen wondered what would happen. She had fallen in love with Jimmy. But was love enough?

Chapter Eleven

Jeannie was confused, embarrassed and painfully happy. She kept going over the events of the barracks dance in her mind. She had stepped outside with Bill for fresh air. They had danced together and she had enjoyed it. She knew how he felt about her. But she thought they had sorted it. They had agreed to be friends. Somehow, the intimacy of dancing had changed the atmosphere. Bill had leant down and kissed her. Jeannie had responded. His kiss was sweet. She had felt an urgent desire to pull him closer, to keep the kiss going. Arthur never kissed her the way Bill did. Even while the delicious sensations overtook her, Jeannie pushed him away. She was breathing fast. Then she glanced over and saw Eileen and Annie's startled faces.

Before she could react, there had come the awful sounds of a fight inside the hall. Rushing in with everyone else, she saw her brother swinging at another man. Jimmy's nose was bleeding. Worst of all, his grey eyes, usually so cheerful and kind, were dark with rage. In all the kerfuffle, Bill had been wonderful. He had half-lifted Jimmy and taken him home to Kiltie Street.

Now, she was embarrassed that her friends had seen her kissing Bill. She was confused about her feelings for Bill and for Arthur. And she was painfully happy when she recalled that kiss. It wasn't right, though. She had kissed him while engaged to Arthur. She shivered. What would

Arthur do, if he ever found out? She had never seen him lose his temper but she was afraid to provoke him. Jeannie's breath stopped for a moment. There, she'd said it. She was a little afraid of Arthur. His self-control was unnatural. If it were ever to break…

She shook her head. She was being ridiculous. Arthur would never hurt her. Images of Helen Dunn flashed before her. Arthur's mother was quiet when he visited. As if she too didn't want to disagree with him. Yet, when he was away, she appeared much happier. Jeannie had gone with Mary and Mrs Dunn to the WVS centre to pick up a pile of clothes to be washed and sorted. The two older women had chatted easily to each other like old friends. Jeannie was surprised that Helen Dunn had walked down to Kiltie Street to get Mary before they had all walked over to the centre. When Arthur came home, she sat on the sofa with a blanket over her legs and barely moved.

It was a week since the dance and Jeannie was at home as it was her day off. She sat on the sofa, feet tucked up under her, flicking through Mammy's copy of *Good Housekeeping*. The sun was streaming in the living room window. Kathy was at work. Isa and Bob were out playing. Mammy was in the back yard watering the vegetables that grew on top of the Anderson shelter. Harry Woodley was there too. Jeannie rolled her eyes. He couldn't help but give advice on everything. She didn't know why Mammy put up with him.

She was on the verge of getting up to tidy the kitchen when a knock came at the door. She opened it to see Bill on the doorstep. Her first instinct was to flee. Her second, to run to him and kiss him. She could barely look at him.

'You've got a nerve, coming round,' she said.

'I came to say goodbye.' He took his cap off and ran his fingers through his hair.

All her indignation faded away. 'Goodbye?'

'Yes, we're moving out.'

'Where? When?' It was as if the sun had gone behind a black cloud.

Bill smiled sadly. 'Tomorrow. As for where, we haven't been told yet. It's likely to be down south, I guess, or abroad.'

'Abroad... you mean... to the fighting?' Her throat was tight.

'Look, Jeannie. I'm sorry about the dance. I had no right—'

'Forget it. I already have,' she cut across him. It came out too harshly and she saw him wince.

There was a silence which Jeannie couldn't bring herself to break. Bill was leaving. She ought to be glad. She had Arthur, didn't she?

'Right, then. I have to go. Say goodbye to your mother for me. And the kids. I've loved being part of the family. It's made a real difference.'

Jeannie said nothing. She gripped the edge of the door as for dear life. She felt if she spoke, nothing would come out but sobs.

He saluted her smartly and walked away. She watched him walk along Kiltie Street. Every impulse made her want to run after him. She'd pull him round, kiss his mouth and tell him she loved him. Instead, she did nothing. She watched him walk out of her life. Tears rolled slowly down her face but she didn't feel them. Not until she tasted their salty wetness did she realise she was crying.

Kathy came storming in a short while later. She finished early on a Saturday unless Franny was in a curmudgeonly mood.

'Did you see Bill? They're leaving. They're all leaving.'

Mary was in the kitchen by now, preparing their evening meal. She looked at Kathy and then at Jeannie. 'Well, that's a pity. We'll miss him, no doubt about that. He didn't come to say goodbye but I suppose he'll be busy.'

'He did come by. I saw him walking out of Kiltie Street. What did he say, Jeannie?'

Jeannie concentrated on scrubbing the tatties.

'Jeannie?' Mammy's gentle voice was almost too much for her.

'He said they're moving down south.'

She felt Mammy's hug. She bit her lip. The tatties had a lot of soil on them. Scrub, scrub, scrub.

'We all know you had a soft spot for Bill,' Kathy smirked.

Mary turned to her daughter. 'That's quite enough. We all liked Bill and that's all there is to it. You know fine well that Jeannie's engaged to Arthur. So stop your stirring and get a move on here with the mop. Do something useful.'

'I've spent all the day working with Franny breathing down my neck,' Kathy moaned.

Her sister's whining was a blessed distraction. Jeannie kept her head down until the tatties shone. If she had wavered, thinking of Bill's kiss and how maybe she was in love with him, then Mammy's words were like a shock of cold water. Mammy was right. She was engaged to Arthur. He was the man she was going to marry. Bill was gone. She resolved to do better. She'd be the best fiancée. She'd fall in love with Arthur all over again.

Arthur came back on a three-day pass before the end of June. Jeannie heard from Mammy that he was back. Mary had been visiting Helen who, with the help of her house-keeper, was cleaning and tidying her house and preparing meals. He didn't visit Jeannie until the second day he was home. She tried not to feel hurt about it. He needed time with his mother, she thought. Helen would enjoy having Arthur to herself. Jeannie had to have patience.

As they walked to a city centre café, Jeannie looked at him carefully. He looked tired. There were lines around his mouth she hadn't noticed before. There were shadows under his eyes. She felt a wash of tenderness roll over her. She would look after him. She'd make him laugh this afternoon and take away the tension under his jaw.

Impulsively, she hooked her arm into his and squeezed them closer.

'Isn't this nice?' She smiled. 'Just you and me. I'm dreaming of a lovely cup of tea and a scone right now. What are the chances of a scrape of jam?'

He stared at her as if she was mad. She flushed. He was making it hard. He had never been very chatty but now he was almost morose.

'Are you all right?' she asked.

'All right? Of course I'm all right. Why wouldn't I be?' he said belligerently. 'Are you saying there's something wrong with me?'

They had arrived at the café and Jeannie took a silent breath of relief. She pushed the door open and a waft of baking filled her nostrils. In the bustle of finding a table at the window and ordering from the waitress, she didn't have to answer him. She put her handbag on the floor at her feet and glanced up. There was a small table in the far corner, for one person. Miss McGrory sat there. She had a pot of tea in front of her and a plate with a small buttered scone. Despite the warm weather, she wore a felt hat. On the chair opposite her sat her neat navy blue handbag, a pair of matching blue gloves lying limply across it.

As if sensing Jeannie's gaze, the woman looked across. Jeannie smiled politely. Miss McGrory's expression changed as she recognised her. In her seat by the bright window, Jeannie recoiled at the hostility she saw there. Arthur shifted in his chair and her view of the supervisor vanished. She poured the tea, her heart thumping. Arthur didn't notice. He seemed wrapped up in his own thoughts. Miss McGrory's face as she saw Jeannie had turned to anger. Jeannie could have sworn it was so. Not just anger but something else. Disgust. That was it. She looked as if Jeannie disgusted her. But why?

I won't think about her, Jeannie decided. I'll concentrate on Arthur, who needs me.

'You look tired,' she said. 'Is it very hard at the camp?'

'I don't want to talk about it. You wouldn't understand.'

I could if you explained it, she thought but didn't dare to say. A tension radiated from him. She wished she could help him relax.

'Your mother will be pleased to have you home,' she tried again.

'Mother is overdoing things. I've told her I don't want her going to the WVS centre again. I blame your mother for encouraging her in the ridiculous notion she has to play her part. She's not well. She should be resting.'

Jeannie gasped. 'Mammy's only trying to help. She and Helen have become good friends. Helen's got more energy than you realise, Arthur. She's much happier of late.'

Arthur's agitated fingers broke his scone into crumbs on the plate as he glared at her. 'Firstly, I'll thank you to show some respect and call my mother Mrs Dunn until invited otherwise. Secondly, I know what's good for my mother, not you. Do you understand?'

Two elderly ladies at the next table looked over at them as Arthur's voice rose. In the corner, Miss McGrory's mouth twisted into a dry smile. She slid on her gloves slowly, picked up her handbag and walked past them without further acknowledgement.

At that precise moment, Jeannie realised she didn't love Arthur. She was able to see him clearly. He was handsome with his fair hair and blue eyes and slim build. She knew women flicked admiring glances at him. She saw them do it when they walked out together. They were envious of her. But now she saw it wouldn't work between them. She was scared of his moods. She had to mind how she spoke, what she said, because she was never sure of what his reaction would be.

'Get your things, I'll take you home.' His tone brooked no argument.

Embarrassed, she fumbled for her bag at her feet. Conscious of the sympathetic looks from the next table, she tried to smile as if everything was all right. Arthur paid for the tea and scones, which Jeannie had hardly touched. They walked home in silence. Arthur's expression was tight and brooding. Jeannie didn't care. She was fuming with him. He'd spoiled what should have been a lovely day. They hadn't seen each other for ages. Surely, a normal engaged couple would have kissed and hugged

161

and said I love you? Instead, he'd provoked an argument over nothing.

She hardly said goodbye as he left her in Kiltie Street. How different he was from Bill. She felt tears threatening. Her throat was clogged. Bill was kind and gentle and she felt safe with him. But she was engaged to a man who frightened her. And there was no way out of that.

Arthur turned up the next morning as if nothing had happened. Mary let him in. He sat in the living room.

'It's nice to see you, Arthur. Will you have a cup of tea?' Mary said.

'Thank you but I've already had tea.'

'Let me get Jeannie for you, then. She's out in the back, weeding.' What a stiff young man he was, she thought, leaning out the back door of the close to call to Jeannie.

'He's here?' Jeannie said.

'Of course he's here,' Mary said patiently. 'He's your fiancé.'

'Oh, Mammy, we had an awful argument yesterday,' Jeannie said, rubbing her nose with the back of her grubby hand. She clutched a bunch of dandelions in the other, pulled from the lettuce bed.

'All the more reason to make it up,' Mary advised, gently taking the weeds from her hand and pushing her towards the close. 'All couples have disagreements. What matters is how you deal with them.'

'Even you and Daddy?'

'Not often because your daddy knew how to make me laugh. I'd be on my high horse and he'd tease me right off it,' Mary smiled, remembering. 'But we had a few cross words. It's normal in a long marriage.'

Jeannie hesitated. Mary took hold of her shoulders and turned her to the close.

'Go on with you. Make it up. Life's too short to hold a grudge. You may not like it, but it's the wife who usually has to smooth things over. If you want a happy marriage, that is.'

'I'm not his wife yet.'

'But you will be soon. Go on, now, love.'

With Mammy's wise words, Jeannie felt her last sliver of hope disappear. What did she think was going to happen? That Bill would magically arrive and whisk her away? This was real life. And Jeannie had to face up to it. She was going to marry Arthur and that was that.

'We can walk through the park,' Arthur told her, giving her a quick peck on the cheek. 'Go and get your coat, it's going to rain.'

Obediently, she fetched her light jacket and an umbrella, conscious of Mammy's words. It was as if they hadn't argued the previous day. Arthur clearly wasn't going to mention it. Should she? The park railings had gone, taken away for the war effort. Instead of colourful flower beds, there were rows of cabbages and carrots and other green-topped vegetables Jeannie couldn't identify.

A light shower scattered over them as they walked but it soon dried up. From the top of the park at the edge of a copse of woods they had a view down to the tennis courts where four girls were bashing a ball back and forth amidst gales of laughter. Jeannie wished she was down there with them instead of with Arthur. He was as sombre as usual.

'That looks like fun,' she said, pointing to the courts.

He grunted but didn't reply.

Suddenly, she felt she had to say something. 'Do you still want to marry me?' The words burst out of her.

Arthur looked surprised. 'What a strange thing to say. Of course I do.'

'Do you love me?'

'What's got into you, Jeannie?'

'I don't know. I… You don't seem happy, that's all. Is it me?'

Arthur sighed deeply. He turned from her, staring up at the crowns of the trees as if there was an answer there. When he turned back, he seemed angry.

'There's a war on, don't you know. It's bigger than you or me. This afternoon, I have to go back. I have to leave Mother on her own. None of this is easy.'

Stung by his words, Jeannie didn't know what to say. He hadn't mentioned her at all. It was as if her worries didn't touch him. They walked down the slope from the woodland, past the carefree girls in their tennis whites and beyond the neatly hoed rows of vegetables. At the end of Kiltie Street, Arthur kissed her briefly, his lips hard on her cheek.

'I'll be away after lunch so I won't see you again on this leave. Goodbye, Jeannie. Take care.'

She watched his rigid back as he strode away from her. 'Goodbye, Arthur,' she whispered.

She touched her mouth, reliving the tenderness of Bill's kiss that night at the dance and how she had responded, passion rising up in her. It felt a like a very long time ago in a different place. She had felt like a different person, with possibilities and the future not yet set. Even if that wasn't really true. She had been wearing Arthur's ring, and sneaking a kiss with Bill was cheating although they hadn't planned it.

She knew what Mammy would say. *You've made your bed and now you must lie on it*. There was nothing more to be done.

Chapter Twelve

Mary was in a deep sleep when the siren sounded. At first it was entwined in her dream as the cry of a stray cat. As the wailing sound persisted she sat up suddenly and clutched at the bed sheet. She slept in the bed recess in the kitchen and suddenly the privacy curtain was flung open and Jeannie was there, eyes wide.

'It's the bombers, Mammy. They must be coming.'

'Get Kathy and the wee ones down to the shelter,' Mary said.

'What about you?'

'I'll be right behind you. Now go. Quickly, now!'

She saw the soles of Jeannie's slippers flapping as she went off, calling her sister. Mary pulled on her cardigan and a wave of dizziness swept over her. She clung to the bedpost until it passed. She went into the hall and picked up the cardboard box that sat there. It held their birth certificates, her marriage certificate and other important documents. With it held under her arm and her gas mask in the other, she hurried outside in the pitch darkness. Another fit of dizziness made her cry out. What was wrong with her! She gripped the boxes and half slipping on the damp grass, she was relieved to find the entrance to the Anderson shelter.

The sickly sweet yet sour smell of damp soil hit her nose. Jeannie had lit the oil lamps and a couple of candles and by the flickering light she saw her children and Martin and Linda O'Leary. Martin got up and shut the shelter door behind her.

'I don't hear any planes,' Bob said, sounding disappointed, from his position cross-legged on the bench.

'They'll come, mark my words,' Martin said gloomily.

Beside him, Linda had pulled her knitting out of a large cloth bag.

'Got to keep my hands busy,' she explained. 'Girls, do you want to learn?'

Mary listened but Bob was right. There were no ominous sounds. Kathy yawned as she accepted two knitting needles and a ball of wool from Linda. Isa snuggled into Mary's side and she put her arm round her. It was cold in the shelter. Jeannie unfolded the blankets they'd stored there and passed them round. They were damp and gave off a wet wool smell but no one complained.

Mary fretted about her dizzy spell. Why had it happened? Was she so weak she didn't have the courage to withstand an air raid? She couldn't bear the thought of being without courage. She prided herself on being strong for her family.

The all clear sounded two hours later. Bob had drifted off to sleep and the rest of them were singing 'Little Brown Jug' for the third time.

'Thank goodness for that,' Linda said, putting her knitting away. 'I got most of a sock done but I'd rather be in my bed asleep. Come along, Martin. Pull me up. My knees have gone stiff with the cold.'

'This won't be the last of them,' Martin said darkly. 'Jerry's got a taste for the west of Scotland and he'll be back.'

Mary forbore to mention that there hadn't actually been any bombing, at least over Glasgow that night. She hid a yawn and prayed that when she stood up, she wouldn't keel over. Luckily, she had no more light-headedness and was able to carry Bob, wrapped in his blanket, up the stairs and into their home. He was heavy and she thought, with a touch of melancholy, that he, the last of her babies, was growing up.

Martin turned out to be right. The sirens went off again in early July and disrupted their sleep for several nights. Mary got used to leaving a flask of tea beside the range and taking it down to the shelter along with the cardboard box and their gas masks. The oil lamps were lit, their repertoire of songs grew and they spent more time with the O'Learys than they ever had before. Harry Woodley in his ARP uniform strode about Kiltie Street, making sure that everyone went to their shelters. Mary felt he was enjoying it all too much. For a bossy sort of man, wasn't this a slice of heaven, she wondered. Ordering people about and they had to obey.

Later in the month, Jeannie leaned her heavy head on the bus window on her way to work. Rain was lashing the glass, despite it being the height of summer and the vehicle shuddered from the blustery winds.

'Sweet Jesus and all the saints,' Elspeth said, sitting beside her and looking outside. 'It's more like October than July. You've got awful dark rings under your eyes, Jeannie.'

Jeannie smothered a deep yawn. 'It's the fact of not getting a full sleep. I'm tempted to sleep in the shelter and miss out the part where I get into my bed.'

'Mum's bought me and herself siren suits. Really lovely, they are. They're warm and fashionable too. You should get yourself one.'

'Aye, if I get a moment to bless myself.'

'What's the problem?'

'It's Mammy. She's not been well the past few weeks. She's having these dizzy spells. I've told her to go and see the doctor but she says she won't waste the money. I've told her we can afford it, what with me working at Fearnmore. It may be hard work but the wages are good.'

'Plenty of folk are getting hysterical over the raids. Mrs Lennox is refusing to budge from her bed and Judith was in tears over it. She came to Ma for advice but what can she do? She can hardly lift Mrs Lennox and carry her down to the shelter, can she now?'

Jeannie and Elspeth exchanged a glance which turned into a giggle. Mrs Lennox was a plump lady with stout legs. The thought of Elspeth's slight mother carrying her over her shoulder down to the back court was hilarious.

Jeannie sobered up and sighed. 'I'm worried about Mammy. I don't think she's hysterical. I really wish she'd see Doctor Graham and put my mind at rest.'

She and Elspeth got off the bus and joined the queue of workers streaming into the factory. The rain was bouncing off people's hats, and shoulders were hunched while feet hurried to get into the buildings.

It was almost tea break and Jeannie was looking forward to a cuppa when they heard the first bombs. The distant hum of an aeroplane, followed by bone-chilling crumps made several of the women scream. They ran to the window. Miss McGrory shouted at them but for a while she was ignored.

'Why hasn't the siren gone off?' Janet cried.

Annie peered out at the rainy day. 'There's smoke over the west end.'

'There's fire, over there,' Eileen pointed. 'See it? Nowhere near us, thank God. But someone's copping it, the poor souls.'

'Get back to work right now!' Miss McGrory cried, stalking towards them.

'Why was there no warning?' Janet persisted, her usually cheerful face white and strained.

'No one can answer you that. It's not our place to question the military,' the supervisor snapped. 'Go back to your place and get those machines moving. Every second lost is a second won for Hitler.'

With no more sounds of bomb blast, the subdued group flocked back to their machines, murmuring to each other. Everyone was shaken. Even Miss McGrory looked unsettled as she went back to her desk. Jeannie thought of Kiltie Street and prayed her family were safe. Had Mammy collapsed again?

–

Over in Franny's Emporium, Kathy was wafting air with a newspaper onto Franny's face.

'Hurry up with that tea, Doris,' Kathy yelled.

'Oh, goodness, my heart's racing,' Franny said, patting her generous chest as it heaved.

There was a crash from the back room and the sound of breaking china. Franny jumped a mile.

'It's not another bomb,' Kathy said. 'It's Doris reducing your tea set. Wait a minute and I'll sort her out.'

She marched into the back room where Doris crouched, picking up pieces of a cup and saucer amidst a widening splash of brown liquid. Kathy poured another cup from the teapot.

'Go and give this to Franny. I'll clear that up. For the love of God, don't spill this one.'

Doris stumbled out and Kathy heard Franny's trembling voice and Doris's soft, whispered reply. She mopped up the mess with a cloth and dropped the broken shards into the bin. She was glum. All the soldiers, including her tall, fair-haired Bert, had gone. He'd kissed her goodbye but she heard him whistling as he set off back to camp. He wasn't heartbroken. Neither was she, as it turned out. She didn't pine for Bert so much as for the lost fun and excitement of sneaking out to meet him and all those stolen kisses in the dark.

She heard the shop bell and wiped her hands. Franny would be expecting her to serve. She went through to the counter and brightened. Two soldiers had come into the shop.

'Packet of Players, love.'

He had dark hair and black brows and stood short and stocky. The other soldier was taller with hair a darker shade of red than her own and a smattering of freckles. Kathy perked up. She felt their admiring gazes as she stretched for the cigarettes.

'Anything for you?' She fluttered her eyelashes at the taller soldier.

He flushed almost the same colour as his hair and stuttered an answer. His friend guffawed and playfully punched his shoulder.

'I apologise for my pal, here. He's not the best at talking to the bonny lassies. I'm Gavin, by the way.'

'Nice to meet you, Gavin,' Kathy gave him her best seductive smile. 'Has your pal got a name?'

'It's Billy. But you don't need to know that when you've got me.'

Franny, tucked in the background on her chair, gave a loud cough and the soldier backed away from the counter with a cheeky wink to Kathy.

'See you around.'

She gave a little wave that Franny couldn't see and smiled inwardly as the two men left the shop. Life was looking better.

'You be careful,' Franny said, 'You don't want to be one of those girls who gets themselves into trouble.'

'I don't know what you mean,' Kathy replied.

She hummed as she tidied the counter top. Gavin and Billy were only two men out of a whole new bunch that must have arrived at the barracks. Over the next few days, she bet quite a few of them would find their way to Franny's for their fags.

–

Back in Fearnmore, the factory girls were also having tea in the canteen. The tea break had been put back as Miss McGrory demanded they finish their shift and make up for the time lost staring out the window.

'She's such an old cow,' Annie complained. 'I was dying for a cuppa and biscuit and then we've had to wait 'til now.'

'The shifts are longer too,' Eileen said. 'It won't be long 'til we're asked to work every day with no time off.'

'Do you think so?' Jeannie said. 'Mind you, it is for the war effort and we all want to do our bit, don't we? It's just hard when you don't get a full sleep.'

'We are all in the same boat, though, which makes it easier,' Janet chipped in.

She had got over her shock at the bombs and was her usual chirpy self. Her biscuit had disappeared and she looked hungrily at the others' plates. Eileen took pity on her and pushed across half her biscuit. They tasted of sawdust anyway. Perhaps they were mostly flour and water, a tiny amount of sugar and definitely no butter. Janet didn't seem to mind. Eileen's biscuit went the same way as hers.

'Actually, I've got something to tell you all,' Janet said, a wide grin breaking onto her small face.

The other three looked at her in anticipation.

'Me and Alan are getting married.'

There were shrieks of delight as her friends crowded round her for hugs and congratulations.

'Have you set a date?' Eileen asked, as they all sat down again.

'Next February. My birthday's the tenth so Alan said we should choose that day,' Janet said shyly.

No one watching could be in doubt that she was a woman in love. It shone from her. Jeannie was glad for her friend but piercingly aware of her own dilemma. With the longer work shifts and the endless air raids, she hadn't thought about Arthur or Bill. Life was focussed around getting up in the morning, going to work and coming home, tired, to prepare for another night of possible disruption.

'It won't be a big affair,' Janet was saying. 'We don't have much money. If I was to have bridesmaids, I'd ask you three as my best friends so I hope you won't be disappointed that I'm not having any.'

'We're just happy for you,' Eileen told her. 'You and Alan choose the way you want it and we'll turn up. Won't miss it for the world, will we girls?'

Jeannie and Annie agreed. All too soon, the bell rang and it was back onto the factory floor.

–

Mary took her seat in the doctor's surgery the next day, feeling like a fraud. There was no dizziness today, no light-headedness. She felt fine. As she had done yesterday morning during the raid. Yes, she had been afraid as she listened to the crashes and booms some distance away competing with the drum of rain on the windows. But she hadn't disgraced herself by falling over.

There were two middle-aged women in the waiting room and an elderly man. The two women were talking about the raid.

The first woman, whose hat sported a brown and white speckled pheasant's feather, leaned over to her companion to share what she knew.

'They bombed near Dumbarton Road. My sister lives in Blawarthill and she says the whole tenement will have to come down, it's so damaged.'

'It's a mercy no one was killed.' The second woman was more sedately dressed, in a black coat that was too thick for the July weather. She was thin and her face was pale with two spots of colour over the cheekbones.

'Where did you hear that?' Mrs Pheasant Feather exclaimed. 'People were killed all right. My sister saw two bodies hauled from the wreckage. She said there were chicken feathers everywhere.'

'Chicken feathers?' It was the thin woman's turn to be confused.

'Aye, because they bombed Blawarthill Farm and all. Took out the hen house.'

'I heard it was Govan as took the main bombing.' The elderly gentleman joined the conversation. 'They hit Tinto Park football ground and houses nearby. Where will the homeless go?'

'I never heard that,' Mrs Pheasant Feather said with the disappointment of an inveterate gossip who likes to be first in the know.

Mary had no idea if any of it was true. She sighed inwardly. They probably wouldn't know the whole event for days and only if the newspaper chose to tell them. The reports were deliberately vague, mentioning only 'Clydeside' which covered a huge area and told nothing.

The elderly gentleman was talking about the Great War now and shaking his head as he forecast worse horrors to come. Mary tried to shut it out. She had enough on her plate. She felt an overwhelming tiredness. The nurse bustled out with a clipboard and called her name. Mary's knees ached as she stood up.

Doctor Graham asked kindly after her family before he checked her heart and pulse and asked her a few questions.

'Do you feel well generally, Mrs Dougal?'

'Apart from the dizzy spells, I do. Well… I'm a wee bit up and down and tired but I don't want to complain about that because everyone is. It's the war and the air raids. It's my nerves. I wouldn't have bothered you but Jeannie insisted I put her mind at rest.'

'What about your monthlies?'

Mary blushed. She knew he was a doctor but it was still embarrassing to talk about such intimate matters with a man.

'Well, nothing to tell…' She paused, frowning. 'Actually, I missed the last one. Sometimes, they're fainter than usual.'

Doctor Graham nodded. He made notes, his bushy eyebrows tufted over the top frame of his black-rimmed glasses.

'What's wrong with me?' Mary asked, readying herself for bad news.

'It's not your nerves, Mrs Dougal. I suspect you've got nerves of steel, being a mother of five. There's nothing wrong with you. It's simply the change of life that every woman goes through.'

Mary felt relief. She wasn't dying and better yet, she was no coward.

'Can it really cause light-headedness?'

The doctor nodded. 'You may feel more tired than usual, you may feel a little dizzy and some women will experience a few hot flushes. Nothing to be concerned about, it's all entirely natural and will pass soon.'

'I'm sorry to have wasted your time, Doctor Graham,' Mary said, picking up her handbag.

'Not at all,' he replied amiably. 'Take care of that family of yours. You'll be right as rain.'

She had mixed feelings as she walked home. She wasn't ill, she wasn't fainting away because she was afraid but her fertile days were finished. It was not as if she could have more babies anyway, with Dennis gone, she thought. But still. It was terribly final. Bob was her last baby and he was six and getting bigger and more independent by the day. She was quite subdued as she filled the kettle and had her pot of tea before starting the housework.

—

When Eileen got home from work, there was a letter waiting for her. It was from Jimmy. She took it upstairs to enjoy. Agnes hadn't asked her who it was from. In fact, her mother had hardly turned from the range to welcome her. A delicious smell wafted from the bubbling pot on the heat. She never went hungry and she had clothes on her back. It was only her emotional needs that went unmet. She thought of Janet who complained, with a laugh showing she didn't really mind, that her mother was so nosy she asked her hundreds of questions about the factory and her new friends and wanted all the details. Never mind. She had Jimmy now who loved her.

The sensor had been at work, blacking out key words, and Jimmy's appalling handwriting didn't help. She guessed he was somewhere hot and he wrote that the food was awful but there was plenty of it. He was happy enough but he missed her. He signed off with '*All my love, Jimmy*' giving her a warm feeling right inside her chest. She'd write back after tea. She'd tell him about the bombing and the nights in the shelter and how hard they were working in the factory with the longer shifts. But she'd do it in such a way that he needn't worry about her. Maybe she'd mention the pink flowers she saw that morning on her way from the bus. Did he like flowers? There was so much she didn't know about him.

The bombing continued on and off until the end of November. Everyone was weary and exhausted and grateful when calm descended towards Christmas.

'We mustn't forget those poor people in London being bombed every night,' Mary said to Jeannie as they drew the blackout curtains on another early dark evening. The London Blitz had started in September and showed no sign of finishing. 'Will Hitler let them have Christmas in peace?'

'What are we doing for Christmas?' Kathy piped up. 'Will we have a tree this year?'

'Don't be so selfish,' Jeannie said. 'Can you not think about someone other than yourself for a change?'

'I *am* sorry about the Blitz but I can't do anything about it, can I?' Kathy retorted. 'And talking about Christmas will cheer Mammy up.'

'We'll have our main celebration at New Year as usual,' Mary said, keeping the peace. 'Jeannie's working on Christmas Day.'

'Franny's shutting the shop Christmas and Boxing Day. Her nephew is coming home. Which means I'll have a holiday too.' Kathy skipped out of the room in glee, reminding her mother that she was still young despite her often grown-up pretences.

'I'll invite Helen to join us. Arthur's not coming home, is he love?'

'No, he told me so in his last letter.' And neither is Bill, Jeannie added silently. Not that she expected him to. There were no ties between them. He hadn't written to her and she had no address to write to him, even if she wished to.

'I'll invite Mr Woodley too,' Mary was saying.

'Mammy!'

'It's only fair,' Mary said. 'After all, he's providing the main course. That pig has fattened and he's booked it in for slaughtering.'

'Oh, Mammy, what will Isa say?' Jeannie asked in dismay, forgetting about Harry Woodley in concern for her little sister who had fed Patty the pig all year.

'She wanted to be a farmer, didn't she, now? Well, this is part of being a farmer. She has to learn.'

On New Year's afternoon, they had a small fire burning in the grate to welcome their guests. Harry had brought them a tree as his gift on Christmas Eve. Isa and Bob had decorated it with paper chains and the treasured glass baubles saved from previous years. A paper angel teetered on the top, one of her wings bent where Bob had been too enthusiastic placing her. They had made more paper chains too and these hung from the picture frames in a cheerful fashion.

Jeannie laid out a plate with thick slabs of fruit cake on the sideboard and poured small glasses of sherry. She was wearing her blue dress and brushed her hair until it shone. Kathy wore a new navy striped dress, her present from the family, which accentuated the burnished copper of her long hair. Isa and Bob wore their Sunday best clothes. Mary's good clothes were currently hidden behind her apron as she cooked the pork and trimmings.

They had given each other presents that morning. Kathy's delight in her new dress had made them all happy. Bob had a jigsaw, Isa got a ragdoll that Mary had made in the evenings and hidden in her sewing bag. Jeannie had clubbed together with Kathy to buy Mary a pair of warm slippers lined with sheep's wool, perfect for the air raid shelter.

As the first knock came on the door, there was a howl and the slam of the bedroom door.

'Kathy, get the door,' Jeannie shouted over her shoulder, hurrying into the kitchen.

Mary was stirring several pots at once, her grey-streaked hair clinging to her damp brow. Bob licked a wooden spoon and grinned at Jeannie. The kitchen was a fug of steam and delicious aromas of gravy and meat. Jeannie's stomach rumbled.

'What's the commotion?' she asked. 'Where's Isa?'

'She found out Mammy's cooking Patty,' Bob said, matter-of-factly.

'Will you see to her? I'm nearly ready to serve up. Is that Helen arrived?' Mary said, distractedly.

Jeannie gently pushed open the bedroom door. Isa lay sobbing on the bed. She looked up at Jeannie with stormy eyes and rolled over so that Jeannie could only see her back. She sat on the bed and stroked Isa's hair.

'I'm sorry, love. That's why we had the pig. She was never meant as a pet.'

That brought another gale of fresh sobs. Jeannie sat helplessly. She touched Isa's back to comfort her but the little girl wriggled away. Isa sat up. Her face was red and blotchy and she wiped the snot away with the back of her hand.

'I'm not eating dinner. I hate all of you. Go away!'

Jeannie had laid the table with care. Granny Dougal's china was set out and Bob had put stems of holly with bright, red berries as decorations. He had 'found' them while out with his pals. Jeannie decided not to ask further. Even Kathy helped to pour drinks and offer food to their guests. Harry had been round the neighbours in the pig club the day before with pieces of pork. His portion had been handed over to Mary along with their own.

'This is a feast, thank you, Mary,' Helen said, appreciatively.

Mary took off her apron and sat down with a happy sigh. 'I'm glad you could join us, and you too, Mr Woodley. It's nice to have friends to share with.'

They tucked into the good food. After a while, Jeannie slipped away with a filled plate for Isa with no sign of pork on it. Isa stared at her mutinously.

'Potato, cabbage and a wee bit of sage stuffing but you'll have to imagine the onion as I couldn't get any.'

Isa sniffled. She took the offered plate and fork and dug in hungrily.

'I am sorry, love,' Jeannie said, softly.

Isa didn't answer until she'd scraped her plate clean.

'I don't want to be a farmer any more.'

'I think that's a wise decision. They have to get up awfully early in the morning, even when it rains and snows.'

'I did like it at Miss Main's cottage. She won't forget me, will she?'

'Of course not. She loved having you and Bob to stay. I tell you what, why don't you write her a letter tomorrow? I'll post it for you.'

Isa snuggled in to her. Jeannie felt the warmth of her body against her side and felt a tender love for her little sister. She kissed the top of her head and hugged her close.

'Come on through now. There's cake, and Mr Woodley and Helen want to say hello.'

Later, they played Old Maid and Pin the Tail on the Donkey and the adults drank more sherry. In the evening, Harry walked Helen home.

'Oh, I'm perfectly fine for walking, dear,' she said, in response to Mary's enquiry. 'In fact, I'll enjoy the exercise and the fresh air.'

'It's fresh, all right,' Harry laughed, having gone out to check the weather. 'Nippy, with fresh snow coming down. Just as well we've both got wellingtons.'

Jeannie heard their laughter as they left the tenement. It had been a lovely day, she thought. It was a whole new year and they had Janet's wedding to look forward to in February. In other parts of the country, they weren't so fortunate. London was being blitzed, night after shattering night. All over Europe and further afield, their boys were fighting the Nazis. A shiver ran over her body. She sent up a loving prayer for Jimmy. And for Arthur and Bill.

Chapter Thirteen

It kept snowing all through January and into early
February. Even Janet's naturally ebullient spirits were
challenged by the daily snow showers, icy roads and mean
winds that cut through winter coats and chilled fingers to
the bone as she prayed with all her might for dry weather
on her wedding day. In an act of surprising generosity,
Miss McGrory had given them all the day off on the
Monday to attend the wedding.

'Not that she managed a smile while she told us,' Eileen
said.

'Who cares?' Annie put in. 'At least we got the whole
day to ourselves. I'm very glad to get a rest from the rotten
old factory.'

'We're glad to be able to celebrate our friend getting
married,' Jeannie said pointedly. 'It's not about getting a
rest.'

'Maybe not for you,' Annie mumbled.

Eileen shook her head in sympathy at Jeannie and then
grinned. 'Never mind all that. More importantly, what are
we giving Janet for gifts?'

The three young women were in Jeannie's bedroom
in Kiltie Street, getting ready for the wedding. Jeannie's
home was furthest away from Clydebank and the girls
were welcome there but Eileen had apologised for not
inviting them to hers and said her mother wouldn't like

the noise and disruption while Annie had said it wasn't convenient at her house. Jeannie and Eileen didn't ask her to explain. They had got used to Annie's mysterious home circumstances.

Mary was only too pleased to have the gaiety of the girls in the flat. Jeannie was glad that Kathy was working and that Isa and Bob were at school. The bedroom was small enough without her sisters and wee brother squeezing in to chat and watch them. They had to get dressed and then catch the bus back to Clydebank to the church early afternoon.

'It was hard to find anything for a present,' Jeannie said. 'The shops have been quite bare after Christmas. I managed to find some pretty soaps. What about you?'

'I'm giving her hair clips. They've got paste diamonds. Actually, they're mine but I thought she'd like them.'

'I'm sure she will,' Jeannie smiled. 'What did you get, Annie?'

'I'm giving them practical things. I've got tins of soup and pots of jam. I'll give them over later as they're too heavy to carry today.'

'Isn't it odd?' Eileen said. 'Before the war, that would have been a strange present but nowadays, it will be gratefully received. What a good choice, Annie.'

Annie looked pleased with herself. Jeannie thought she looked pretty today. Her thick dark hair was brushed and held back with a red bow. She wore a dark, wine-red velvet dress which was old-fashioned but suited her heavy looks. Jeannie looked at Eileen. No need to worry about her being well turned out. Eileen looked as beautiful as ever. Her curls were styled and set. Her face was made up with her eyes accentuated and her lips painted a coral pink. She wore a pale blue jacket over a matching skirt and had a pair of high-heeled shoes which were unsuitable for the icy pavements.

Catching her looking, Eileen laughed. 'Borrowed finery for today. These are my cousin's clothes. She's working in London and my aunt said I could use them. My red dress is too ordinary for Janet's big day.'

Jeannie wished she had a cousin with such lovely clothes to lend. She was wearing her blue dress yet again. She smoothed it down with a silent sigh. It was her only outfit for special occasions and she was fed up with it. Never mind. It was such a cold day, she'd keep her coat on and no one would notice. At a wedding, everyone looked at the bride, didn't they?

Arriving in Clydebank, Jeannie thought the Holy City tenements looked exotic somehow, with their pale walls glinting in the daylight and the rows upon rows of chimney stacks showing just how many families were crammed into the space around Radnor Park.

The church was packed but the three friends managed to slip into a pew at the back. From the faces and accents it was clear that most of the wedding guests were relatives of Janet's. Jeannie tried to work out who her eight brothers and sisters were. An older couple sitting on the other side of the aisle must be Alan's parents. They would have had to travel up from England for their son's wedding. Jeannie wondered what they thought of it all. Janet's family were noisy and boisterous until the priest arrived and the ceremony began.

Afterwards, the reception was held in the church hall. The tables were draped in a variety of tablecloths and a buffet was set out on long trestles under the stage. There were plates of sandwiches, trays of biscuits, a bowl of chicken in aspic and the centrepiece was a small fruit cake.

The noise levels almost rattled the old window frames as Thoms of all ages got into the spirit of celebrating young Janet's special day. Alan looked dazed but ecstatic as he put his arm around his bride proudly and they mingled amongst their guests.

Janet came towards them, her faced flushed with happiness. Alan had been cornered by a large beefy man with a ruddy face, holding a pint of beer and a fish paste sandwich.

'You look so beautiful,' Eileen cried. 'What a bonny dress, too.'

'It was my sister Bridget's wedding dress,' Janet said, and waved her small bouquet of wax flowers. 'The flowers were Bridget's too. I've bought a lovely going-away outfit, though. You'll see it at the end of the afternoon. Alan's friend has lent us his flat in Glasgow for our honeymoon. Alan's got two days' leave before he has to return to his regiment.'

'It's a wonderful wedding,' Jeannie said, hugging her petite friend. 'We're so glad for you both.'

'I'm so happy, I could burst,' Janet giggled. 'Now, listen. You must eat or my mum will be offended. She and my aunties have clubbed together with the neighbours to provide all the food and make the wedding cake. There's no icing because they couldn't get the sugar but it'll be tasty and you'll all get a wee slice to take home.'

'The chicken looks delicious,' Annie said.

'Chicken? That's not chicken. My brother Paul got a couple of rabbits from a pal of his and Mum made "chicken" out of them. But don't tell her I let the secret slip.'

A tall man with dark hair swooped down on the bride and made her scream as he swung her round and set her down.

'Did I hear my name?'

'Paul! Watch my dress. Bridget will have my guts for garters if I tear it.' But Janet's voice was fond as she scolded her big brother.

'And who are these gorgeous ladies?' Paul asked, his dark, merry eyes scanning them.

'I'm Annie. Janet was just telling us about the rabbits.' Annie moved forwards, almost bustling Jeannie and Eileen out of the way.

'Shhh,' Paul said, mock-sternly. 'Don't mention the rabbits. Please remember that is chicken in that bowl.'

'I won't tell if you don't,' Annie said coyly.

'Would you like to try some? What do you want to drink?' Paul took Annie's arm and drew her away towards the buffet table where a crowd had gathered.

'He's a bit of a flirt,' Janet said. 'I'm so glad Miss McGrory gave you the day off to come to our wedding. It means such a lot to me. You're my best friends.'

Janet's words were so honest, they pulled at Jeannie's heart. She realised Janet was right; Eileen, Annie and Janet had become her very best friends and she felt so lucky to have them.

'Where's the bride? Her husband's searching for her,' a tiny, bird-boned woman in a purple dress shrieked as she clutched at Janet's shoulders, nearly dislodging her veil.

'Och, Mum, don't be daft,' Janet grinned, 'Alan's only over there. He's been button-holed by Uncle Iain but he's been waving at me every few minutes.'

'Come along now, let's get the two of you for a picture. Dad's got the camera ready.'

'Excuse me,' Janet breathed as her mother steered her away.

'What a lovely family,' Eileen said wistfully. 'There are so many of them.'

Jeannie agreed, although she had the beginnings of a headache from all the noise and hubbub in the hall. A band was tuning up in the corner and it looked as if a ceilidh was going to take place soon. All of a sudden she wished Bill was there. Wouldn't he love a ceilidh! It would be a lovely Scottish memory to take home to Canada. And what about Arthur? Shouldn't she be wishing he was there, instead?

Jeannie remembered the bag she'd left at the edge of the stage. Mammy had sent a sponge cake for the newlyweds. She should add it to the buffet. When she told Eileen, her friend's face dropped.

'What's the matter?' Jeannie asked. 'Did your mum send something too? Did you forget to bring it?'

'Oh, Jeannie, if only it was that. My mum… she's so different from yours. Or from Janet's. I told her about Janet and Alan getting married and she wasn't interested at all. It never occurred to her to make food and send it with me. And then, today, it hit me all over again. Your mother saying how pretty our dresses are when we were getting ready at your house, and bringing us cups of tea and biscuits and asking us all about the wedding. My mum just doesn't care about me at all.'

Jeannie was taken aback as all this poured out of Eileen. She'd had no idea that Eileen felt this way. Her friend always seemed so sure of herself, and happy, and full of fun.

'I have to tell you something. It's a secret but I don't understand it.'

'All right, let's sit over here away from the dancing.'

Jeannie led Eileen over to a small table at the far end of the room, away from the stage and the sweating band blasting out folk tunes and the couples dancing and whooping and stamping their feet in time to the music.

'I've always felt that my parents don't love me,' Eileen said. 'When I was wee, I suppose I thought everyone's parents were like mine. They don't hug me or kiss me and they don't talk to me very much. Mind you, they don't talk to each other much, either. When I got older and visited friends, I saw how different their parents were. Like yours, Jeannie. Your mum is so interested in what you're doing and it's obvious she loves you. Janet's mum asks her a dozen questions every evening about her day.'

'Maybe they are just shy, quiet people. My grandparents were like that. My grandfather never spoke much and my granny was known for being dour. They were kind in their own way but not given to showing much affection.'

Eileen shook her head. 'There's more. I've never been allowed into their bedroom. But I went in when I was ill recently, to get a book. And I found... I found a photograph of a wee boy.' She stopped, remembering her father's response.

'Who was he?'

'I have no idea. I asked my dad and he was very odd about it. His reaction scared me. He told me to put it back and never to mention it to my mother.'

Jeannie's brows wrinkled. She was out of her depth. How was she to best advise Eileen?

'Perhaps you should ask your mum. Even if your dad said not to. It sounds like she knows the answer.'

'You don't know my mum. She'd blow her top if I said the wrong thing,' Eileen said miserably. 'Oh… I wish Jimmy was here.'

Jeannie smiled despite the strange conversation. 'You really love him, don't you?'

'I love him with all my heart,' Eileen said and her eyes shone. 'I'm not alone any more now that I have Jimmy.'

'Oh, Eileen, you were never alone. Not since you met me and Janet and Annie.'

'I love you all, too. Now I'm getting maudlin. Come on, let's go and dance. That's the Gay Gordons starting up. I think I can remember the steps to it. Up you get, Jeannie Dougal!'

Eileen's bright, cheerful expression had returned as she teased Jeannie into standing for the dance but Jeannie was no longer fooled by her friend's jolliness. She understood now that underneath the happy-go-lucky exterior, there was a girl who was sad and lacked confidence in spite of her attractiveness. Jeannie vowed to herself to help. She wasn't sure how but she'd be there when Eileen needed her.

–

Annie was having a marvellous time. Paul hadn't left her side since he cut her a slice of the rabbit and got her a drink of fruit cordial.

'Take it easy on the cordial,' he advised her with a cheeky grin. 'My brothers, Thomas and Andy, were in charge of adding a nip or two of a wee something to it. I seem to recall a large bottle of whisky from Dad's pre-war stash being hauled out.'

'Mmm, it's delicous,' she laughed and then coughed as the first sip caught the back of her throat.

Paul roared with laughter as he thumped her on the back until she stopped coughing. Annie had never met anyone like him before. He was larger than life. A tall, broad-shouldered man with a loud, infectious laugh and merriment in his dark eyes, he was always on the lookout for amusement. His two brothers, twins, looked a lot like him and the trio provided half of the noise in the hall, she reckoned.

'Thick as thieves, we all are,' Paul told her as they watched the dancers, from the side of the hall. 'Thomas and Andy are next to me in age and we've always been a gang, getting into all sorts of scrapes. My poor wee mum despairs of us.'

'Janet said there's nine of you. Is that right?' Annie didn't much care whether there were nine or none or ninety-nine, she simply liked watching him laugh and talk.

'Aye, that's right. The three of us are in the army, based up at the barracks in Glasgow. It's a bit of a miracle we all got passes for the wedding, to be honest. The sergeant is all right and he likes us so that helped. Then there's Janet, who's working, and Bridget who's married. The other kids are school age but they're not at school today, as you can see them tearing around the hall here.'

Annie was thrilled that Paul seemed to like her. He asked her to dance and they stayed on the floor for the Dashing White Sergeant, Strip the Willow, the Canadian Barn Dance and then a slow waltz. She was flushed and laughing when he guided her to a table and brought her another cordial.

'Excuse me a moment,' Paul said. 'Mum wants me to take Auntie Vera onto the dance floor for a whirl. I'll be back so don't disappear on me now, will you?'

Annie promised she wouldn't and watched his tall back as he walked away. She saw him bending down to a tiny, white-haired elderly lady and offering his arm. She glanced about for Jeannie and Eileen. She ought to go and chat to them. But instead, she sat where she was, luxuriating in the thought of Paul. He liked her, she could tell. Sipping the fortified cordial, for a short while she felt strong and emboldened. She knew she looked good this evening with her hair freshly washed and brushed a hundred strokes and her red, velvet dress stolen from her mother's wardrobe.

But then her spirits subsided as her constant worry nagged in her brain. What would the others say if they knew her secret? They would hate her. And what about Paul? He looked so smart and handsome in his army uniform. If he knew, she was certain that look of admiration in his dark eyes when he gazed at her would turn to pure disgust.

Chapter Fourteen

'Ooh, look at the size of that moon.' Kathy leaned out of the window and sniffed the air.

It had been a lovely, warm spring day and now the evening's sweet fresh air lingered as it wafted into the room. Kathy's make-up was perfect and her hair was swept back fashionably. She had announced that she was going over to Judith's to keep her company again. Mary thought that Kathy was very kind to do so when the old lady was asleep or dozing in her armchair. Jeannie was more suspicious. She kept meaning to ask Judith if Kathy visited her but was so busy she never got round to it.

'That's a bomber's moon.' Jeannie shivered now as she joined her sister at the open window.

All of a sudden she felt sure that Jerry was coming back. They had had three months of peace from bombing. The last bombs in late November had destroyed tenements in Eveline Street in the East End of the city and then... nothing.

'Is your box packed?' she asked Mary, who was sitting sewing in the big armchair. Not waiting for the answer, she went through to the kitchen to boil the kettle. A flask of tea might be in order.

'Don't go out tonight,' Jeannie begged Kathy. 'Stay here. I have an awful feeling that something bad's going to happen.'

'Don't be daft.' Kathy threw Jeannie's hand off her arm. 'I've told Judith I'll be round. I can't change my mind. Mammy, tell her not to be nagging at me.'

'What is it, Jeannie? Why are you so agitated?' Mary said, setting down the blouse with a tear in the sleeve where Kathy had carelessly caught it on a loose nail on a shelf in Franny's shop.

Before Jeannie could answer, the eerie sound of the siren began to wail over the city.

'I knew it,' she shrieked. 'Mammy, you take the box and the gas masks, Kathy, the flask is ready. Be quick. I'll wake Isa and Bob.'

She didn't wait to see if her orders were being followed. She ran into the bedroom and shook the children awake. She helped them dress, all the while listening for the sound of enemy planes. If they were coming tonight, would they reach the north-west of Glasgow?

As they stumbled in the darkness down into the maw of the Anderson shelter, the drone of aeroplanes got louder. Jeannie glanced up and a shaft of terror pierced her. She saw the outlines of the bombers and saw the first streaks of fire as the incendiaries began to fall. The ack-ack guns were firing now and the air was full of noise and smoke and beams of light criss-crossing the orange sky. Martin and Linda hurried towards her, their faces pale with fear. Jeannie helped them down the steps and then pulled the door shut after her. As she pulled it close, she heard Harry Woodley's bellowing voice and then the sharp sound of his whistle on Kiltie Street. He was on ARP duty tonight, making sure all Kiltie Street's residents were moving towards shelter. She hoped he stayed safe.

Kathy had lit the oil lamps and candles in the shelter and the light flickered and bounced off their faces, all turned up towards her. Jeannie felt a tender love for them all squeeze her heart painfully. If anything should befall them… but she mustn't think like that. She put a smile on her face for Isa and Bob.

'Who's up for a game of Old Maid?' she said with forced cheerfulness.

It was a long night of terror. The raids began at nine p.m. and would not finish until five thirty the next morning, by which time the town of Clydebank, north of Glasgow, would lie in ruins with hundreds dead or made homeless, and the West End of Glasgow would be hit by many stray high explosives. The River Clyde acted as a silver ribbon guiding the German bombers to their targets. Flares and incendiaries showered down before the high explosives were let loose. By nine thirty, the huge timber yard at Singer was alight, along with the Dalnottar oil storage tanks and two whisky distilleries.

In their shelter on the edge of the city, Eileen and her mother sat opposite each other on the cold, wooden benches. They had brought in blankets but Eileen felt cold seep into her limbs. Every crump and boom made Agnes flinch. Eileen wanted to sit next to her and put an arm around her but knew that her mother wouldn't like that. If only they were a family that showed emotions, she thought, gripping her own hands tightly. She could do with a hug right now. She thought of her friends and prayed they were all safely in a shelter or cellar. And most of all, she prayed for her dad. He wasn't on duty that night and Agnes had told him not to go. But he had ignored her, put on his jacket and gone out to help.

Eileen watched him leave as she helped her mother pack their important papers and make hasty sandwiches in case it was a long night. Robert Boyle went out the door calmly, as if he were headed to a day at an office. Her father wasn't one to make a fuss. He was a quiet man. In fact, she felt she didn't really know him at all. What if he died tonight? Before she had a chance to get him to open up about… everything? By 'everything', she meant that photo. But, also, she was desperate to ask if he loved her at all.

Another loud boom made her shake. It was close. The shelter rattled and shook on its foundation and a layer of dust came down onto her head, making her sneeze. Agnes was praying out loud now. The noise outside was ear-splitting and Eileen pressed her hands over her ears.

'He shouldn't have gone,' Agnes burst out. 'It isn't his turn. He's not on duty tonight. I told him not to volunteer. He had that heart attack a few years ago. It should be someone else's job.'

'It's Dad's nature. He couldn't leave it to others. He'll be all right,' Eileen said, hoping it was true.

Now, she reached across to take her mother's hand, expecting to be pushed away and told not to be ridiculous. But Agnes clutched it like a lifeline. Eileen felt the roughness of her skin. A work-coarsened hand that made meals and cleaned their little house and kept them warm and safe. A hand that touched her brow when she was sick but didn't soothe or stroke. For some reason, Agnes wasn't capable of that. Anyway, it was enough. Eileen's shoulders sank down and her fear subsided.

They stayed that way for a while, not drawing closer but not drawing apart, either. There was a short lull in the terrible sounds outside. Eileen waited for the all clear but it didn't come. Please God, let that be it.

At that moment, Agnes gave a loud scream.

'What is it, Mum?'

Agnes ignored her. She scrabbled beside her on the bench and picked up a book.

She flicked through it. 'It's gone!'

'What's gone? Please, Mum, calm down. What's gone?'

Agnes moaned and the book slipped from her grasp. Eileen bent to pick it up. It was the book she had borrowed from her parents' bedroom and immediately she knew what her mum was looking for.

'I'll get it for you, Mum. I know what it means to you.'

She didn't know who the little boy in the photo was but Agnes's distress was more than Eileen could bear. She got up and opened the door of the shelter. Staring out, she saw that the sky above her was red and huge planes passed overhead. There was a roar of not-so-distant thuds and explosions. She ran across the grass and there it was. A square piece of paper lying on the muddy lawn. The boy's face stared up at her. She picked it up and turned back to the shelter. Before she had taken a step, there was a strange whoosh, as if the air had been sucked out of the garden and she was flung head-first into the corrugated iron.

Eileen felt an intense pain in her head and shoulders and then mercifully it all went black. When she came round, she was back in the shelter. Her head was in her mother's lap and Agnes was sobbing.

'Mum… Mum…'

'My darling girl, you're alive!'

'My head…'

'Don't move until you're ready. You took quite a blow. If only your father was here. He'd know what to do. Keep still, Eileen. Let me see your eyes. You're likely concussed. I have to get you to hospital but it's still going on out there. There's no sign of it stopping. Oh dear, what will we do?'

'It's all right… Mum. I'm going to be fine. I know it.'

Eileen lay in wonder as Agnes kissed her forehead and stroked her arm in comforting movements. Her head ached and she felt sick but none of that mattered. It was as if she was dreaming. Her mother loved her! Finally, Eileen was getting what she had passionately wished for. Agnes was demonstrating her affection.

'You do love me,' she whispered weakly.

'What?' her mother's voice was suddenly stringent and familiar. 'Of course I love you. What nonsense you're mumbling. I've always loved you. You're my daughter.'

Eileen strained to sit up. Agnes, taken aback by her words, let her. Eileen leaned against the bench. Her head throbbed horribly but it didn't matter.

'Who is he?'

'Never mind that just now. Why did you do such a silly thing? Opening the shelter when the bombs are going off?'

'Because I know how much he means to you. I just don't know why.'

Agnes gave a deep sigh. 'I never wanted to tell you. Your father said we should but I didn't want to. I thought it would spoil your childhood, knowing.'

'Not knowing has been worse. I've… I've never felt that you loved me. I found the photo recently and Dad said I wasn't to say to you.'

'His name was Ronnie. He's your brother. If he was alive he'd be twenty-four. I suppose I might have lost him anyway, caught up in this dreadful war. As it was, I lost him when he was three. I had a difficult birth and I was ill for a long while afterwards. Then, when I got better, Ronnie got ill. He never recovered. When I had you, I decided not to love you too much in case I lost you, too. I thought… I *knew*… I wouldn't survive that. I kept myself close. And your father supported me. Perhaps if he'd done it differently, if he'd told me to snap out of it, I might have been able to be a better mother. I don't know.'

'You are a good mother,' Eileen said, tears rolling down her cheeks. 'I love you and Dad so much. I wish you could've shown me you loved me too. But it doesn't matter. I know now that you do.'

Agnes groaned and pressed her hand to the small of her back.

'What is it?' Eileen asked in alarm.

'I think I've put my back out, pulling you into the shelter.'

'Oh, Mum,' Eileen said sympathetically but then a rumble of laughter began to build inside her until it burst out in a snort and giggles.

Agnes looked affronted for a moment until the corners of her mouth twitched and she began to laugh too until she winced. 'No, really, I have. You're not as light as you look.'

Well, that just set Eileen off again. Her head throbbed as she laughed but as her body shook with it, all her tension washed away, leaving her weak and floppy but contented.

'My head hurts,' she said.

'I'll fetch the warden. He can get an ambulance.'

'No, don't go out. Don't leave me.'

'I'll be back as soon as I can,' Agnes promised.

Eileen caught her hand and held on fiercely. 'Not yet. It's too dangerous. I'm not losing you just as I've found you. Wait a wee while until the all clear. Promise me?'

'All right. But if you worsen any, I'm away.'

'That sounds reasonable. Can I have a blanket? I'm that cold.'

Eileen felt the wonderful sensation of being tucked in by her mother and the gentle touch of her fingers on her temples. 'Mum?'

'Yes, dear?'

'I didn't tell you about Jimmy...' Eileen's voice trailed away and her eyes closed. She was ever so tired and her head felt heavy on an aching neck.

There was a high-pitched whistling sound followed by a moment of ominous silence before an enormous explosion shook the shelter from its earth foundation. It was as if the whole corrugated shell jumped up in the air before crashing down again. Both women screamed and everything went black.

In Kiltie Street, Jeannie was running out of her reper-toire of songs but Linda O'Leary remembered tunes from the Great War and kept the singing going. Soon, Martin, Linda and Mary were leading them in yet another vigorous rendition of 'Pack up Your Troubles'. Bob lay asleep on Mary's knee while Isa was curled up on the wooden bench next to them, her blanket tightly around her so that she resembled a sausage roll. In the midst of the booms and gunfire outside and the singing inside, Jeannie was able to speak to Kathy without anyone else hearing.

'Are you really going to Judith's these evenings?'

'Of course. I said I was, didn't I?' Kathy was sullenly defensive.

'All dressed up? Don't think I haven't noticed you stealing my lipstick. There's only a stump left.'

'It's not as if you need it. Arthur doesn't like you wearing make-up.'

'That's hardly the point,' Jeannie said, feeling defensive herself. 'Why would you need to get all dolled up to go round to the neighbours?'

In the low light from the oil lamps she wasn't sure if Kathy blushed. Something clicked in Jeannie's mind.

'You're seeing someone, aren't you?'

'I am not.'

'Mammy'll have your guts for garters, I'm telling you,' Jeannie warned.

Kathy's shoulders slumped. 'You won't tell her, will you?'

'Not if you promise me you'll stop. Who is it, anyway?'

'No one you know.'

'Will you promise?' Jeannie persisted. 'You're not old enough to be stepping out.'

'I'm sixteen now, for God's sake,' Kathy's voice rose angrily. 'I'm old enough to get married.'

She quietened down as Mary glanced round at her. Luckily Linda had started a rendition of 'Keep the Home Fires Burning' and Mary joined in.

'And is that what he's offering? Marriage?' Jeannie said.

'Och, what do you know? You've only ever been out with Arthur. And he's hardly exciting.'

'Well, exciting is all very well but just watch out it doesn't lead to something you ought not to be doing,' Jeannie said, stung by Kathy's comment.

The terrible noises outside the shelter built to a crescendo until they couldn't hear themselves sing and a huge boom and crash made them clutch one another.

'That was too close.' Martin stood up shakily. 'Someone's taken a hit nearby.'

'Sit down, Martin. We cannae do anything,' Linda shook her head wearily.

'I can do something,' Mary said in a low voice. She gathered the sleeping Bob in her arms and looked over at Isa, still curled up under her blanket.

How they slept through the sounds, Jeannie couldn't understand.

'What are you saying, Mammy?' she said, scared of Mary's expression.

'I'm going to send them away again. It's not safe here.'

'But where to?' Jeannie knew it was for the best but she couldn't bear the thought of the family being split up further.

'I've got a cousin, Martha. She's married to a farmer out in East Kilbride. I'll write to her. I'm not doing it through the school this time. I'll sort it myself.'

The all clear went in the early morning and they staggered out, Martin complaining of his stiff knees and Linda blowing her nose and saying she'd caught a cold from the damp. Mary looked exhausted and Bob was grumpy at being woken so early. Isa was like a little white ghost, clinging to Jeannie's side and yawning in a dazed fashion. Only Kathy was bright and chirpy and she was happy because she reckoned Franny wouldn't expect her in to work that day.

'It's not that bad here,' Jeannie told her. 'Clydebank's been hit hard but we can go to work.'

There was smoke over the city as Jeannie and Elspeth took the bus out to Fearnmore. They could see the orange glow of the fires at Singer's timber yard and where the oil depots burned. At the factory, many girls were missing including Eileen, Janet and Annie. Miss McGrory was absent too and the atmosphere was subdued as the women hurried through their tasks and ate hasty lunches in the canteen. Production was being speeded up, they were told, as the war effort demanded. The supervisor standing in for Miss McGrory didn't explain how they were to do that with people missing.

The bombers came back that evening for another night of destruction. With a sense of déjà vu, Jeannie gathered their belongings and herded her family into the shelter. It was another long night and they were tired from the previous night. Martin and Linda looked old and frail and even Mary looked worn out, Jeannie thought with a pang. She realised she depended on Mammy's strength and calm.

When the all clear finally went, they came out to a scene of devastation. Kiltie Street was intact but tenements further over were in a bad state.

'Kilmun Street's taken a hit,' someone shouted.

A bulky figure loomed out of the fog, covered in white plaster dust. It was Harry Woodley. Mary ran to him and Jeannie turned away, shooing Isa and Bob into the flat and telling them to wash. Kathy lit the range and put the kettle on without being asked. For once, she was quiet, seeming as shocked as Jeannie at the damage to homes nearby.

Mary came in, wiping dust from her coat. 'Mr Woodley says to tell you, you'll not get to work today. The buses aren't running from here. There's a crater in the road and it gets worse further west. Fearnmore was hit. Mr Woodley doesn't know how bad.'

'What about Kilmun Street?' Jeannie said. 'Did he know—'

Mary shook her head. 'It's awful; there's people dead there. Mr Woodley said he's seen things to make him weep. He's been with others all night, using their bare hands to lift the rubble. They got a wee girl out alive. Like a miracle. But her mother and sister didn't make it.'

'Oh, Mammy, come away and sit down. Kathy'll bring you tea,' Jeannie said softly. 'I'm going to walk up to Helen's and make sure she's all right.'

There were people standing around on the streets as Jeannie walked up the steep hill. A pall of smoke and dust hung in the air. From the road she saw the bomb damage over in Kilmun Street, dark gaps like missing teeth in the sandstone rows, and uniformed figures running back and forth amongst the smoking rubble. The poor souls who had lost their lives and their homes, she thought. With relief, she saw that the houses on Helen Dunn's street were untouched.

'I didn't go to the shelter last night,' Helen said, bringing her in to the living room. 'I simply couldn't bear another chilly, damp seat in that blasted place. I stayed right here and felt if my name was on that bomb then so be it.'

'Arthur wouldn't like you to sit here when there's a raid,' Jeannie said, horrified.

Helen clasped Jeannie's hands in hers. 'I've been thinking. In fact, I had the whole evening to think.'

'What is it? Do you feel ill?'

Helen ignored her question. She looked Jeannie straight in the eye. 'I'd like you and Arthur to set a date to get married. Life is very short. It can be gone just like that. I'd like to see you both settled. I know you'll be good for him. He can be... difficult, my son but you're good for him, Jeannie. You'll make him happy.'

Jeannie sank into the armchair, her legs suddenly weak. How could she explain that she was having second thoughts? That when she tried to think of Arthur, Bill's face appeared in her dreams instead?

'I've taken you by surprise,' Helen said. 'I'm sorry. You don't have to answer me now but please consider it. Plenty of young people are marrying quickly these days.'

Jeannie made her escape as soon as possible after making sure Helen had everything she needed. She'd been unable to answer, unable to assure Arthur's mother that she'd do what she asked. Instead, she felt as if she was being trapped. Slowly and surely without a way out.

When she got home, Mary met her at the door.

'You've got a visitor.' Her face was troubled but Jeannie didn't notice, still mulling over Helen's words.

'Jeannie…'

But Jeannie was already past her and into the parlour. She stopped. For a moment she didn't recognise the tall dark-haired young man in army khaki standing there. Then she placed him.

'Hello, Paul,' she said, surprised. What was Janet's brother doing here?

He twisted his cap, unable to meet her eyes. But when he did, she was hit by the anguish in his dark gaze. Her heart began to thump hollowly in her chest.

'It's Janet, isn't it?' she said.

'They're all gone. Janet and Mam and the wee ones. The whole street's gone, nothing but bricks and a bloody great hole in the ground. My dad was out working and me and Thomas and Andy were at the barracks. Bridget's legs are smashed up but she survived in her wee house the other end of town. God knows how. The whole place is a mess,' his voice cracked.

'I'm so sorry,' Jeannie whispered.

She couldn't believe it. Janet was gone. Sweet Janet with her lovely, bright smile and her hearty appetite. Always with a cheerful word for everyone. Always looking on the bright side and giving comfort when anyone was down.

'She liked you,' Paul said. 'Talked about how kind you were to her. How you were the leader of your wee gang, as she put it.'

Had she really said that? Jeannie wanted to cry. She'd had no idea Janet felt that way about her. She touched her cheek. Her birthmark had always made her shy and self-conscious. And yet, she'd managed to make three good friends since the war started. Irreplaceable friendships. Jeannie started to sob. She'd never see Janet again.

Paul drew her to him and held her while she cried onto the rough material of his army jacket. When she stood back, she saw his dark eyes were damp and his face white and strained. Neither noticed Mary peek into the room and quietly go away.

'I'm so sorry for all of you,' she said. She could barely imagine what Paul was feeling. He had lost half his family. 'I heard it was bad in Clydebank and I saw it burning.'

'Aye, it's bad. Those that are left have nothing. They're leaving if they can. The centres can't house them all. People fled to the hills the second night of the bombing and came back to hell.'

'Annie—'

'She's all right. I checked on her and she and her mother are homeless but unharmed.'

There was a silence between them then. Jeannie heard a crow cawing outside. In the rest of the flat there were voices, Isa and Bob arguing and Kathy telling them to shut up. Life went on. Even when devastation occurred and nothing could be the same again.

'Will you take a cup of tea, Paul?' she asked. Her own throat was so dry, she felt she could drink a gallon of the stuff and still be thirsty.

He shook his head. 'I must away. Bridget needs me and so does my dad. He just sits there. Won't eat or talk. I've got compassionate leave and I'll need it to sort things out.'

'Oh, what about Alan?' How could she have forgotten him? Her mind wasn't working properly. Now it flitted back to the wedding and the young couple's happiness so plain for all to see.

'He knows. It'll take him a couple of days to get up here. He's based on the south coast just now.'

'How will he bear it?' Jeannie said.

Paul placed his cap on his dark hair. 'How will any of us bear it? But we'll have to. This bloody war still goes on. I hope I get transferred overseas as soon as possible. I'll kill as many Nazis as I can.'

Jeannie was chilled by the savage tone of his voice. He didn't say more and she showed him out, worried about him and the rest of Janet's family. Bob came in, telling her about his comic and pointing out Desperate Dan. Isa brought her paper dolls and played on the floor in front of the fireplace. Their chatter washed over her while she nodded and answered. They didn't notice anything wrong and Jeannie found their presence comforting.

Life was short. Helen had told her that. And now Janet was gone.

Chapter Fifteen

Jeannie found Eileen in a hospital bed halfway down a long ward. She was asleep so Jeannie sat beside the bed. Mary had sent biscuits. Jeannie put the paper packet on the cabinet, and waited. Eileen's face was pale with purple shadows under her eyes and bruising across her cheeks. She was propped up on pillows and there was a sling across her left shoulder.

Her eyelids flickered and she smiled faintly. 'Jeannie, is that you?'

'How are you? Annie sent a message that you were in here.'

'I've got a concussion and had a dislocated shoulder. I'm all right really but they've kept me in because of these dizzy spells and I feel quite sick.'

'Poor you. It must've been awful.'

Annie had written from the village of Cardross, on the coast north of Glasgow, where she and her mother had been billeted and were living on a farm with another family that the farmer and his wife had taken in. The letter spoke of Janet and Paul and that she had met Mr and Mrs Boyle at the community centre and found out that Eileen had been injured and taken to hospital. It made no mention of Annie's own circumstances or feelings except giving the address of the farm if Jeannie wished to write back. If not, Annie would see her at Fearnmore once it opened again from the bomb damage.

'It's funny but I don't remember hitting my head. Our house is completely gone, Mum says. Is she here?'

'I didn't see anyone else. I think I'm your only visitor this afternoon.'

'I forgot; she and Dad went back to the centre to fill in some forms. They're trying to find us a place to live. I'm a bit confused, so don't mind me if I say something odd,' Eileen said.

'Mammy sent some food and clothes. I'll go there after and hand them over.'

'Your mum is so kind.'

'You'd do the same for us if we needed it,' Jeannie smiled.

'I'm glad I got hurt.'

'Now that is an odd thing to say.'

'No, really. And it's not the bump on the head talking. I have to explain. I discovered that my mum loves me but she had her reasons for not showing it.'

Jeannie listened as Eileen told her what had happened in the Anderson shelter.

'I remember all that,' she finished up, 'but I don't remember the bomb landing and I can't remember being in the ambulance or ending up in hospital. Maybe it'll come back but if it doesn't, I don't care. I know the important parts.'

'I'm so glad you've found each other finally,' Jeannie said, her heart glad for her best friend. 'What a pity your mum couldn't show her love. But now you can make up for lost time.'

She thought of Janet and how there was no time left for her and her family. Did Eileen know?

'Annie told me,' Eileen said quietly. 'You're thinking of Janet. I can see it in your face. Oh, Jeannie, it's so awful, isn't it? Here we are, chatting, and we'll never chat to Janet again. I'm going to miss her so much. She won't be there staring hungrily at me in the canteen when I eat my bread and jam. I won't ever get to share it with her again.'

Jeannie swallowed a lump in her throat. She'd shed so many tears already. She seemed to have an endless supply of them.

'It is awful and we'll never forget her. We have to keep going, for her sake, so it wasn't all in vain. We've got important war work to do, making munitions.'

'Is the factory open again? Annie told my parents to tell me it was closed because of bomb damage.'

'I don't know. I heard the same. I'll try and get there tomorrow only the roads were blocked so I hope they've been cleared. It'll be a while until you're back at work, I suppose?'

'I'm hoping to get out today or tomorrow. But the nurse has said I must rest for a few days. Don't worry, I'll get back as soon as I can and keep you company. Annie will be there; she can catch a train from Cardoss.'

'She didn't say much in her letter about being bombed out or how she is.'

'She's a bit of a mystery, our Annie. Never mind, one day she'll trust us enough to tell us her secret.'

'Secret?'

'Oh, yes. She's definitely hiding something.'

Jeannie thought Eileen's head injury was confusing her and decided not to say any more.

'Are you tired? I should leave you to rest,' she said, concerned at Eileen's pallor.

'I'm a wee bit tired but don't go just yet. It's lovely having you here. I'll sleep in a while.'

'I can't think of much more to tell you,' Jeannie said, 'except that Mammy's decided to send Isa and Bob away to the country for safety. She blames herself for bringing them back from Perthshire. Most of the kids came back to Glasgow around the same time when it seemed nothing was going to happen.'

'You'll miss them, but she's doing the right thing,' Eileen comforted her. 'There could be more bombing.'

'We had a letter from Jimmy, did you get one?' Jeannie changed the subject as the notion of the children's evacuation felt too raw.

'I did. Mum brought it yesterday. The censor's been all over it so it doesn't tell me much but he's put SWALK at the bottom before he's scrawled his name so I'm happy.'

'What's SWALK?'

'It means "sealed with a loving kiss". I didn't know either but Nurse Jennings told me. She has two boyfriends, one in the army and one in the navy. She's good for a giggle but only when Sister isn't around.'

Jeannie felt a tiny flare of envy which subsided almost at once. She could never imagine Arthur signing off his letters like that. He wasn't one for showing his love. In fact, he thought it rather vulgar and had told her so when she'd tried to kiss him while out walking. What about Bill? She had told him in no uncertain terms that he had no right to speak of being in love with her. She had sent him away. She hadn't had a single letter from him so there could be no SWALK from Bill. And it was all her own fault.

–

The rest centre was in the secondary school in the Vale of Leven, eleven miles north of Clydebank and, it was hoped, out of range of bombing raids. It was full of families, with children running up and down the corridors and worn-out adults sitting or lying on rows of palliasses. There was a stink of unwashed bodies and overflowing toilets. Jeannie passed a man asleep on his back with a canary in a cage balanced on his stomach. The canary's trilling song was lost in the crying, shouting and general hubbub.

'Is there a Mr and Mrs Boyle here?' she asked as she went past people, who shook their heads.

Eventually, a thin woman wearing a flowered apron and a lemon-yellow turban called out, 'Over there, hen, in the corner. I'm their neighbour. Or I was, when I had a home.'

'Thank you.' Jeannie headed over to the corner of the hall where she saw a woman who looked like an older, faded version of Eileen. 'Mrs Boyle?'

'Yes?'

'I'm Jeannie. I'm a friend of Eileen's. I went to see her this afternoon and she said you were here. My mother sent some food and clothes. We didn't know if you had managed to salvage anything.'

'A friend of Eileen's? I'm so glad she has nice friends. Will you take a seat? The mattress isn't the most comfort-able but there we are. We have to make do.'

Jeannie sat beside her. Mrs Boyle was right about the mattress. It was lumpy and itched her legs as she stretched them out in front of her.

'Why would your mother think of us?' She sounded dazed.

'It's what friends do. I'm sure you'd help us if we'd been bombed out.'

Mrs Boyle stared at her. 'I don't have any friends. Somehow, I let them all go when Ronnie died. It's too late now, isn't it?'

'It's never too late to make friends,' Jeannie said. 'I didn't have many before I worked at Fearnmore and met Eileen and Annie and… well, now they are my best friends.'

She wouldn't mention Janet. This poor woman looked as if she'd snap in two in a strong wind.

'Are you Jimmy's sister?' Mrs Boyle asked.

'Yes. I'm glad Eileen's told you about him. They're very much in love. Jimmy was never one for writing letters but he writes to Eileen a lot. That's love for you,' Jeannie laughed.

A small smile broke across Agnes Boyle's face. Jeannie felt it was a face that hadn't smiled very much for a long time. She thought of what Eileen had told her about being lonely and her parents' lack of love. It wasn't too late. Not for friendship or for love. Thank goodness, Eileen's mother had discovered that at last.

A tall man approached them. His suit was dusty and his nails black-rimmed but he carried himself with quiet dignity.

'This is Eileen's father,' Mrs Boyle said. 'Robert, this is Eileen's best friend, Jeannie.' There was pride in her voice as she introduced Jeannie.

Mr Boyle gave a distracted nod. He waved a piece of paper in his hand. 'There are no more billets close to home. Upstairs – you should see them, Agnes – there's a long queue of desperate people, willing to snatch anything.'

'What will we do? We can't stay here forever.'

Agnes Boyle's gaze took in the squalling children nearby, the rows of palliasses and scattered belongings and the pervasive smell which wafted in the stuffy air.

'I've decided we'll go and ask Uncle Herbert if we can stay with him.'

'Your Uncle Herbert?'

'Of course my Uncle Herbert. How many Uncle Herberts do you know?' Mr Boyle's tone was gentle but exasperated.

Jeannie was embarrassed. She should go. She got up. Eileen's parents were too absorbed to notice.

'He's never liked you.'

'That's by the by. The man has a four-bedroom house in Greenock, overlooking Lyle Hill. He lives by himself since Lily died and they have no children. He's family, Agnes, and he must take us in. It's the only chance we have.'

Greenock. It was on the other side of the Firth of Clyde. Jeannie's heart sank. If Eileen moved to Greenock, she wouldn't be able to work at Fearnmore. Mumbling her goodbye, she made her way through the clusters of tired families, thinking about that. She almost didn't hear her name being called.

'Jeannie Dougal, is that you?'

Miss McGrory stood in front of her, barring her way. The supervisor was usually impeccably dressed with her mousy brown hair pulled back into a neat bun and her glasses perched on her nose. Now, she was dishevelled, wearing a faded red jacket, a size too large, over a torn, smeared skirt. There was a crack in the left lens of her glasses. Her hair, always so neat, looked greasy and unkempt.

'Are you all right?' Jeannie said, catching her arm as Miss McGrory wavered on her feet.

'I feel a little faint.'

'Come along, we'll sit over here,' Jeannie said, taking control and amazed at herself for doing so.

She was wary of her supervisor. Especially since she'd been taken in for a dressing down that time at the factory for being late. Now, here she was, ordering Miss McGrory about. What cheek, Jeannie Dougal, she thought to herself with an inward grimace. She braced herself for a reprimand. But Miss McGrory meekly let herself be led to the nearest palliasse. They both sat on its thin weight.

'This isn't mine,' Miss McGrory said vaguely. 'There's a young woman, on her own, who lies here all day usually. All her family were killed and their house is in smithereens. I wonder where she's gone?'

'I'm sure she won't be far. When she comes back, we can move,' Jeannie said, soothingly.

'Why are you here? Have you got relatives in the centre?'

'I brought food for Eileen Boyle's parents.'

'That Agnes Boyle. She and I went to school together, did you know that? Nowadays, she's too uppity to be friends.'

'I'm sure that isn't true,' Jeannie said. 'She's lonely and would like company.'

Miss McGrory sniffed. 'This isn't my jacket, you know. It's too big and I don't like red. Too gaudy.'

'Do you need more clothes? I could bring you some.'

Miss McGrory took off her spectacles and rubbed her eyes. She blinked at Jeannie and set them neatly back on her nose.

'That's very kind. I'm afraid I've been very harsh on you girls.'

'It has felt like it but you must've had your reasons.'

'I was bitter. That's the truth of it. I'm a bitter old maid.'

When Jeannie politely protested, the supervisor waved her away.

'I can't make any excuses for myself. I was jealous of you all. You were so young and carefree while I... I was engaged to be married, you see, and we were very much in love. He was killed in the last week of the Great War. I don't think I've ever quite forgiven him for that. If he'd only held on for seven more days, we would've got married and had our little family and been quite content for the rest of our days together. Instead, I never married and I'm quite alone except for my sister and her family.'

'So you took it out on us?' Jeannie thought how sad her story was but was also angry that she and her friends had suffered under the supervisor because of it.

'It was very wrong of me. I hope you'll forgive me. It didn't help that I knew Agnes Boyle was Eileen's mother. I was sorry to hear about Janet. She didn't deserve that. None of us deserve all this.'

Jeannie's anger deserted her. Poor Miss McGrory looked crumpled and unwell.

'Work will be much more pleasant if you're nice to us from now on,' she smiled. 'You should go over and talk to Mrs Boyle. Something tells me she'd be pleased to see you.'

'Perhaps I will. Thank you, Jeannie. You're a kind girl. Just like your friend Eileen, and Annie too.'

'What will happen to you? They're trying to clear the rest centre. Where will you go?'

'My sister will take me in. She lives in Partick and her oldest girl is getting married and moving in with her husband's parents. So, there'll soon be a room for me. It's not ideal but I'll be better off than most of these poor folk.'

A thin, colourless girl came towards them.

'We'd better move, dear,' Miss McGrory said. 'My mattress is further down the row and I don't feel faint any more.'

Jeannie walked with her to the middle of the room. 'I'll see you at the factory, then.'

'I'll see you there tomorrow,' Miss McGrory smiled firmly. 'Despite the repairs, the factory's operating again. I'll expect all the workers to turn up. You make sure and tell Miss Boyle and Miss Morris.'

She was brisk and business-like again but Jeannie knew there was a softness to her. Work would be much more pleasant from now on.

–

It was left to Jeannie to take Isa and Bob to the farm in Lanarkshire. Mary had one of her dizzy spells and Kathy was working that Saturday.

'Be good, do what Martha tells you,' Mary told them, hugging them tightly.

'Do we have to go?' Isa asked.

'Why aren't we going to Miss Main's cottage?' Bob piped up.

'I've told you, my loves. Martha is my first cousin. She and Angus have a farm with lots of fields. They've no children of their own so they'll be glad to have you. Out in the countryside as they are, there'll be plenty of food. And no bombs.'

Bob perked up. 'Will they have sweets?'

'Mammy means proper food,' Jeannie said. 'Butter and eggs and…' Her imagination deserted her for a moment. 'Pies.'

'Pies. I can't wait,' Bob said happily.

'I'm old enough now to stay at home,' Isa pleaded. 'Please, Mammy.'

'I need to sit down. My head's swirling. Jeannie, it's time you went.'

'Don't worry, Mammy. I'll get them there safely. They'll be just fine,' Jeannie comforted her. 'Get your coats on, you two. Remember, Isa, it's your job to look after Bob. He can't go alone, now, can he?'

Their journey involved a bus, a tram ride, another bus and finally a lift on a cart drawn by a large, placid horse when Angus met them on the south-eastern edge of the city.

'Martha's very keen to meet you,' he said, chewing on the stem of a clay pipe and sending up a blue column of smoke into the fresh country air.

Angus was a short, broad man. His muscular shoulders strained at his work jacket seams. His strong, gnarled hands gripped the horse's reins. He had given them a warm greeting as they had stood uncertainly on the pavement at the start of the fields. At their backs were the sandstone tenements with children playing in the narrow lanes and back courts. In front of them were grazing cattle and a flock of grey partridge nibbling at the grass.

'It's a wee bit like Miss Main's field,' Isa said quietly.

'There you are, then,' Jeannie said, making her voice cheerful. 'You loved it there. And you'll love Martha's farm.'

'But I'll miss Mammy and you and Kathy. And Jessie, too. Who's she going to play with now?'

'I suspect Jessie will be evacuated again, too. Elspeth told me her mother's considering it. You'll have to write to each other.'

'I'm hungry. Do you think Martha's got lunch ready?' Bob knelt on the ground and ripped up clumps of grass.

'I'm sure she has. Get up, your knees will get muddy.'

'Look at that giant horse,' Bob shouted, pointing at the horse and cart making its way slowly towards them along a path between the fields.

Now, they trotted along with the cart wobbling and creaking. It was peaceful, though. Jeannie lifted her face to the sunshine and thought how blue the sky was. At moments like this, it was hard to believe there was a war on. The birds were chirping in the trees, the cattle were mooing and Angus was humming a tune as he puffed on his pipe.

After an hour on the cart, she was thankful when Angus finally turned the horse up a low hill to a stout, stone-built farmhouse. Around them were fields of sheep and others of tilled earth and crops. The front door of the farmhouse was open and a woman stood there. As Jeannie got down from the cart, she rushed forward.

'Hello, you must be Jeannie and these two must be Isa and Bob.'

Martha was short and plump with a lovely, dimpling smile and twinkling brown eyes. She leant down to the children.

'Do either of you like scones and butter?' She held her hands out to them. 'Come along and we'll see what's for lunch.'

Jeannie watched Isa and Bob take her offered hands and skip along either side of her into the farmhouse. She turned to find Angus watching her with a kindly smile.

'You don't have to worry about those two. Martha loves kids. We weren't blessed ourselves but she's been looking forward to this since Mary wrote. We'll take good care of them, lass.'

It felt odd travelling home without them. The buses and tram weren't much fun without their chatter. The flat was empty without their noise and mess. Jeannie sat on her bed. Mary was lying down with a headache in her bed recess in the kitchen with the curtain draped across it. Kathy wouldn't be home for a while. Their home was silent.

'Don't be daft about it,' she told herself sternly. 'It's for their own good. And it's not as if they didn't go away before.'

But there was a big gap in the family and she knew they'd be away for a lot longer this time. She'd almost got used to Jimmy being away. She'd have to get used to this too. It felt unreal. Janet was gone forever and Eileen might be moving away. Helen had asked her to bring forward the wedding.

Jeannie lay down on the bed. This terrible war. It had changed everything. What else was going to happen before it was all done?

Chapter Sixteen

Eileen thought that Janet's funeral was the saddest event she'd ever been to. To see poor Alan stumbling through it looking lost almost broke her heart. She had nearly lost her nerve and decided not to attend.

'I can't bear it,' she told Jeannie, as the two young women dressed in black in Jeannie's bedroom in number four, Kiltie Street. 'I finally feel loved for myself. Mum is so loving these days she's like a different woman. And I know that Jimmy loves me too. Dad cares too, only he's such a quiet man he's not given to hugging but I know he does. To be surrounded by that love and then know that Janet won't ever feel that again… it's too awful.'

Jeannie had arranged with Mary that Eileen would come and live with them for a while. There was room in the flat with Isa and Bob gone to the farm. Eileen had been only too grateful. She didn't like Uncle Herbert any more than her parents did. Besides, she really didn't want to give up working at Fearnmore and lose her friends' company.

'It's not about us, though. The funeral is about Janet's family laying her to rest. We must go and pay our respects whether our hearts are breaking or not,' Jeannie said firmly.

Eileen stared at her. 'Goodness, Jeannie Dougal, you've changed. When I first met you, you wouldn't say boo to a goose. Now look at you, taking charge and putting me in my place.'

'Is that what I'm doing? I'm sorry, I didn't mean to.'

Jeannie looked so dismayed that Eileen giggled. The laughter helped dispel some of the tension in her midriff at having to go to the funeral. She'd rather remember Janet as she was when she was alive. A lovely, cheerful girl with a huge appetite and such kindness to everybody.

'You can be quite bossy these days.'

'Well, I don't mean to be, but then I feel I have to look after everyone. With Jimmy away fighting and Isa and Bob living on the farm our family's scattered to the four winds. There's only me and Mammy and Kathy. Mammy's so tired these days and still getting dizzy spells. As for Kathy... she worries me.'

'Why do you say that? She seems chatty enough to me.'

In fact, when she was at home, Kathy dogged Eileen's footsteps, which amused her. She asked about Eileen's clothes and make-up and styled her hair just like the older girl's.

Jeannie sighed. 'Och, I don't know. It's hard to pin down. More a feeling than anything. Never mind me. Are you ready to go?'

'I don't think I'll ever be ready. But I'm dressed and I've got my coat and shoes on. I'll have to do.'

'You look beautiful and neat as always. I wish I looked like you.'

'You don't need to look like me. You're gorgeous as you are.'

Eileen tucked her arm into Jeannie's and squeezed. It was so good to have a best friend. And Mary had turned out to be like a second mother to Eileen while she stayed with them. Kathy was like a younger sister. Apart from the awful event they were about to go to, Eileen felt very contented.

Annie met them at the church before they went in. She was wearing a shapeless black dress which did nothing for her large figure and looked glum. Eileen heard very little of the funeral mass. Janet and her mum and younger brothers and sisters were all being buried. How tragic it was for the remaining Thom family. She wondered how they could stand the pain.

At the wake, Alan sought them out. He stood awkwardly with a cup of tea in his hand. He didn't drink it but turned it and turned it in its saucer until Eileen gently took it from him and set it on a nearby table.

'How are you?' she asked softly.

'I miss her.' His voice broke and tears welled in his eyes.

Before Eileen could move, Jeannie stepped forward and put her arms around him. Eileen didn't hear what she said but Alan nodded. Eileen found her clean, pressed handkerchief and silently gave it to him.

'We're so sorry, Alan. We miss her too.'

'I've asked to be sent overseas as soon as possible,' he said. 'I won't come back to Scotland. There are too many memories.'

He walked away and they let him go. Eileen and Jeannie's gazes met. There was nothing to be done. They said their condolences to the family and decided to leave as most other people had done. The Thoms deserved time alone with each other to grieve. Eileen noticed Annie looking miserably at Paul's turned back. What was going on there? Still, she knew better than to ask. Annie wasn't one to share much of herself.

Back at work the next day, Annie's mood hadn't improved. She snapped at Ruby who was working the machine next to her and complained to Miss McGrory when their break time was late. In the canteen, she sat heavily next to Eileen and Jeannie and almost flung her tray down on the table.

'Watch out, you'll break that plate,' Jeannie said.

'Who cares? You're such a Goody Two-Shoes. Why don't you mind your own business?'

'That's enough, Annie,' Eileen warned. 'It's not Jeannie's fault you're so grumpy. Now, instead of taking it out on us, why don't you tell us what's wrong?'

Annie had the grace to look shame-faced. She picked up her sandwich, inspected its contents and made a sour face. She ate it before she spoke again. Eileen held her breath. Would Annie really confide in them? She'd known she had a secret for some while. Were they about to find out what it was?

Annie stared at them both. Eileen kept an encouraging smile on her face. Jeannie was frowning. She'd never clicked with Annie. Eileen was closer to her, if you could call it that. No one was close to her. She wouldn't let them be.

Suddenly Annie's brown eyes blinked rapidly and she wiped the back of her hand against them.

'I'm ashamed. I've never told you what's going on with my family and that's why. I thought you'd all hate me for it. It's too late now, anyway. Everyone knows, or will soon.'

'We don't know. Will you tell us? We won't hate you for it, whatever it is. Will we, Jeannie?' Eileen said.

'Of course not,' Jeannie said, reaching out and touching Annie's quick-bitten fingers. 'We're your friends.'

Annie looked startled. 'You might change your mind when I've told you.'

'Tell us and let us decide.'

'I live with my mum. She's an invalid. My dad's dead, he died when I was a baby. My brother Brian is in the army.' She stopped and swallowed.

'Go on,' Jeannie said. 'We won't judge you, I promise.'

'Brian is a deserter. He was called up early on and went to the Borders for training. Then one day he came home and said he wasn't going back. He was being bullied by his sergeant and the others in his regiment. He was frightened and depressed. At first, we hid him at home. Mam wouldn't hear of me telling the authorities. She was glad he was there. They played cards in the evenings and during the day he hid in the back bedroom.

'Then it got too dangerous. The neighbours were getting suspicious and asking questions, and the military police kept coming and asking if we'd seen him. He fled to the hills during the days and came back in the middle of the night for food and to get dry clothes. That's why I'm always so tired. I had to be up to make a meal for him. We were always tense and anxious in case we got found out.

'But they caught him. It was after the bombing. He came back and the house was in ruins and we were gone. The police got him and he's going to jail for a long time.'

'Oh, Annie, I'm so sorry. How awful for you all,' Eileen said.

'That's not even the worst of it,' Annie's voice caught on a sob. 'Paul's not speaking to me. We've been stepping out and I told him, thinking he'd understand. But instead, he looked as if he was disgusted by me and he's avoided me ever since.'

Jeannie shook her head. 'You need to speak to him again. It's come as a shock to him, that's all. He probably needs time to adapt. If he loves you, he'll forgive all this.'

'I love him,' Annie burst out. 'Nothing he told me would make that stop. So why can't he do the same for me?'

'People react differently to things,' Eileen said. 'Jeannie's right. Give him time and then ask to see him. I bet he loves you, too. I'm sure he's embarrassed at how he reacted.'

Annie's secret was a revelation to Eileen. No wonder she was so often grumpy and bitter. What a load she'd had to shoulder alone. It sounded as if her mother wasn't much help.

'Thank you,' Annie said. She sat up straighter and ate her last offending sandwich. 'I do feel better for telling you. I don't know why.'

'A problem shared is a problem halved, as my mother always says,' Jeannie grinned. 'Now, promise us you'll speak to Paul?'

Annie nodded. 'I promise. I only hope he'll listen to me and that he's able to forgive me. He's so proud of being in the army himself and that his brothers are too; this is like a slur on him.'

'I have a feeling that Paul's a better man than you know,' Jeannie said wisely.

–

Agnes Boyle came to visit Kiltie Street the next Saturday.

'It's very kind of you to let Eileen live here,' she said to Mary.

'We love having her here. And we've got the space now my wee ones are away in the countryside. Besides, I should be thanking you for the rent money and of course Eileen's brought her ration card.'

'You have a lovely home, Mrs Dougal,' Agnes said primly, taking an offered armchair in the parlour.

'Call me Mary. This is my friend Helen Dunn. Helen and I are running a WVS canteen this afternoon down at the local rest centre.'

Helen, who was sitting in the other armchair, greeted her with a kindly smile. 'Jeannie is engaged to my son, Arthur. I consider her my daughter-in-law already. And Eileen is a credit to you, Mrs Boyle, she's a lovely young lady.'

'She's my pride and joy,' Agnes said, with a swift smile to Eileen as the two girls settled onto the sofa to join the older women.

'Are you settling in over in Greenock? You must miss your own home. It's a terrible thing, this war,' Mary said.

'We can't grumble. We're very lucky that Mr Boyle's uncle has taken us in. But I do miss my wee house. I don't know when we'll get back to Glasgow. There's no talk of rebuilding as yet.'

'Hitler's not finished with us yet, I'm sure. The Clyde and the shipyards are just too tempting for his bombers. It makes me shiver now when the moon is full. They say it shines down and its light on the river makes a pathway perfect for the bombers,' Helen said.

'We'd best be going,' Mary said. 'We've that many tea urns to fill and sandwiches to be made. There are still families in the centre waiting to be rehoused. You'll want some time with Eileen so there's no hurry. Stay as long as you like. And come and visit as often as you like. It's nice to meet you finally.'

Mary and Helen slipped on their coats, hats and gloves and hurried away. Jeannie got up, too.

'I'll leave you two alone to catch up. I've some shopping to do for dinner.'

Eileen and Agnes were left in the Dougals' parlour.

Nervously, Agnes smoothed down her skirt. She may have told her daughter that she loved her but old habits died hard and she still found it difficult to show her emotions readily.

'I can't stay long,' she told Eileen. 'I had a letter from Hannah McGrory inviting me to tea. She's living in Partick now so I can walk over from here easily enough.'

'Miss McGrory? My supervisor at Fearnmore?'

'As it turns out, yes. I had no idea she was your supervisor but then… that's my fault as I never asked you about the factory. I went to school with Hannah and we'd lost touch. It was my fault. I let all my friendships slide after… after Ronnie died. But we met again in the rest centre at the school. She wouldn't take no for an answer but that I must go and visit her at her sister's house.'

'That's great, Mum,' Eileen said, enthusiastically. 'You'll soon pick your friendship back up. And Jeannie's mother and Mrs Dunn are nice people, too. You'll see them again when you visit me. Soon, you'll have lots of friends.'

'Aye, well. We'll see. Enough about me. How are you doing?'

–

Later that evening, while Mary, Jeannie and Kathy listened to the wireless, Eileen excused herself and went into the bedroom. She sat on the bed and took out Jimmy's letter.

She wanted to be alone to enjoy it. She'd written to tell
him about the bombing and where she was living now.
She took it out of the envelope carefully. The paper was
creased and grubby and she tried to imagine him writing it
in spare moments away from the front line and the shelling
and the danger.

> *My dearest Eileen*
>
> *I hope this finds you well. I am doing fine.
> The grub is plentiful if not tasty. I miss Mammy's
> cooking. I was right sorry to hear about your home.
> I'm glad you're safe with my family. I'm glad too
> you've made things right with your ma. Family is
> the most important thing. I've always known that
> but I feel it keenly now.*
>
> *Thank you for the photograph. You are so
> beautiful. I know that but now the lads know it
> too. One of my pals asked if he could keep it. I
> won't tell you my language when I said no!*
>
> *We've not known each other that long but for
> me I feel I've known you forever. I love you,
> Eileen, and I always will. There's a black cloud
> hanging over me. I can't seem to shift it. The days
> are all the same, dodging bullets and the sounds of
> the shelling and always the forward march.*
>
> *They call me Lucky Jim. But now I'm not so
> sure.*
>
> *Anyway, what I wanted to ask is, will you
> marry me? I don't know when I'll be home again.
> But when I do, will you be ready?*
>
> *With all my love*
> *Jimmy xxx*

'Of course I'll marry you, Jimmy Dougal,' Eileen said out loud.

She kissed the letter, her heart singing. She got up off the bed and did a little pirouette of happiness. But then she sank back onto it and re-read the letter. Her happiness mingled with dread. On a second reading, a sense of Jimmy's depression emerged. He sounded scared and fatalistic.

'You must come home to me,' she whispered. 'Please, Jimmy. Please make it home. Don't give up. You're my Lucky Jim. We've a whole life together to look forward to.'

She couldn't bear to think of the alternative. She refused to. If Jimmy wanted to marry her, she'd reply right away and accept. Then she'd start to plan their wedding and look for a wedding dress.

–

'Cough it up, then.' Judith Lennox stuck her hand out.

'I'll give you a penny,' Kathy said.

'You will not. You'll give me what you owe me and nothing less. Thruppence it is. Hand it over.'

Reluctantly, Kathy slipped her fingers into her jacket pocket and took out the coin. She pushed it into Judith's greedy palm. The other girl magicked it away smartly.

'There you go. Not so hard, was it?'

'And you'll say I was at your house all evening?' Kathy reminded her.

'Aye, of course I will. You get what you paid for. My silence.'

The smirk on Judith's face made Kathy want to slap her. But she couldn't. Judith was too important. If Mammy ever asked where Kathy was of an evening, she only had to mention the Lennoxes and Mammy's face relaxed. Not only did that leave Kathy free to her own devices but she knew Mammy thought her a very kind, helpful girl to keep Judith and her elderly aunt company so frequently.

Jeannie was more suspicious but since she knew Kathy was stepping out with someone and had said her piece, she hadn't asked about it since. Anyway, Jeannie was too wrapped up in her own problems since her friend died. Of course it was awful about Janet but Kathy couldn't help being relieved that it meant Jeannie wasn't on her back all the time.

'Where are you going?' Judith asked, leaning on the close banister.

'None of your business, you nosy cow.'

Kathy stuck out her tongue and clattered away down the stone steps before Judith could get her. The other girl had a schoolyard reputation for being handy with her fists.

She soon forgot about her as she hurried up Kiltie Street and turned the corner onto the main road. It was the beginning of April and the days were light until nearly nine p.m. She'd have to be home by then. She patted her hair. It was freshly washed and dried. She'd tried to curl it just like Eileen's hair. Her lips felt sticky with Jeannie's lipstick and she'd borrowed some powder from Mammy's pot to cover her freckles. Rounding the corner, she slipped the ring onto her fourth finger and felt the metal, cold and loose. It didn't fit but he'd said they'd get it tightened.

Gavin was waiting for her halfway up the road. She made her hips sway as she walked, pretending that she hadn't seen him until the last minute when she looked up and smiled alluringly just like her favourite film star, Maureen O'Hara.

'Let's nip in here.' Gavin took her elbow and guided her into a side lane.

The lane was a dead end, littered with cigarette stubs and smelling of tomcats. A wire fence separated it from the back of a warehouse whose entrance was on the next street up. On the other side of the fence they were hidden by columns of barrels, stacked up high. It was a quiet place and Kathy knew it well by now. She and Gavin had been meeting there for weeks.

'I don't know why we can't go to a café or to the cinema like other couples,' she complained.

'We'll go to a cinema another day. Give your old man a kiss and stop whining. It's not pretty behaviour from a pretty girl.'

Gavin leaned in and gave her a hard kiss. Kathy opened her lips and let his hot tongue press inside. A flicker of excitement started in her stomach. She pushed his seeking fingers from her breasts.

'I'm wearing your ring,' she said, showing him. 'You said we'd get it measured. I'm worried I'm going to lose it.'

'You've not worn it at home, have you?'

She was taken aback at his sharp tone. 'Of course not. I promised you I wouldn't. I keep it in my pocket so Jeannie won't find it.'

'That's my girl. Give me another kiss.'

'Wait a minute.' Kathy finished the kiss, her mind momentarily on other things. 'Now that we're engaged, are we going to take it to the jeweller's? And when are you coming to meet my mother so we can tell her? I can't wait to see Jeannie's face when she finds out I'm getting married before her!'

'I told you, I want to get to know you first before I meet your family. That's nicest, isn't it? How can I get to know your mother and sister when I don't know everything about you yet? Come here and let me find out more,' he murmured, pulling her close.

Kathy didn't resist. She let him unbutton her blouse and touch her breasts. The stroking movements gave her a thrill and a yearning for more. She knew what he wanted. She wanted it too but she had been brought up properly and knew she had to have a ring on her finger before giving him 'it'.

Being secretly engaged was exciting. She had it all planned out. She was going to wear a proper wedding dress, white with a row of buttons down the back, and a hat with a veil. Gavin would wear a suit. They'd eat roast chicken at their wedding lunch and everyone would admire the sponge cake with pink icing. She thought they'd live with Mammy for a few months while they saved to rent a place of their own.

She couldn't wait to tell Jeannie. Couldn't wait to see the look on her face. Jeannie was always telling her she was too young. She'd show her! She'd be married before Jeannie and boring, fuddy-duddy Arthur. Arthur might be good-looking but he didn't have Gavin's passion.

Now Gavin's fingers were under her skirt. They teased her soft flesh. She moaned and twisted and rubbed up against him but it wasn't enough. Now they were getting married, it was all right to go further.

Gavin hadn't asked. He fumbled with his trousers. Barely knowing what she was doing, she moved until he groaned and her excitement rose. She had the power to make him want her. She smelt his hair oil as he pressed his head next to hers and their bodies moved together.

She stood there, his weight heavy against her, pinning her to the wall. She felt the cold roughness of the bricks on the back of her head. Around her, the lane was quiet. A rumble of engine echoed loudly as a bus went along in the street beyond. Gavin stood back from her and adjusted his clothing. She buttoned her blouse. She felt grown up. She'd done 'it'. She bet Judith Lennox hadn't.

'Shall we go for a walk now and talk about the wedding?' she said.

Gavin lit a cigarette. He didn't offer her one. He blew out a stream of blue smoke. 'Sorry, darling. I need to get back. Billy's covering for me. You don't want me to get into any bother, do you?'

Hiding her disappointment, Kathy forced a smile. After all, wives did have to look after their husbands. She might as well practise now.

'I understand. We'll go to a café next time we meet, right? We can share a pot of tea and I'll bring a pencil and paper so we can list the wedding guests.'

He rubbed his nose. Strands of his slicked back hair stuck up. There were large pores on his nose and thin, red veins either side of it. He wasn't handsome like Arthur. Or like his pal, Billy. She'd wanted to go out with Billy at first. After the two of them came back to Franny's for their cigarettes and started coming regularly, she'd flirted like mad with Billy. But then, after a couple of weeks, he'd told her he had a girl back home.

Gavin was quick to say he didn't have a girl back home. After that, he'd asked her to meet him and she'd agreed. Out of Franny's hearing. Not that she was doing anything wrong. The first few times they'd met, all they had done

233

was walk around the local streets, talking. She liked him but didn't fancy him. She was flattered by his interest in her. When he kissed her, she let him and enjoyed it.

There was power in being a woman. Kathy hadn't realised that before. At home, she had to do what she was told by Mammy and Jeannie. It was worse when Jimmy was there. He acted like he was Dad, bossing them all about. It was so annoying. But with Gavin, it was different. He treated her like a lady and gave her what she wanted. At least, he had at first. She had asked to go to cafés and he had taken her. If she was honest with herself, she liked that better than meeting in the smelly lane for kisses.

She couldn't wait to get married. She'd be in charge of her own wee home, not answering to anyone else. She'd put her ornaments just where she wanted them. She'd make delicious meals and have them on the table for Gavin at six o'clock sharp every evening. Conveniently, she dismissed the war in this daydream. She imagined Gavin wearing a suit and tie and coming back from his important job in the bank. She was in their perfect home with two neat children, ready to greet him.

'What job did you have before the war?' she asked him.

'What?' He was frowning and stubbing out his cigarette on the dirty brick wall.

'Your job. Were you in the bank?'

'The bank? What are you on about? See this here brick – that's what I did for a living. I was a brickie. And that's what I'll be going back to after this bloody mess is done.'

'Oh.' She was deflated. 'Couldn't you get a job where you wear a suit each day?'

Gavin laughed, shaking his head. 'You're a funny one, all right. Me in a suit? I don't think so.'

Never mind. He didn't entertain the thought now but he could change. Kathy was sure of that. It was a wife's duty to support her husband and to improve his prospects. If Jeannie's Arthur worked in a bank, then her Gavin could, too.

'You're a nice girl, Kathy. I…' He gave her a strange look then shook his head again. 'Forget it.'

'I'll walk you up the road,' she suggested.

'No. I'd like it, don't get me wrong, but if the sergeant was to see us, well, it wouldn't be good.'

'Haven't you told them we're getting married? Surely that must make a difference.'

'I'll tell them soon.' He smoothed down his wayward greased hair and put on his army cap.

'I don't want you to go,' Kathy said, pursing her lips into a moue and trying to hold his interest. 'It's still early. We could walk about a bit.'

'Now you're being silly. I told you, I have to get back or Billy will get in trouble. I'll meet you next week back here. All right?'

Kathy glanced back at the shabby lane entrance and shuddered. 'I don't like this place.'

Gavin put his arm round her. 'Hey, don't say that. It's our special place. And you're my special girl. Now, say you'll meet me, usual time next week.'

Kathy nodded. Of course she would. After all, this was the man she was going to marry. Before long, she'd be Mrs Kathryn Greenlaw with all the respect of her family and neighbours that came with it. She waved to him as he strode off without a backward look at her.

Hugging herself with happiness and the joy of her very own secret, Kathy headed for Kiltie Street and home.

Chapter Seventeen

'I don't understand. The papers should be full of it. But no. They say there were raids over "a central Scotland district" and "central Scotland town". They mention high explosives and incendiary bombs—' The newspaper rustled as Jeannie read out the article.

'At least they got that part right,' Eileen said. 'There were certainly high explosives. We couldn't miss that from the Andie, could we?'

The raids in the second week of April had hit Clyde-bank again and other towns north-west of Glasgow. In the city itself, there was serious local damage near the Trongate and also north and south of the river at Hyndland and Shawlands. It was hard to find out much about it all though, as the papers were being deliberately vague.

'The powers that be must think the Germans will be reading the *Daily Record* too,' Eileen suggested. 'That's why they don't want to give details.'

'But surely people deserve to know what's going on?' Jeannie shook her head in disgust. 'It's not right. Ordinary folk are being bombed and killed, losing their homes like you. The least the government and the newspapers can do is let everyone know.'

'It's all about morale,' Mary said gently. 'We must keep people's spirits up.'

It was a Thursday evening and they were all in the parlour. Mary had lit a very small fire in the grate with the last of the coal ration. Although it was April, it was a cold evening. She sat knitting army socks. The wool bounced and shook her cloth knitting bag with every click of the needles. Jeannie always found it comforting, sitting with Mammy while she knitted. The clicks and bounces were part of her childhood. Before the war, the wool had been brighter colours and not dull, endless khaki but that seemed the only difference.

She and Eileen were sharing the sofa. Eileen was writing a letter to Jimmy while Jeannie was attempting to write one to Arthur. She found it difficult to know what to say. She could mention the bombing but that was depressing and perhaps it was better not to worry Arthur. She had very little else to say. Work at the factory was monotonous and tiring, made bearable only because she had Eileen and Annie there. Lunchtime at the canteen was the high spot of the day. At weekends, she was busy helping Mary clean the flat, shopping for food which was ever scarcer and queuing wherever there was a queue in the hope of getting something edible, if not tasty. Everything lacked flavour these days.

Arthur didn't need to hear all that. Jeannie picked up her pen again, chewing its top until Mammy frowned at her. Whatever she was going to write to Arthur, she had better get on with it. After that, she was going to write a reply to Isa and Bob. They had had a lovely letter from the two youngsters full of excitement at spring on the farm. Jeannie smiled fondly. She really missed them but Mammy was right; they were better off out of the city.

Kathy sat on a cushion in front of the fire, her legs tucked under her, flicking aimlessly through one of

Mammy's *Good Housekeeping* magazines, much smaller and thinner than they used to be because of the paper shortages. The frequent evening visits to Judith upstairs had stopped and Jeannie wondered why. She made a mental note to ask Kathy, when Mary wasn't around.

A knock on the door made them all look up.

'I'll get it,' Jeannie offered, levering herself up from the sofa and glad to let her half-written letter flutter down onto the sofa cushion.

She opened the door, expecting it to be Judith from next door looking for Kathy, or Helen who occasionally dropped in for a chat with Mary. Instead, it was the last person she ever expected to see.

Bill MacKenzie stood there, crisp and neat in his army uniform with his hair brushed neatly and a light in his eyes when he saw Jeannie.

'Bill, what are you doing here?' Jeannie cried out.

A warmth flooded her chest and it was all she could do not to rush into his arms. The memory of their kiss, never far from her mind, rose up and her lips tingled.

'I've been back at the barracks for a few weeks but this is the first day I've had leave. How are you Jeannie? You look good.'

Oh, the sound of his soft Canadian accent! She'd missed that. She drank in the sight of him. His light brown hair and warm, hazel eyes. The little lines on either side of his mouth. Was she imagining it, or were they more defined than before?

'Who is it, Jeannie? There's a cold draught here. Invite them in, for goodness' sake,' Mammy called.

'Come away in,' Jeannie smiled. She led the way to the parlour. 'Mammy and Kathy are here and you remember Eileen, don't you?' And to the others gathered in the small, cosy room with its scents of coal smoke and beeswax, she said simply: 'It's Bill. He's back.'

They exclaimed over him, giving him the armchair by the fire and bringing him a cup of tea and a butter-less scone with apologies for its taste and texture.

'Are you here for long?' Mary asked, putting her knitting into its bag and tucking it down beside the wireless cabinet.

Bill shrugged, good-humouredly. 'Gee, Mrs Dougal, who knows? The army works in mysterious ways. I had no idea I'd be stationed up here again, that's for sure. I guess I'll find out a day before they move me on, just like last time.'

He glanced at Jeannie and she felt a flush of heat on her face, remembering how he'd come to say goodbye and how she'd told him he had a nerve coming round. She hadn't even wished him well or said a proper goodbye; she'd been so stunned that he was leaving. Oh, but it was lovely that he was back. Even though they could only be friends, she reminded herself. The partial letter for Arthur was now on the mantelshelf beside the clock, she noticed. Mammy must've moved it to keep it safe.

'It's good to see you, Bill. I'll excuse myself now. I'm taking a few of these scones round to Harry. He looks exhausted from his night duties looking after us all and making sure we get into our shelters during the raids,' Mary said.

'When did it become *Harry* and not *Mr Woodley*?' Jeannie whispered sternly to Mary, following her into the kitchen to get the offending scones.

Mammy leaned in and kissed Jeannie's cheek.

'What was that for?'

'I love you, Jeannie Dougal. You're my oldest daughter and you're keeping us all straight. God knows, I need you more than ever, these days.'

'Mammy?'

'Just pass me the scones, will you? Fill up the teapot and give Bill another cuppa. I'll see you in a wee while.'

With Mammy gone and Jeannie unsure whether to be annoyed with her or amused, Eileen stood up and made a show of stretching and yawning.

'You don't mind if I call it a night, do you? I'll finish my letter to Jimmy in the bedroom.'

Kathy made no move at all. She hadn't said much and the magazine lay open on her lap.

'Kathy, why don't you come with me? I've got another piece of paper. You can write to Isa and Bob.'

Usually, Kathy's response would be to roll her eyes and make a sarcastic reply, but she quietly got up and followed Eileen into the hall. Jeannie frowned. Something was wrong with her sister but she didn't know what.

'Where are Isa and Bob?' Bill asked. 'I know they're not here otherwise I'd have a toy plane flying around me and someone leaning on me asking questions.'

'They're evacuated out to a farm. We really miss them but it's a relief to know they're safe. The raids last week show Mammy was right to send them. Kiltie Street didn't get hit but we spent some nights in the shelter listening to the bombers going overhead and praying they didn't stop. It makes you feel guilty hoping they'll go elsewhere. And then reading the papers about who died and whose homes were destroyed.'

'Yeah, it's bad. And gonna get worse.'

'Oh, Bill, you don't know about my friend, Janet, do you?'

Bill shook his head. Jeannie had to take a deep breath before telling him. It didn't get any easier. The raw pain of loss had passed but now it was like a wound that didn't properly heal. She and Eileen and Annie had made a promise to keep talking about Janet so that they never lost her but it was hard. Very hard.

When she'd finished, Bill reached over and held her hand. She felt the comfort of it. His hand was strong and capable and warm and alive. She let hers rest there before gently removing it. She had to remember that she mustn't love Bill. She had to remember Arthur, who for all his faults said he loved her, and whose ring she wore.

'I'm sorry for your loss,' Bill said.

'What happens now?' Jeannie said, simply.

He didn't pretend to misunderstand her. 'Can we continue as we were before I left? We can be friends, can't we?'

Her thumb rolled her engagement ring on her fourth finger. She felt its cold, smooth metal dig into her skin. Bill glanced at her hand and his mouth twisted wryly.

'I'd like that,' she said. 'I'd like to be friends.'

'Great.' He stood up to go. 'Thank your mom for the tea. Will you go to the cinema with me, Jeannie? It's Friday tomorrow and they're showing *A Little Bit of Heaven* at the Grand Central. Sounds like your kind of film.'

'I'd like that,' Jeannie said, her eyes shining. 'I really would.'

Mary chose that moment to appear in the doorway. She unbuttoned her coat.

'You can't go to the cinema with Bill,' she said abruptly. She turned to face Bill and her usually kind face was set.

'Jeannie's fiancé is training to go fighting overseas. It's not appropriate for her to flaunt herself with other men.'

'Mammy!' Jeannie cried, aghast. 'I'm not flaunting myself.'

Bill cut in politely. 'Your mother's right. I apologise, Mrs Dougal. I meant no disrespect. I'll take my leave now and say goodnight.' He put his cap on and tipped it to them. 'Thank you for the tea and scones. I do appreciate it.'

He walked smartly out and Jeannie followed him, feeling embarrassed and humiliated. At the door, she opened her mouth to say sorry but he stopped her.

'I shouldn't have come. I couldn't help it, I had to see you. But it was wrong. You're engaged to be married to another man. We can't be friends. Not really. I don't want to be your friend, Jeannie. And what I want... you can't give me. I wish you all the best for the future. Goodbye.'

He turned on his heel, clipping down the stone steps and was gone into the dark night before she could let out one sob.

'Don't let the lights show,' Mary said sharply, coming up behind her and shutting the door.

'You sent him away. How could you?' Jeannie stormed.

Mary tried to hug her but Jeannie pulled away out of her arms. She'd found Bill again and lost him all in the course of a couple of hours. The anguish was like a stab to the heart.

'What did you expect?' Mammy was saying quietly. 'Don't think I didn't notice how you looked at him. I was glad when he moved on before. He's a nice boy but he's not for you.'

Jeannie groaned. Mary led her into the parlour and shut the door.

'Helen's right. You and Arthur should get married soon.'

'You've discussed me with Helen?'

'She's concerned about you both, too. She feels it'll be good for Arthur. She's worried about him. I know she told you that. She wants to see you both settled.'

'We agreed on a long engagement,' Jeannie said, feeling the walls pressing in on her. 'Arthur agreed to that.'

Mary threw her a look. 'He may have agreed but it was you wanting that, love. Arthur would marry you tomorrow if you allowed it.'

Was that true? Jeannie tried to be honest with herself. Arthur's behaviour when she last saw him had been strange. There was the argument which had distressed her. He said he still loved her. Her thoughts were all over the place. It was so long since she'd seen him and his letters weren't regular. She knew he wrote to his mother more than he wrote to her.

Mary patted the seat beside her on the sofa. 'I want to see you settled and all. These dizzy fits, they haven't gone away—'

'The doctor said they weren't serious. Are you getting worse?' Jeannie felt a ripple of fear run up her spine.

'They're not worse and I know it's a natural part of growing old for a woman. But it makes me realise I won't be around forever. If and when you marry Arthur, you'll be safe for life. You'll live in a nice, big house and have plenty of food – at least once the war's over, you will. You won't lie awake at night worrying if you've enough for the rent or if you can afford to heat the flat that week.'

'Oh, Mammy. You mustn't worry so much.'

'It's easy to say that but I do worry about all of you. I'm your mother, it comes naturally to me. Just wait until you have babies of your own. You never stop with the worrying, whatever their age.'

Babies of her own. Jeannie couldn't imagine it. She didn't want that. Not yet. Maybe not ever. She wanted to have a job and some freedom after the war was over. But she couldn't say that. Not to Mammy and certainly not to Arthur. They wouldn't understand. Besides, she was old enough to know that babies followed weddings. There was no stopping that.

'I'm getting old, Jeannie. I want to know you're happily married and I'd like a grandchild or two. Will you promise me to set a date with Arthur?'

There was no escape. She was promised to Arthur and she had to marry him. She wished with all her heart that she'd met Bill first. She shouldn't have been so quick to step out with Arthur after she met him. She'd let him sweep her off her feet with his expensive clothes and nice accent. He hadn't given her a choice. He'd always acted as if they were going to get married right from the start. And she, silly young fool that she was, had gone along with it until it was too late to back out.

'What about Bill?' she said faintly.

'It's wrong to string him along when there's no future in it,' Mary said. 'And I don't want the neighbours getting the wrong idea either. He's not welcome here any more. You can write to Arthur tomorrow and tell him you want to get married on his next leave.'

Jeannie was numb. She pushed up from the sofa, knowing Mammy was right and that she'd do exactly what she asked. Even if she was crying inside.

In the girls' bedroom, Eileen was sitting up in bed, dressed in her nightclothes and with her hair in curlers. She was scribbling like mad as Jeannie came in. Beyond her, Kathy was a shape under the blankets, her back to them. Jeannie wondered if she was asleep or just pretending to be.

'Do you think Jimmy's getting our letters?' Eileen asked Jeannie.

Jeannie sat on the edge of the bed, her heart leaden. Slowly, she began to undress, ready to get into her nightdress.

'Jeannie?'

'Sorry, I was miles away. I hope he is. We have to keep writing and hope so.'

'It's been weeks now since I had a letter from him. His last letter was so... I don't know. He asked me to marry him and that was happy but the rest of it was... dark, somehow. And you haven't had any family letters either. What if—'

'Don't!' Jeannie put her palms up to stop Eileen's next words. Hearing them out loud gave them power. It let dark thoughts free like the genie from the bottle, and they couldn't be stoppered again.

'I'm sorry,' Eileen said. 'I'm that worried about him.'

Jeannie hugged her. 'We all are. But we have to try and not be. He's Lucky Jim. He's all right, I know it.' He couldn't be otherwise. Her body and mind couldn't take it if anything happened to her big brother. 'Mammy's that thrilled about your engagement. Aren't you fed up yet with her talking about the wedding plans?'

'How can I be when I'm that excited myself?' Eileen laughed.

Jeannie was glad to see her friend's expression brighten. They had to keep cheerful. Had to get through these awful days, weeks and months. God help them, surely not years as well. The war had been raging for eighteen months. It had to be over soon.

'I've to set a date with Arthur.'

Eileen grinned. 'We could have a double wedding.' Then she paused. 'What do you mean you *have* to set a date? Don't you want to?'

'Mammy wants me to. So does Helen. And Arthur will be happy. It was always me wanting a long engagement.'

'Ah. I see. Bill has set the cat amongst the pigeons.'

'I've not to see him any more,' Jeannie said. 'Mammy's right. I have to do the right thing.'

'What does your heart tell you?' Eileen asked, folding her letter up and slipping it under her pillow.

Jeannie was envious of her in that moment. It was all so simple for Eileen. She loved Jimmy and he loved her right back.

'Sometimes it doesn't matter what your heart tells you. I made a promise to Arthur and I intend to keep it. I won't bring shame on our family. I won't hurt Mammy.'

Beyond Eileen, Kathy moved under the blankets as if someone had poked her.

—

Dear Mother

I hope that you are keeping as well as can be expected and taking care not to overdo it. It is important to eat at regular hours, something I know you are reluctant to do. Do cover up and try to sleep. You are an invalid and must acknowledge that to yourself. I've told you often that I will look after you as a son must since Father died.

It is unlikely that I will be able to come home on leave for quite some while. Days off are taken

locally trying to find meals and enjoying the coun-
tryside. It is quite different here from Scotland. I
can say no more. Loose talk can cost lives, as they
say.

    I remain your loving son
    Arthur

If Helen had been the sort of woman to roll her eyes, she would have done so. Dear Arthur. He was her son but in many ways he was more his father's son. She loved him but wasn't blind to his faults. The sooner he got married, the better. He could focus his attentions on caring for his wife. It was exhausting being the focus of Arthur's concerns. Besides, she felt so much stronger since he'd left. She never sat around with the blanket over her knees. And he was wrong about her eating habits. She ate well at breakfast, lunch and dinner now that she set her own meal times and ate the food she wished to, within the confines of the rations available, of course.

She sighed. No, she decided firmly. It was in everyone's best interests for Arthur and Jeannie to marry quickly. She'd speak to Mary about it again very soon. Perhaps at the next WVS centre meeting the following day.

—

Annie hated the farm. The air reeked of cow manure and she couldn't step outside without mud clinging to her shoes. Her mother wouldn't hear a word against Farmer Gillan and his wife Clare who had taken them in after the blitz. The other evacuated family had two small children who cried and hit each other. Annie was glad to go to work at the factory to get away from them. Anyway, today, none of that mattered. It was Saturday and Paul had agreed to meet her in a café in Glasgow.

She was nervous as she approached the corner café. Her palms were damp. She wiped them on her dress. Her shoes squeezed her toes. She was wearing her posh pair with the shiny patent leather. They'd cost her a fortune when she bought them before the war. Her hair was pinned back in a loose bun. She pulled tendrils down over her ears to soften the effect.

Paul was sitting at a round table for two. He stood politely as she went in. She tried to read his expression but he gave nothing away. His smile was a tight line.

'What do you want? I've ordered a pot of tea for two. The vegetable soup's good here. It's even got some vegetables in it.' He winked and the air sagged out of her with relief.

He wasn't angry. At least not with her, right at this moment. He spoke of Janet and of missing his mum and younger brothers and sisters and he was angry about all of that. It was clear from his flashing dark eyes and the grim set to his mouth. In the lull after the waitress poured the tea and left them alone, Annie plucked up the courage to speak.

'About my brother, Brian...' she said.

'I was angry with you. That's why I've been avoiding you.'

'I know.' Annie was hurt and there was a tremble in her voice that she couldn't hide.

Paul reached over and squeezed her hand gently. His touch sent a tingle of awareness that ran right along her arm and made the little hairs on the back of her neck stand up.

'I was wrong, Annie. I was wrong… but you see, it made me furious that good men were dying fighting the Nazis while your brother was skulking in a warm house. I was angry with you for harbouring him.'

'I'm sorry.' The tears rolled in fat drops down her cheeks. Annie rubbed at her face, smearing them away.

Paul took out a crisp, white handkerchief and gave it to her. 'You don't have to apologise. It's me. I have to say sorry to you. I was being unfair. It all got mixed up with my grief for my family. When I calmed down, I asked myself, what if it was Thomas or Andy who deserted? And I know I would hide them. You'd do anything for your family. I know that. I feel it even more strongly now that half of mine is gone.'

Annie's eyes stung where she'd wiped Paul's handkerchief on them. It was now damp and balled in her fist under the table. Paul's gaze sought hers and she tried to meet it.

'Most of all, I was upset that you didn't tell me. You didn't trust me enough to confide in me.'

'I couldn't. What if you'd told the police?'

Paul nodded, his mouth twisted down. 'You didn't know me well enough.'

'It wasn't my secret to tell. There was such a risk and my mother was terrified she'd lose Brian,' she tried to explain.

There was a silence between them. Annie's heart thumped. Paul looked so serious. Was he about to tell her he never wanted to see her again? That because she hadn't trusted him, he couldn't trust her? That he didn't love her? He hadn't said that he did love her, Annie thought. She had imagined he did. The waitress brought a fresh pot of tea and took their soup bowls away. It gave Annie time to compose herself for whatever Paul had to say.

'Can we start again?' Paul asked.

'What do you mean?' she said, startled.

'I'll introduce myself. I'm Paul Thom, I'm a private in His Majesty's army and I have two brothers, my sister Bridget, and a dad who keeps us in order. May I ask who you are?'

Getting the idea, Annie smiled. 'I'm Annie Morris and I work at Fearnmore munitions factory. I've got one brother, Brian, and my mum's an invalid.'

'You're a very beautiful girl, Annie Morris. I'd like to take you out to the pictures or, if you prefer, a dance. What do you say?'

'Oh, Paul, I'd like that very much,' Annie breathed happily.

She poured the tea for them both. 'We haven't really had much time to get to know each other. What with Janet…' She stopped, scared she would set off his anger again.

But Paul nodded with a wistful smile. 'Aye, that's true enough. It was a lovely wedding Janet had, made even better for me by meeting you.'

'I remember you swinging Janet round and her scolding you for creasing her dress, but she didn't mean it. Janet was the most cheerful, loving girl I've known. She always had a positive way of looking at things even when I felt they were gloomy.'

Paul laughed. 'That was Janet, all right. She took after my mother in personality. I'll tell you a story about her when she was just a wee girl…'

They sat at the table, sharing memories, Annie watching Paul's mobile face hungrily. He was a handsome man and he was hers. She hadn't had much luck with men in the past but now that had changed. She vowed to herself that she was going to do what she could to keep him.

—

Kathy's stomach churned. She barely made it to the shared privy before she threw up all the bubble and squeak that Mammy had fried up for breakfast. It was one of her favourite meals, too. At least it used to be. Now the sight and smell of it made her queasy. She sniffed away her tears. It was all too much getting a tummy bug on top of feeling miserable. Blast this war! After she'd let Gavin go all the way with her, she was desperate to see him the next week to talk about their wedding but the bombing raids had put paid to that. The following week she went to the lane but he didn't turn up. She'd wandered around, shivering in the April drizzle, before dejectedly heading home.

Eventually, she'd gone looking for him at the barracks. The soldier on the gate wouldn't let her in or take a message but then she saw Gavin's pal Billy and shouted to him. The soldier shrugged and turned away into the guard box and Billy came over. He blushed as bright red as his hair when he saw who it was.

'Where's Gavin?' Kathy cried. 'He hasn't come to meet me in weeks and he hasn't answered my messages.'

'He's… I'm… He's not here,' Billy stuttered.

'Well, go and get him then,' Kathy said, stamping her foot in frustration.

'No, you don't understand. He's not here at the barracks. He's been transferred down to the Borders.'

Billy's thick country accent made her want to box his ears. The shock of what he said made her head swim and she staggered back from the fence. Gavin was gone? Without a word to her? It wasn't possible.

'He must've left me a message,' she wailed. 'He can't just have gone.'

'I'm sorry,' Billy said.

'Did he tell you we're getting married?'

Billy's expression suddenly seemed older as he stared at her. She couldn't bear the sympathy she saw on his plain features.

'Gavin's a married man. I thought… I hoped he'd tell you himself.'

'He told me he didn't have a girl but you did.' Kathy's emotions were tumbling from anger to bewilderment to fear.

'He didn't have a girl but he has a wife, Maureen, and a nipper too.'

She stumbled away from him, her fingers pressed to her mouth to stop the scream that threatened to pour out of it. She'd let him have his way and now he was gone. He had a wife and a child. She wanted not to believe it but she did. There was no reason for Billy to lie. Back at Kiltie Street she told Mammy she wasn't feeling well and went straight to bed. In the days following, she found it difficult to pluck up any energy. She didn't even fight with Jeannie or beg to use Eileen's curlers or face powder.

Lying in bed the evening Bill had come to see Jeannie, she'd overheard Jeannie and Eileen chatting before going to sleep. Jeannie was saying how she'd never bring shame to the family or hurt Mammy. It made Kathy's tummy ache to hear that. What she'd done was so much worse than not marrying stupid Arthur quickly enough. What if Mammy and Jeannie found out what a terrible thing she'd done?

For weeks, her secret had gnawed away at her. It was making her ill. She wanted to blurt it out and let Mammy comfort her and tell her everything was all right. She didn't actually miss Gavin but she missed the glamour of having an older boyfriend. She ought to be interested in the new soldiers coming into Franny's shop but somehow she wasn't.

There was a sharp rattle of knocks on the privy door. Kathy huddled over with a groan.

'Kathy, are you in there?' It was Mammy's concerned voice. 'Are you ill?'

Kathy undid the lock and fell sobbing into Mammy's arms.

'Let's get you back inside. Smartly, now, before the neighbours come out and ask questions.'

Mammy's hand gently but firmly guided her back into the flat and straight into the busy parlour where Jeannie and Eileen were knitting and listening to the wireless. Sounds of soft jazz music pulsed merrily in the May evening air.

'Eileen, will you leave us for a wee while, please,' Mammy said. 'We've family business to discuss if you don't mind.'

'Of course. I'll take my knitting into the kitchen and I'll put the kettle on, too. Shout when you want a pot of tea made for you.'

Kathy sat on the sofa in Eileen's vacated seat. Jeannie was beside her, mouth open in astonishment, a half-knitted khaki scarf on her knee. Mammy took the armchair.

'Who is he?'

'I don't know what you mean,' Kathy lied.

'I wasn't born yesterday, my girl. When did you last have your monthlies?'

Kathy thought about that. A few weeks ago? It should've been two weeks ago but she was late. Come to think of it, she hadn't had a show in April either.

'I can see the answer in your face.'

'What's going on, Mammy?' Jeannie asked, looking from Kathy to their mother and back again.

'Your sister's having a baby. That's what's going on.' Mammy's harsh tone made Kathy flinch. She'd never heard her speak like that before. Not even when Kathy had done something wrong or been cheeky.

'Oh, Kathy. What have you done?' Jeannie said. 'How could you?'

'That's enough. It takes two. Someone has taken advantage of my wee girl and I want to know who.' Mammy's voice was suddenly soft again and it brought tears to Kathy's eyes.

The whole sorry story tumbled from her lips and by the end of it, Mammy's arms were rocking her to and fro and their heads were pressed together. Jeannie sat, looking shocked and dismayed.

'You won't throw her out, will you?' Jeannie asked. 'For bringing shame on the family?'

'Now, listen here, both of you,' Mammy said fiercely, 'the Dougal family sticks together. Through thick and thin. Aye, and this is the thin of it, all right. But it's not Kathy's fault. That man was older than her and knew what he was doing with his cheap ring and sweet talk. It makes me sick to hear of it.'

She kissed Kathy's cheek and sat back, tapping her fingers to her chin in silence. Kathy could hardly take a breath for waiting to hear what was going to happen next. She was having a baby. It was awful! She didn't want a baby. She wanted everything to go back to normal. She wished she'd never met Gavin and Billy and all the soldiers she'd flirted with at Franny's. Oh, why had she wanted to be so grown up? It was all her own fault for wanting to rival Jeannie.

It wasn't a tummy bug, after all. She hadn't ever considered she could have a baby. She and Gavin... it had only been that once and she'd never been with anyone else. How could it have happened so quickly? Horrified, she pressed at her stomach, wishing she could press the baby away. She didn't want to be a mammy at her age. All her friends had their freedom to go out to work and meet up for a giggle while she'd be at home looking after a wailing baby. Oh, it was too much to take in.

'She can't stay here, though, can she?' Jeannie was saying. 'I mean, it's going to be obvious in a few months that she's having a baby.'

'She can stay here until she starts to show.'

'And then?'

Yes, and then? Kathy thought but didn't dare say it out loud. Please God, let Mammy say I can stay here forever. Please don't send me away.

'I know just where she can go to have the baby.'

Chapter Eighteen

The baby was pressing on her bladder again. Kathy put on her coat and rammed her beret down over her ears. It was late autumn and chilly at night. She stumbled down the crooked wooden stairs, bumping her head on the low ceiling. Not bothering to try to be quiet, she opened the back door and stomped across the wet grass to the rickety wooden shed that housed the privy. She shuddered in disgust as the damp, earthy smell rose up to her nostrils. At least she didn't feel sick all the time now. Something rustled behind her in the hedgerow and she squealed, pulling the door shut. When she was done, she cautiously peered out but it was so dark she saw nothing.

Sitting at the table for breakfast, she yawned loudly. Miss Main glanced round reprovingly at her but said nothing. Kathy drummed her fingernails on the surface of the pine table. If she did that at home, Mammy told her off or Jeannie told her to stop it because it was driving her crazy. Here, the old woman didn't even seem to notice. She had her back to Kathy, cooking up porridge on the black range. Kathy stuck her tongue out at her. She let Miss Main set the table with two woven mats, two silver spoons and a pot of steaming tea. A bowl of porridge appeared under her nose. Her appetite these days was huge and Kathy picked up the spoon and began to eat. The old woman sat down slowly, clasped her hands together and said Grace before picking up her spoon and taking small spoonfuls of the porridge.

When the silent meal was done, Kathy sat and rubbed at her swollen belly. Miss Main picked up the bowls, the spoons and the china teacups and took them over to the sink where she poured a kettle of hot water over them and washed them up. She paused, as if waiting for Kathy to pick up the tea towel. When that didn't happen, she took the towel from its rail on the range and dried the crockery. Kathy felt a momentary pang of guilt. At home, Mammy would've skelped her if she didn't help. She could almost hear Jeannie's nagging voice telling her it was shameful, the way she was behaving.

But she hadn't asked to come here. She hadn't asked to be sent away from home for what was going to be months on end with no word of when she could come home again. Here she was, in a stranger's home and bored out of her mind. The cottage was tiny and cramped, so was the village. She hardly walked for minutes before she was met with fields and trees. She missed Glasgow. She scowled. Miss Main ignored her. Kathy pushed her bulky body up from the table. What now?

She went upstairs slowly, feeling sorry for herself and lay on the bed with its candlewick coverlet. An unfinished letter home lay on the desk along with an ancient *Woman's Weekly* magazine that Miss Main had offered her. Tears blurred her view of the low ceiling with its plaster cracks and dripped down her cheeks onto the pillow. It was like living in the dark ages here. There were no light switches, only oil lamps and at night she had to take a candle up to her bedroom to see her way.

A ripple pulsed through her belly. She pressed on it. Mostly, she tried not to think about the baby. When she did, it was terrifying. There was a living creature *inside* her and at some point it had to come out. She shied away from it. If there was one thing she was sure of, it was that she didn't want it. She'd written to Mammy telling her that. She wanted it to be adopted. Mammy's letters, always regular, hadn't replied to that. There was time to think about it, she wrote. Whatever happened, Kathy wasn't to worry. The Dougals would find a way through this.

She rolled over with difficulty and got off the bed, bored and listless. Her bedroom window overlooked the village lane but there was nothing of interest to see. She went across to the bedroom opposite. Its view was of the back garden and the fields. Beyond the fields were dark patchworks of woodland, the trees lit up in yellow and brown and quite a few bare-branched where the wind had torn the leaves away.

Below her, she saw Miss Main with her old, wicker basket, searching for eggs. The black hens ran around her skirts with their comical high-stepping legs like yellow stockings. Kathy grinned in spite of herself. The cow lumbered over to the fence, greeting the old woman as if it were a dog. Miss Main turned and looked up. She waved at Kathy. Kathy took a step back into the bedroom and out of view.

–

Picking up the eggs, Agatha Main felt her bones raw and her joints ache. It felt as if Penny and her other ladies were deliberately being mischievous in laying in odd places, challenging her to find their brown, speckled offerings.

'Penny, dear, I've got bigger problems right now,' she told the black hen, who clucked affectionately at her voice. 'What am I to do with that girl up there? I've tried to get through. I've tried to make her feel at home. To be honest, I thought she'd be company, you know? I missed my Isa and Bob so much it felt like a blessing to be offered their sister. As if God was listening to an old lady's loneliness and wishes. Now, I'm not so sure. They say you should be careful what you wish for, don't they just?'

Penny pecked thoughtfully at the ground where Agatha had scattered grain earlier. The wicker basket was heavy. If Isa was here, she'd have taken the basket and found all the eggs. She had the makings of a country girl in her. Bob would've been running about, his socks wrinkled to his ankles and his knees scabbed from climbing trees and falling off. He'd forgotten one of his *Beano* comics and she'd left it in their room in case he ever came back. She needn't feel sorry for herself. Isa and Bob had written to her from the farm they lived on now. They were happy and so she was happy for them. But how was she to make Kathy happy?

Agatha and Mary had kept in touch after Isa and Bob went home. Mary's letters told her how the two children were doing. Although she was disappointed that they hadn't returned to her for their second evacuation, she understood when Mary explained she wanted them to be closer to home, and with her own family. Organising their evacuation herself instead of through the school, she'd been able to find them somewhere but she wanted Agatha to know how grateful she was to her for the care she'd shown them.

Then the letter about Kathy had arrived. Mary's letter was apologetic as she explained the problem and asked for Agatha's help. She had leapt at the chance to take Kathy.

Perhaps she ought to be shocked at the girl being pregnant with no husband on the horizon. However, having reached the grand old age of seventy, she found there was very little left to shock her in the world except this awful war. The idea of a brand-new baby, by comparison, whatever the circumstances of its birth, seemed like a bright spot.

Heaven help the wee thing with such a grumpy, resentful mother-to-be. Anyhow, Agatha couldn't think on it now. There was work to be done and no help to do it. She kept her thick woollen shawl on over her coat and fetched her bag. There was food to shop for and meals to be made. An expectant mother needed milk and orange juice and eggs and meat to make a strong, healthy baby. Kathy's ration card had allowances for some of that. The rest were not too hard to find in the rural areas.

In the greengrocer's, she purchased apples.

'Miss Main, the very person I wanted to see. How are you today?' It was Dorothy MacFee, whose farm lay at the back of Agatha's field and who was a good neighbour.

'I'm very well, thanks. How are you? Is Ted's back better? Have you heard from your lads?'

'Ted's back out on the tractor as fit as a fiddle. I've told him he is not to lift so much. That's why we have the land girls, two of them, to help. As for the boys, not great letter-writers but they're still out there as we haven't heard otherwise.' Dorothy sighed then smiled. 'We've got something to show you. I've got the cart if you'll come and I can drop you back afterwards.'

There's no fool like an old fool, Agatha told herself later that morning after Dorothy had left her at her blue-painted front door with her small burden. She went through the gate and round the back and in at the kitchen door.

'Is that yours?' Kathy said. She was sitting at the table doing nothing much as far as Agatha could see. The devil and idle hands came to mind.

'It's a she and yes, apparently she's mine. She's called Breagha.'

Agatha set the collie pup on the floor. For a small animal, she was quite heavy. The puppy wriggled excitedly, pink tongue hanging out and soft ears cocked.

'That's a funny name. Why did you call her that?' Kathy stooped as far as her belly let her to stroke the soft fur.

I haven't heard so many words out of your mouth since you came to live with me, Agatha thought.

'Breagha means "beautiful" in the Gaelic. I didn't name her, my friend did. She's weaned and ready for a new home and Dorothy was minded to gift her to me.'

'She is beautiful. You are Breagha.' Kathy smiled at the puppy and at once Agatha saw the resemblance to Isa and to Jeannie. Kathy was a pretty girl when she wasn't scowling and sullen.

'Her tongue's like fine grit on my skin,' Kathy laughed. 'How old is she?'

'She's a baby so she still needs looking after. Dorothy's given me food to get us started.'

Breagha settled on Kathy's shoes and fell asleep.

'Babies do that. They're playful and then all of a sudden they have to sleep,' Agatha explained, bringing a fresh pot of tea to the table along with two slices of an apple cake which had kept well in greased paper and an airtight tin since September 1939. Pre-war but only just.

Kathy stared at her teacup at the mention of babies. Agatha waited. She concentrated on eating the cake and sipping her tea.

'I don't want to have a baby,' Kathy said. Her fingers tightened on the cup.

'But you are having one. That's a fact and you have to face up to it,' Agatha said, not unkindly.

'Aren't you disgusted by me? I'm an unmarried girl who's pregnant. I've had to leave home because of it.'

'You've left home to have your baby but you'll go home afterwards,' Agatha corrected her. 'And no, I'm not disgusted. These things happen. Not to me, of course. No man ever offered for me. I was never a beauty; my nose is too hooked and my chin sticks out. I'd have liked to get married and have children.'

'Well I don't want to have a child. Not now, at any rate. I'm too young and the father... he said we'd get married but it turned out he already had a wife and a child. I want everything to go back the way it was. I want to have fun and see my friends and have my job at Franny's back.' Kathy sniffled and wiped her nose on her cuff. She looked at Agatha curiously. 'I thought you were a widow because you're always dressed in black.'

At least she was thinking of someone beyond herself. That was progress.

'I wear mourning for my nephew. He died when he was five, many long years ago. I wore it until it's become a habit, I suppose. It's a way of remembering him, and I'm too old to change now.'

She got up stiffly, the aches in her joints flaring hot and sore. Talking about him was bitter-sweet. You could say it kept his memory alive but she had no need of words for that. He was inside her heart, each and every day.

She took the empty pot and rinsed it. Breagha slid off Kathy's feet and slept on. Agatha reached for the dirty teacups with their tea-leaf dregs.

'Let me wash those,' Kathy said. 'You have a seat and keep Breagha company. I'll dry them and hang them on the cup hooks too.'

–

There was a bench near the entrance to Kiltie Street overlooking a patch of scrappy grass. Mary never sat on it. She was always too busy coming back with her shopping or going out to visit Helen or going to the WVS centre. Even before the war, she had never sat there. The local kids used it as a climbing frame and the older ones for courting. But today, she did sit. She let her two shopping bags slide down onto the ground beside her aching feet. A few autumn leaves scooted along the pavement in the breeze. There were no onions to be had and their rations of eggs and cheese weren't going to go far for meals so her bags were lighter than usual. Her mind, however, wasn't on the meagre food. It was on Kathy and her latest letter.

Where did I go wrong? The words circled in her head. She and Dennis had brought their children up to know right from wrong. That man had taken advantage of a young girl but Kathy knew it was wrong to do what she did before the wedding ring was firmly on her finger. The Dougals would get through this together but Mary still felt the humiliation of it. She was sure Franny suspected the truth although she hadn't made any remark. Mrs Lennox had asked about Kathy and Mary stuck to her story, that she'd been evacuated like Isa and Bob. Martin and Linda had accepted that. Mary wondered if the rest of

263

Kiltie Street was talking about them. Would she ever live it down? Kathy said she didn't want the baby and now she had written that she wanted it adopted. Mary's own grandchild. She couldn't bear it and yet it was the answer to all their problems.

'Penny for them?' A familiar booming voice broke into her swirling thoughts.

'They're not worth a penny.' She forced a smile, hoping Harry would keep walking but he sat beside her, running his hand over his hair to smooth its springy shape.

'It can't be that bad, can it?'

'The worst possible.' The words were out of her mouth before she could filter them.

'They say a trouble shared is a trouble halved,' Harry said.

'You're full of sayings today,' Mary said and then regretted her waspish tone. It wasn't Harry's fault that her world was collapsing.

He looked at her and Mary couldn't meet his gaze.

'Mrs Dougal, we've been friends, you and I, these past two years since the war started. Before that, we were neighbours for three years. I think you ought to trust me with whatever's bothering you. I've never seen you so down in the dumps.'

Had they really known each other for five years? She supposed so. Five years ago she was grieving for Dennis and about to give birth to a wee boy who would never know his father. So, she reckoned she'd forgive herself for not remembering Harry Woodley moving in.

'It's Kathy,' she said, keeping her voice low although no one was out in Kiltie Street on this breezy, cold day. 'She… she's got herself into trouble and I've sent her away to a friend up north to have her baby. She says she wants

264

to have it adopted; she doesn't want it. Which is the right thing to do… except… that's my grandchild, whatever the circumstances. To give him or her away… I don't know what to do.'

She stopped, searching for her handkerchief. Harry's large hand appeared in front of her lowered face with a clean, ironed handkerchief. She took it gratefully and mopped her eyes.

'It's the shame of it all, too. My neighbours must suspect something. I can't bring the baby home. It's hard enough being a widow with five children. They'll say I didn't bring them up properly. Och, I shouldn't care what they think, but I do. I have to live here in Kiltie Street the rest of my days. I want to be thought well of, to be respectable. Is that wrong?'

Harry didn't answer. He got up and walked round the bench, pausing as if to say something. Then he shook his head and walked away over to his tenement close and vanished. There was a pain in the pit of her stomach and her chest ached. She'd lost Harry's friendship by telling him. In that moment, she realised how she felt about him. He was nothing like Dennis. He was loud and boisterous and annoying, always full of advice and sure that he was right. She'd found him irritating at first. But now she had come to rely on him. She relied on his companionship, his blustery good humour and yes, even his endless advice. He could never replace Dennis in her heart but maybe there was enough room in her heart for another love?

There was no use crying about it. Life went on. Mary took the handles of her shopping bags to pull them up.

'Mrs Dougal, please sit where you are.' Harry was back. His face was red and his hair wilder than ever, as if fingers had been run through the strands over and over.

'I thought you disapproved. That you couldn't bear to be near me after what I've just confessed.'

'Couldn't bear to be near you? The opposite, dear Mary. May I call you that?' He began to pace in front of the bench, churning up what little grass there was left into mud. 'I have a solution to your problem, if you'll listen.'

'I'll listen if you stop pacing, you're giving me a headache. Will you sit?'

He sat next to her, leaving as much gap as possible.

'I have a solution,' he repeated.

'Go on with you, then. Because I can't think of any and I've been awake many nights trying to find one.'

'Kathy doesn't want her baby, and who can blame her? She's a young girl with her whole life ahead of her. You want to keep the baby and have a home and love to give it. And I... well, Mrs Dougal, Mary, I admire you greatly and always have. I've always thought you to be very attractive and these last couple of years, as I've got to know you better, I've found you to be kind and generous and good-hearted. In fact, I've fallen in love with you, Mary. Will you marry me? We can bring up your grandchild together as our child.'

Mary was stunned. Harry Woodley was in love with her. Who would have thought it? And, she had feelings for him too. Emotions that had crystallised right there and then when she believed he was abandoning her.

'You would do that for me?' she wondered.

'If I'm honest, you'll be doing me a favour. I'm being selfish. I'll get a lovely wife and a ready-made family out of it. My wife died of flu shortly after we got married so we never had a chance to have children.'

'I've become very fond of you too,' she said. 'I'll be honest, Dennis will always have a special place in my heart but I think I've enough love left to say yes.'

'You will?' His voice boomed happily.

'I will.'

He leaned towards her and planted a kiss on her lips. It was a long while since she'd been kissed, and only ever by Dennis, who had been her childhood sweetheart, but Mary decided Harry's kiss was nice.

'Will people believe that I'd be having a child at my age?' she murmured, letting him put his warm arm round her. 'The dates of a wedding and the age of the baby won't add up either.'

'You're young enough yet. Besides, people believe what they want to believe. We've got good neighbours. They don't wish us ill. They want what's best for us.'

Mary remembered Mrs Mulligan from two streets down. She had announced her pregnancy in the summer and she was fairly certain they were the same age. Women often got caught in their forties, thinking their child-bearing days were over. If Dennis were alive, perhaps she too would've had a late baby.

Her heart leapt a little. She was going through the change of life but that didn't mean life was over. Here she was, getting married again and having a baby which was her own flesh and blood, if not from her own body. And, if Kathy changed her mind and wanted to keep her baby then she would give her all the support she needed.

'When shall we set the date?' Harry said. 'There's no reason to wait and plenty reason to be quick.'

'Come in for a cuppa and we'll decide together.'

The paper rustled in Jeannie's hands as she read the letter again.

> *Dear Jeannie*
>
> *I'm glad that you have come to your senses and see that there is no point in a long engagement. We can get married at Christmas as I'm due leave then. I will leave it to you to arrange the banns and the licence. We will get married in the church where my parents were married. You are to find a suitable outfit which I will pay for. I prefer you to wear a two-piece costume, perhaps in a serviceable colour like blue which is practical and can be worn again. I'll be in my uniform so no need of expense for a new suit.*
>
> *Once we're married you can move in with Mother.*
>
> *Yours*
> *Arthur*

He had it all worked out. There was no discussion with her. He hadn't asked her if she liked his plans or had other ideas. Was this what marriage to Arthur was going to be like? He would do the telling and she would do what she was told? There were plenty of married couples who lived like that. After all, Arthur would be the man of the house and wives had to obey, didn't they?

Only, she'd always hoped that when she got married, it would be different – that she and her husband would share every decision and compromise when they couldn't agree. If she was marrying Bill… She shied away from that treacherous thought. Bill was gone. There had never been a choice for her, not really. Mammy was right. Marrying Arthur was sensible. She'd never want for money or comfort and that had to count for something. She'd have to learn to keep the peace with him. She folded the letter carefully. War time was full of difficult decisions and heartbreak. She knew that from seeing their friends and neighbours struggling on. This was no different. Now it was her turn to face the future and make it as good as it could be.

Chapter Nineteen

Mary and Harry were married in a quiet civil ceremony by the local registrar on Christmas Eve. On the morning of their wedding, Mary was surprised to find herself feeling nervous.

'It's ridiculous. There's nothing to worry about,' she told Jeannie, sitting in their tidied parlour that morning. 'It's a simple wedding with a few, dear guests and afterwards we'll have an early Christmas and New Year celebration.'

'Have you changed your mind about Harry?' Jeannie asked.

'Not at all. I hope you're pleased for us, love. I know you haven't always seen eye to eye with him.'

'I can see his good points now. Besides, he must have something special or you wouldn't be marrying him,' Jeannie grinned.

'I am very fond of him. He'll never replace your father in my heart but I think it's all right to have a second love.'

'It solves Kathy's problem too.'

Mary glanced at her eldest daughter. Jeannie had taken so much responsibility on her slender shoulders during the war. It was a great help, especially when Mary felt so shaky some days and so very tired on others. But she didn't want Jeannie to worry so much about everything.

'Kathy's still adamant she doesn't want the baby,' Mary reminded her. 'This way, we keep our family together.'

'Oh, Mammy, you're so good to us all. Is that why you're marrying Harry? For respectability?'

'Partly, but it's not the only reason. I do actually love him and it'll be very nice to have someone to share my life with and stop me being lonely. There's Jimmy away and no sign of him coming home any time soon. Isa and Bob are safely in the country until this is all over. And you'll be moving to Helen's after your wedding.'

'I could stay here with you.' Jeannie sounded hopeful.

Mary shook her head. 'That's not fair on Helen or Arthur, love, and you know it. When you marry Arthur, you promise to love, honour and obey. If Arthur wants you living with his mother, then you have to do that. It's quite a normal arrangement after a wedding for young couples and it makes sense for you, especially when Arthur's going to be away. I'm glad to see you settled, as you know.'

Jeannie shifted on her seat. 'The neighbours are going to know it's not your baby. Kathy's due in early January, isn't she? And here you're getting married late December. They're bound to guess.'

'It's winter so I've been wearing bulky clothes deliberately the last few months. I think they'll be kept guessing. Perhaps they'll think me and Harry tying the knot is a shotgun wedding. One way or another, the Dougals are causing a minor scandal but it'll stay within Kiltie Street; that I do know. People here are loyal.'

–

The neighbours came out onto Kiltie Street to wish them well as they left, waving and calling good luck in spite

271

of the drizzling rain and overcast skies. At the registry office, Mary smiled at their guests. Jeannie sat in the front row with Arthur and Helen beside her. Martin and Linda O'Leary were there and so was Eileen and her mother, Agnes. Mary was glad they had come to see her and Harry's happy day but she was only too aware of those that were missing. Her beloved Dennis – she caught herself at the thought: of course he wouldn't be there to see her marry another man! But he had been there with her through all the other important moments in her life and it was natural to think of him. Jimmy, Kathy, Isa and Bob were all missing. She'd written to them all about the forthcoming wedding. She'd write again to describe the day.

After the short ceremony, they had their photos taken on the top step of the registry office before heading for home.

'How are you doing, Mrs Woodley?' Harry whispered in her ear.

That's right; she was Mrs Woodley now. She'd have to get used to that. She wasn't Mary Dougal any more. She turned to her new husband and kissed his cheek fondly.

'I'm fine, Mr Woodley. Just fine. Looking forward to my Christmas dinner and wedding feast all rolled into one.'

'Me too,' Harry beamed. 'Me too, Mrs Woodley.'

–

Jeannie took off her coat and hung it on the hook. She hurried into the parlour and lit the fire. She and Mary had worked hard getting the celebratory dinner ready for days. Ingenuity was the order of the day, she thought, as food was increasingly scarce and certain items impossible to find at all. And not only food. There was no Christmas tree and no Christmas wrapping paper. It had been hard finding gifts, too. She'd unravelled a jumper and made gloves and socks for her family. They were wrapped in newspaper on the sideboard for giving out after the meal.

Eileen came in, her blonde hair glistening with raindrops. She rubbed her hands.

'It's freezing out there. Can I give you a hand?'

Eileen and her parents were now living back in Glasgow, in a rented house not far from where they used to live. Jeannie missed her company but was glad to get her bed back to herself.

'You can pour the sherry, please,' Jeannie said, pointing to the sideboard where she'd set the sherry bottle and glasses out that morning. 'I hope there's enough to go round as I couldn't get any more.'

Eileen squinted at it and nodded. 'This will do, especially if you and I have a lemonade instead. Anyway, more importantly, guess what's arrived?'

'What?'

'A huge bundle of letters from Jimmy!' Eileen's face shone with excitement. 'Oh, Jeannie, he's safe and alive. I kept writing but I never had a reply and I thought the worst had happened. Did you get any?'

'I'd have told you right away if we did. But that's wonderful news. You have to tell my mother. That's the best Christmas present ever. We've been so worried. Surely, we'll get a letter soon. I wonder what happened to them all that time and where they went missing?'

Eileen shrugged. 'I don't care. I'm just glad they finally got here.'

The others had arrived in by now and the room smelt of coal smoke and damp wool, perfume and sherry and the sweet incense scent of pine. Eileen had brought two small tree branches with green needles on them which she'd broken from a small tree growing on the ground near their new house on the edge of the city.

'It's not a Christmas tree but it's the next best thing,' she said, giving them to Jeannie before they went to the wedding.

Jeannie looked at them all. Harry had his arm around Mammy and was kissing her cheek. He looked proud and happy. Martin was sipping at a large sherry while Linda watched him shrewdly. Agnes, neat in a pale, pink tweed suit, sipped at a much smaller glass and stood on the edge of the group with a faint smile. Arthur had shepherded his mother to an armchair and was bending down solicitously to her.

Jeannie felt guilty. She hadn't had time to talk to Arthur on his own, not properly. She'd walked with him and Helen to the registry office and back again. At the short ceremony, she'd whispered to him, 'That will be us soon,' expecting him to share her delight in the day. Instead, he'd shushed her as if she was making a scene and she'd shut up. There was a tension to him that was almost audible. It was as if his body was buzzing. She could feel him next to her, his sleeve brushing her arm, the muscles tight. What was going on? He was thinner too.

'A toast, a toast!' Harry boomed. 'Will you raise your glasses to my lovely wife, Mrs Mary Woodley, before we all have some cake to celebrate.'

They raised their glasses to the happy couple and Jeannie hurried through to get the plate of carefully sliced fruit cake to offer round. There wasn't as much fruit in it as normal and it was made more from breadcrumbs and creativity than traditional ingredients but everyone said it was delicious. After an hour of conversation, Agnes and Eileen and the O'Learys said goodbye.

Eileen hugged her as they left. 'Have a lovely celebration and I'll see you tomorrow. It's a pity we don't get tomorrow off as well but Miss McGrory, even though she's softened towards us, is still strict when it comes to the rosters.'

'See you tomorrow. Thanks for coming. Even though Jimmy can't be here, at least his fiancée and my best friend was able to.'

'We'll be sisters-in-law imagine that. We're so lucky, aren't we?'

'We really are.' Jeannie waved to Eileen and Agnes as they went off into the night with their torches, feeling so glad that she had made such a very good friend who was soon to be family. She slipped back into the flat, making sure she didn't let the light escape. Harry might be her stepdad now but he was still the ARP warden.

The rabbit casserole was cooking nicely in the range where it had been left at midday before the ceremony. The potatoes, cabbage and carrots were scrubbed and ready to boil. Jeannie set them on the range. There was also a pudding wrapped in muslin which was to be steamed. It had suet and candied peel and sultanas in it. Mary had added an egg beaten in hot water to make up for the two eggs which should've been used. There was no milk for custard but Jeannie stirred in water and hoped it wasn't too thin a sweet sauce.

Mary bustled in. 'Thank God your friend had those rabbits. I was afraid we'd have no meat for the meal without a turkey or chicken to be had.'

'It was kind of Annie to think of us,' Jeannie agreed. 'Paul's a dab hand at finding things but it's best not to ask too many questions about where they come from.'

'They're not stolen, are they?'

'He's got a friend who goes hunting,' Jeannie said vaguely. 'Did Eileen tell you about the letters?' She changed the subject.

'The best Christmas present or wedding present I could get. I only hope we get a letter ourselves soon. I'll write again.'

'Isa and Bob will be well fed, going by their latest letter,' Jeannie said, stirring the custard sauce and squashing out the lumps with the back of the wooden spoon. 'They're excited because they helped Uncle Angus, as they call him, to dig up a tree and it's in the corner of their living room all decorated with candles and glass ornaments. Bob's drawn a picture of the goose they're apparently having on Christmas Day and Isa wrote about buttered scones and helping Auntie Martha make jam preserves.'

'I'm glad they're happy but I miss them terribly. I haven't read their letter, I've been that busy with organising today but I'll sit down later and read it.'

'I miss them too, and Kathy.' Jeannie stopped her stirring, thoughtfully. 'Mammy, can I ask you something?'

'Of course. Whatever is it?'

'It's about Kathy. I feel I ought to tell Arthur, but…'

'There's no buts about it, love. You can't have secrets from your husband-to-be. Besides, Arthur's practically family now, what with your wedding next week.'

'Does Helen know about Kathy's baby?'

'I haven't told her yet because of all the things to do with my wedding and getting ready for yours but I'll be telling her soon. I'm not worried about that. She's turned out to be a good friend and I know she'll stick by us.'

'So, I should tell Arthur?'

'Yes, you must, but ask him to keep it to himself. It's all right within the family but we don't want it getting outside. All this will blow over and what with the war, there's plenty of distraction for folks but even so…Yes, it'll all work out fine. Now, help me with the plates. Everyone will be wondering when their dinner's coming.'

It was odd having their meal on Christmas Eve instead of New Year's Day and strange to think it was Mammy's wedding meal too. Jeannie glanced around the table, happy to see everyone seemed satisfied with the food. There was hardly any rabbit casserole left. Harry had scraped the bottom of the pan and served it up, spoonful by spoonful until everyone had their fair share. The portions were modest but the steamed pudding and custard was filling enough.

'How's army life treating you, Arthur?' Harry asked as he cut the pudding and divided it between the best china bowls. Jeannie had poured the custard into a jug ready to serve along with it.

Arthur was sitting next to Jeannie and again, she felt that strange vibration coming off him. His left leg jiggled under the table at Harry's question.

'Very well, thank you,' he said curtly.

'I served in the Great War but worked in the army stores,' Harry went on, making conversation. 'Never got further than the south coast. But no doubt after training, you'll be in the thick of it, you lads.'

'Mother, would you like custard?' Arthur said loudly, grabbing at the jug and pushing it towards Helen.

'Thank you, dear.' Helen looked taken aback but duly poured a little of the thin, yellow liquid onto her portion of pudding.

'Perhaps Arthur doesn't want to talk about the war,' Mary said to Harry meaningfully.

Poor Harry, Jeannie thought. He's gone quite red. He was only being polite and Arthur's taken it the wrong way. What is wrong with him? I can't imagine what he's going through but he's being really rude to Harry and at his wedding meal, too. Below the edge of the table, where no one could see, she tried to take Arthur's hand to calm him. Arthur pulled his fingers away abruptly.

Jeannie sighed. Their own wedding was only a few days away and yet sometimes she felt as if she didn't understand him at all. She was dreading the marriage. There; she'd said it. But she'd never let Mammy know that. It was hard enough with the baby coming and all the gossip that was bound to ensue. She wasn't going to let Mammy down by breaking it off with Arthur. And she wasn't going to think about Bill. That was all over. There was a tight spot inside her chest lately that didn't loosen. The only way she got through the days was by putting on a bright smile as if everything was all right.

After the meal, Mary got out the Snakes and Ladders board and the Old Maid playing cards and they played games. Jeannie made a pot of tea and brought out the last of the cake with a pot of jam. Even Arthur joined in with the games and Jeannie relaxed. She sat next to Helen on the sofa.

'Your mother and Harry are good together,' Helen said as they watched the other three play cards. 'You will be thinking of your own wedding coming up. I'm so glad you and Arthur are getting married so soon. I wish you could have a bigger wedding but with the war on…'

'A small wedding will suit us just fine,' Jeannie smiled.

One good thing about marrying Arthur was having Helen as her mother-in-law. She got on very well with her. Anyway, she was telling the truth. She didn't care to have a big wedding at all. She just wanted to get it over with.

'Arthur wants you to move in with me once you're wed. Is that what you want?' Helen asked.

Arthur hadn't asked her what she wanted. He'd dictated that, just as he'd dictated what she should wear. Jeannie had wanted a white wedding dress as pretty as Janet's but that wasn't to be. Still, she had to make the best of it. There was a war on. Arthur was right; the blue suit she'd used her clothing ration points on was practical and something she'd get good wear out of. But it wasn't romantic.

'I'll be very happy to move in with you,' she said now and was rewarded by Helen's smile.

Later, they listened to the wireless. Jeannie wanted to catch Arthur on his own before he and Helen left to walk up the road. There was no point in waiting to tell him about Kathy. She leaned over to him and whispered, 'Can we talk outside for a wee bit?'

'Now?' He looked annoyed, and her stomach flipped nervously.

She nodded. This had to be done. There was no time like the present, as Mammy often said. Frowning, Arthur stood up and followed her to where the coats hung. Jeannie put on her wool coat and waited for him to do likewise.

'What is it, Jeannie? Whatever it is, why can't you say it inside where it's at least warm?'

'I'd rather we went outside, if you don't mind. We don't have to stay out long.'

'Very well,' he grumbled.

They went out into the darkened street, pulling the door closed quickly to keep the light and warmth inside. She waited for him to take her arm, to pull her close and kiss her. Surely, her fiancé should want time alone with her? A moment to make a joke, or a soft touch to the skin to lighten the mood and indicate some intimacy between them? But, nothing. Arthur stood there sullenly, rubbing his hands together to show how cold he was and what an inconvenience this was.

'I've got something to tell you,' Jeannie began, swallowing a lump in her throat. 'It's only fair that you know before we get married.'

'What are you on about? Hurry up, will you, so we can get back to the fire.'

'You haven't asked where Kathy is.'

In the dim, veiled moonlight she saw Arthur's eyebrows rise. 'That's because your mother said she'd been evacuated. I assumed she was with your little sister and brother.'

He'd assumed that because he wasn't interested enough to find out. Jeannie's mouth twisted wryly. She wasn't going to start an argument. Not when Arthur was strung as tightly as a bow as it was.

'She's having a baby.'

'She's what?'

'You heard me. She's having a baby. She got herself into trouble and the baby's due next month. Mammy and Harry are going to bring it up for her. But I wanted you to know, Arthur, before we get married. I don't want any secrets between us.'

'She should wed the father.'

'He's married already.'

'Your sister's a little slut, that's what you're telling me. And you sound as if you're on her side.' Arthur's voice was ice-cold.

'Don't call her that! She made a mistake.'

'A mistake. That's calling it something. She opened her legs for some man, or a few of them, and now she's been caught.'

'Arthur, please, that's a horrible thing to say.' Jeannie felt quite sick the way he was talking.

He lifted up his shoulders, suddenly standing taller, looming over her. Jeannie took an involuntary step back, almost tripping.

'What's the matter with you, Jeannie? You've changed. You used to be so sweet and shy. Now, you're... you're brash and bold.' He spat the words out and she flinched at the anger radiating from him.

Some fighting spirit rose up in her. A need to contradict him and to defend Kathy. She might find her sister annoying and immature but she was family and Arthur had no right to disrespect her.

'If I'm brash and bold, it's only because I've had to grow up fast these last two years and look after my family,' she cried. 'As for me being so sweet and shy, all that means is you feel you can tell me what to do and what to wear—'

The blow came out of nowhere in the dark. It stung her cheekbone and the tender skin around her eye and she cried out in pain and astonishment. She stood stock-still for a moment, trying to make sense of it.

'I won't bring your dirty secrets and shame to my mother,' Arthur snarled. 'Consider our engagement over. You were never good enough for me. I don't know why I chose a shop girl for a bride. Once lower class, always lower class and breeding will out. You're as bad as your sister.'

Jeannie spun on her heel and ran towards home. Her vision was blurred as she raced to her bedroom, not heeding the merry calls from the parlour. She untied her shoelaces, kicked off her shoes and slid under the blankets. After a short while, she heard voices in the hall and realised with relief that Helen and Arthur were leaving. What had Arthur told them? She didn't care. Her face was throbbing. If he hadn't broken their engagement, then she would have because he'd hit her. She sobbed until she drifted into sleep. She woke to hear Mary open her bedroom door.

'Are you awake?' Mary whispered.

'Mammy,' Jeannie wailed and threw back the blankets to hurl herself at her mother.

She cried some more until she was choked up.

'What is it? What happened?' She felt Mammy's fingers on her chin, turning her face to the lamp. 'Your face. Did Arthur do that?'

'He hit me,' she whispered, still appalled by the events that had unfolded. 'How could he?'

'We'll talk about it in the morning,' Mammy said quietly. 'I'll tell Harry we're stopping here tonight.'

They had been planning to go to Harry's flat for their honeymoon night.

She turned down the lamp and tucked Jeannie back into bed. As she tiptoed to the door, Jeannie looked at her.

'It's over, Mammy. There'll be no wedding now.'

—

The next morning, Jeannie's eye had bloomed into a livid purple bruise. She covered it with face powder as best she could and hurried up the road to the Dunns' house. She had to speak to Helen and try to explain what had happened between her and Arthur. It was only fair to do so after Helen's kindness and her eagerness for Jean to join their family.

She rang the bell and Helen answered. She looked sympathetically at Jeannie.

'He won't see you. I'm so sorry, dear.'

'Did he tell you why we argued?'

Helen nodded. 'It doesn't matter to me. Mary's been a true friend and we all have our troubles to bear. But Arthur won't listen to me. He's afraid that we'll be tarnished by association, as he puts it.'

'He's broken off the engagement.'

'Perhaps it's for the best. I shouldn't say this about my own son but for your sake, it's best.'

Jeannie touched her tender eye. Had Helen suffered the same from Arthur's father? She wanted to ask but didn't dare. It was too personal. She slipped the engagement ring from her finger and gave it to Helen.

'I'm sorry,' she said. 'Please give this to Arthur. I don't know what's made him so angry; he was so even before I told him about Kathy but I do wish him well in spite of all that's happened.'

Helen closed the door. Jeannie stared at the large house. Next week she was meant to have moved here and called it home. Next week she was to be Mrs Arthur Dunn, comfortably off and never to worry about money or security, which was to make Mammy happy, even if it didn't matter to Jeannie. Now everything had changed.

On the walk home, she stopped halfway down the hill and took in a deep breath of cold air. The slate roofs and chimney stacks of the tenements were so clear in the frosty morning she felt she could reach out and touch them. She felt a sudden rush of tenderness for Kiltie Street and the place she called home. The tight spot in her chest loosened a little and she hurried down the slope, thinking to put the kettle on and make a pot of tea for Mammy and Harry.

Chapter Twenty

Kathy was fed up. She couldn't see her feet and her back ached. She lumbered around like an elephant. She was so huge she didn't want to go out walking in the village. It was horrible when people stared at her. She knew they wondered if she was married. Miss Main said to ignore them but it was impossible. It was easier to stay inside and sit with Breagha. She rubbed her back. It was worse today. Outside, the snow fell in big, soft snowflakes.

'Shall I put the kettle on for tea?' she called to Miss Main.

'Is your back sore?' Miss Main frowned.

'Och, it's always sore. I wish all this was over.'

'And I wish I had married and had children. Then I would know what to expect. As it is, I have no experience to draw on. My dear, I think your baby may be coming soon. I'm going to get my gumboots on and go and find the midwife. She knows you're due but I think it won't hurt to have her check you over.'

'What? No, don't go. I'm fine, really,' Kathy cried in alarm. It couldn't come now, could it? 'I want Mammy.'

'Don't fuss,' Miss Main said in her stern, teacher voice that she sometimes employed when Kathy was lazy or didn't dry the dishes properly. 'I won't be long. Dorcas Cole only lives a street over.'

Kathy groaned as another ripple of pain went across her back. This one reached round to her belly too. She bent forward, gasping.

'Right, that's it. Breathe. I'll be back very soon.'

Kathy barely noticed her go. The pain, when it came, was all-encompassing. Great, sharp ripples that punched the wind from her. When the pain stopped, she drew in a deep breath and prayed that was the last one. There was a respite for a short while and she thought it had all been a mistake. She put the kettle on and made a pot of tea. Tea was rationed but she didn't care. But on taking the first sip, she cried out as the spasms came back.

Breagha padded around her with a low whine. Her big, brown eyes stared at Kathy. She managed to bend down and stroke the dog's soft head.

'I can't do this. I don't want to do this.'

She'd put the idea of a baby out of her mind while staying with Miss Main. She pretended it wasn't happening. She never even thought of Gavin any more. All she wanted to do was to go home to Kiltie Street and the city. The wide open fields and damp woodland frightened her. She had almost got used to the chickens chasing after her when she went into the back garden and the cow that lumbered over to the fence in curiosity. She and Miss Main had become friends of sorts. And Breagha, she loved. But she wished that none of this had happened.

'I was stupid,' she told Breagha, fiercely. 'I was taken in by him. He gets to waltz off none the worse for it while I… I'm stuck here like this. Oh—' She doubled over with the pain.

Breagha barked. There was a sharp rap at the front door. Kathy stumbled to it. Thank goodness, Miss Main had brought the midwife. But when she opened the door,

Mammy stood there. Kathy let out a sob and ran into Mammy's open arms.

–

Mary's journey to Perthshire was long and tiring but strangely enjoyable. She missed Harry of course and had left plenty of instructions for Jeannie on making meals and keeping house.

'When will you be back?' Jeannie asked.

'I'll stay as long as I'm needed. Then I'll bring the baby home. Kathy'll stay with Miss Main that bit longer.'

'Will she be all right?'

'Of course she will. Miss Main has written that there's a local midwife, Mrs Cole, who's delivered all the village babies for years. If there are any complications, there's a doctor but hopefully we won't need to call for him.'

'Me and Kathy… we bicker and you tell us off for that. I find her annoying and she doesn't like me bossing her about, but…'

'I know. You love each other really. It's called family. She's going to be fine. I promise you.'

She might have reassured Jeannie with those words, but Mary knew it wasn't a promise she could really keep. Not if things went wrong. She was afraid inside for Kathy. There were plenty of women who died in childbirth, even these days. She confided her fears in Harry, glad to have him to turn to.

Harry kissed her. 'She's got you, and that's the biggest help she needs.'

'You don't mind me going, then?'

'I'll miss you but you need to be with her. Right now, Kathy needs you more than I do.'

'I love you, Mr Woodley. You know that?'

'I suspected it, Mrs Woodley, but I may need convincing. How about another kiss?'

–

Harry and Jeannie came with her on the bus to the train station and waved her off on the train. Once the train was moving, Mary had a flicker of excitement. She was going on a journey. It was a change from the everyday tasks she had. She felt immediately guilty. She ought to be thinking only of Kathy right now. But as she stared out the window at the unfamiliar countryside, she realised she hadn't felt as bright in ages. As long as Kathy got through this, there was a lot to look forward to. There would be a whole new member of the family.

She found her way easily enough on the local bus which dropped her off in the centre of the tiny village, recalling her previous visit. Mary took a deep breath of the clean, fresh air and felt revitalised. It felt as if the war hadn't touched this place at all. She looked over at some distant woodlands, a patchwork of fields closer by and a lovely lane of cottages like something out of a film set. It was nothing like Kiltie Street but she felt strangely at home. She walked briskly along until she found the cottage.

'Mammy!' The blue front door of the cottage opened suddenly and Kathy howled and ran straight at her.

The force of her body, swollen and huge with child, almost threw Mary backwards. She grabbed Kathy and hugged her. She smelled her hair and skin and a wave of love washed over her. This was her wee girl and she needed her mammy.

'Come along, let's get you inside. It's freezing out here. We're both going to be like snowmen with these snowflakes on us.'

She ushered Kathy inside and shut the door. Inside, the cottage was warm and snug. There were scents of beeswax and old wood.

'Where's Miss Main?'

Kathy cried out and pressed on her belly. 'It's coming, Mammy. The baby… it's on its way.'

Mary managed to make out that Miss Main was fetching the midwife while she shepherded Kathy into the kitchen, intending to make tea and boil a kettle and find towels. She was pleased to see a fresh pot and a cup already made and, on the kitchen table, a neat pile of towels.

The back door opened and two older women arrived in with a flurry of snow.

'Mrs Dougal, you made it. And just in time, too,' Miss Main said. 'This is Dorcas Cole, our midwife.'

The other woman, slightly younger, had a round, rosy-cheeked face and eyes like blackcurrants almost lost in laughter lines. She nodded to Mary and then went over to Kathy.

'Looks like things are happening. Let's get you comfortable upstairs, shall we?'

'Perfect timing,' Miss Main said to Mary. 'Only a mother is needed at a time like this. I was prepared to do whatever was necessary but I am somewhat relieved that you and Dorcas are here to take charge.'

'She's early,' Mary said. 'I came today because I wanted to be here for a few days before the baby came.'

'That's nature for you. Keeps you on your toes. Why don't you go up to her and take up some tea? Dorcas says it'll be a while yet.'

'Thank you, Miss Main. Not only for taking in Kathy but for looking after my Isa and Bob.'

'Call me Agatha and I'll call you Mary. Now's no time for standing on ceremony. Besides, I feel almost part of the family. I should be thanking you for all the interest your children have brought to my life.' Agatha reached out to her and they shared a short, fierce hug.

Mary took the pile of towels and went up the crooked stairs to the bedroom. Kathy was pacing the small room while Dorcas unpacked her bag. There was a small dog watching it all, head cocked to the side.

'Should I take the dog out?' she said.

'Probably best,' Dorcas said calmly. 'Now dear, between contractions, you must breathe. Come and let me examine you so we can see how you are coming along.'

Mary felt helpless. Apart from shooing the dog out the door, there wasn't much she could do. She wished she could take Kathy's pain away. Instead, all she could do was sit beside her, holding her hand and murmuring comfort and reassurance, while Dorcas busied about.

Kathy's baby boy was born that evening, shortly before five o'clock. Dorcas offered him to his mother but Kathy shook her head. Mary cradled him, marvelling at his tiny hands and drinking in the sight of her first grandchild. Sure, didn't he have the look of her Dennis? Tears of joy and relief stung her eyes. He was whole and healthy and she sent up a prayer of thanks for that.

'He'll need a bottle if she won't feed him,' Dorcas said, shaking her head.

'What will you call him?' Mary asked Kathy.

Kathy's hair clung damply to her forehead and her gaze was sleepy as she looked up at Mary. 'You name him, Mammy. He's yours.'

'Don't you want him, love? We don't have to do it this way. I'll support you, so will Harry and Jeannie and Jimmy. All of us. If you really want to be his mother, we can do it.'

Kathy shook her head firmly. 'He'll be a bastard. I won't have that for him. I want him to have what I've always had, to be part of a good family. I want you to be his mammy and I want...' Her voice broke a little before she went on. '...I want to be me again. Just me. I know that's selfish but I want to work at Franny's and go to the cinema with my friends and be a girl, not a mammy.'

Mary kissed her hot forehead. 'As long as you're certain. I'm going to take him and feed him now.'

Sitting in Agatha's warm kitchen, the baby swaddled in a soft shawl in her arms, sucking on the bottle, Mary felt completely contented. Agatha came in and put the kettle on to boil.

'He's a bonny wee boy. Have you got a name for him yet?'

'Dennis Robert Woodley. Dennis for his grandfather and Robert for my father.'

'That's a good, strong name. There's a telephone at the corner shop if you want to let your family know.'

Once Dennis was fed and tucked up asleep in a chest drawer that made a good, snug cot, Mary put on her coat and boots and walked along the lane to the corner shop. It was closed for the day but Agatha had said that if she knocked, Miss MacLachlan who lived upstairs, would let her in. The snow had stopped and the fresh snow underneath her boots crunched squeakily. She made a call to Helen who was the only person she knew with a telephone in her home.

'That's wonderful news,' Helen said, her voice tinny over the crackly line. 'I'll walk down now and let Harry and Jeannie know. I'm so glad that mother and baby are both well.'

'You're a good friend. I'm so sorry we won't be family now. It's a pity that Jeannie and Arthur couldn't make it up with each other.'

'I'm sorry for that, too. I'd have liked Jeannie as my daughter-in-law. Still, there's nothing to be done about it and I hope our friendship hasn't suffered because of it.'

'Never,' Mary said. 'We're friends for life.'

'I sent him packing, you know.' Mary heard Helen's sigh at the other end of the line.

'Arthur?' Mary asked in surprise.

'We had a big row. I could tell you it blew up out of nowhere but that would be a lie. It's been a long while in the making but I've been too cowardly to stand up for myself. When I saw what he'd done to Jeannie's beautiful face, I was shocked. I knew Arthur was like his father but I'd hoped he was a better version of him. On top of that, he kept controlling me and, well, I didn't tell you but it was getting worse. I was being smothered by his attention and I snapped. I told him to go back to his unit until he sorted himself out. And I laid down the ground rules.'

'Helen!' Mary said, full of admiration for her courageous friend.

There was laughter at the other end of the line. 'I know. Who would have thought I'd have it in me?'

'Still, he's your family so I hope you make up with each other.'

'Yes, he is my only son so I hope so too but this time it's going to be on my terms. I've got a lot of years left in me yet and I don't intend to spend them being miserable.'

'I'll come round when I'm back,' Mary said. 'It'll be nice to catch up over a cuppa.'

'I look forward to it. The centre's busier too so I'm going to put myself down for more shifts to help out. I've got more energy these days and I want to use it to help end this war.'

Mary smiled as she walked back to the cottage, watching the snow sparkle on the ground. Wasn't it funny how things turned out? And how people could change and adapt to circumstances? No one wanted this awful war but it certainly made some folk stronger and brought out the worst and the best in others.

–

The greengrocer's had a sign across the window which stated 'no oranges, tomatoes or onions'. Jeannie queued anyway and came away with carrots and potatoes and a small, bruised cauliflower. She thought about Kathy as she walked home, a bag in each hand. It was a cold, bright, late January day with a nipping wind that stung the tip of her nose. Mammy's letter said she was due home on the train today, bringing baby Dennis while Kathy was to stay on for a few weeks with Miss Main. Jeannie missed Kathy. It was odd. They argued and bickered when they were together but this whole situation made Jeannie realise how much she loved her sister. She hoped Kathy wouldn't be too changed by having a baby. She was a mother now, how strange.

At home, she called out a greeting to Harry on her way to the kitchen. That was something else to get used to. Harry had given up the rent on his flat and moved in to the Dougals' home which was larger.

'I'll bring you a cuppa,' she called through, lifting out the vegetables onto the work surface.

'Thanks, love,' Harry bellowed back.

He'd fitted easily into the role of stepdad and although she'd never call him 'Dad' and he could never replace her own real dad, Jeannie was becoming fond of him. Besides, he was good for Mammy and made her laugh. Mammy seemed like a different person these days with Harry at her side. Her eyes often sparkled and Jeannie heard her humming a wee tune as she cooked and cleaned.

Perhaps that's what love did to you. Jeannie glanced at her bare left hand. She'd written to Arthur but had no reply and now had to accept that her engagement to him was finally over. Arthur wasn't going to forgive her or her family and, to be honest, she couldn't forgive him either. The tight spot in her chest had vanished and she knew that it was for the best. She didn't love him and now she wondered if he had ever really loved her; he'd been so quick to give her up. No, it was best she forgot everything and moved on.

She had a lot to be thankful for. She enjoyed her job at the munitions factory and she had good friends in Eileen and Annie. She never forgot Janet when thinking of her friends. Miss McGrory was a friend of sorts, too, now and often joined them in the canteen for a brief chat or wished them a good weekend as work finished on a Friday. Eileen was busy planning her dream wedding. She and Jimmy hadn't set a date yet but if he got leave in the summer and made it back to Glasgow, they'd marry then. Jeannie was looking forward to being chief bridesmaid. Eileen had Jimmy, while Annie had Paul. It wasn't right to be envious but she couldn't help it.

As for her… Jeannie sighed. She had no right to wish for more. Mammy was coming home with baby Dennis and she was excited about being an auntie. Except she had to remember to be his big sister. How confusing.

She put aside her wishes and yearnings. She scrubbed the vegetables and set them to boil while she made a potato pastry. Lord Woolton Pie was a popular dish and that's what they were having for tea when Mammy came home. Despite the recent rationing of rice and dried fruits, Mammy's cupboard stores allowed for a small rice pudding with raisins for dessert.

When the food was prepared, she left it covered and went through with a cup of tea for Harry. He was dozing in an armchair, the newspaper over his face. On the sofa, there was a pile of knitted baby clothes.

'Where did those come from?' she asked.

The newspaper slid off Harry's face and he rubbed his eyes. He took the cup of tea gratefully, taking a gulp of it before he answered. 'Helen Dunn brought them round while you were out shopping. Said she'd been knitting for the baby since Mary told her. Very kind of her, isn't it?'

'They're beautiful. Much better than the hat and socks I've knitted,' Jeannie laughed. 'I don't think I'll ever be good at knitting. I'm better with a needle and thread.'

'Ah well, I'm sure baby Dennis will be delighted with whatever he gets. He's a lucky boy to have such a lovely big sister.'

'Kathy's sure about it, then?'

'It's the only answer, if you think about it,' Harry said kindly. 'This way, Dennis grows up with a mum and dad and three big sisters and two big brothers. The other way, he gets called all sorts of nasty names and plenty of folk won't invite him into their homes. As for Kathy, she'd have a miserable life too and no chance at marriage and a home of her own.'

'I want to kill that Gavin.'

'You're not the only one.' Harry looked suddenly fierce. 'I went looking for him but he'd gone. The coward. Only a cad does that to a girl. And him married, to boot.'

'Harry, you really are taking us on as family,' Jeannie marvelled.

He looked sheepish. 'I hope you don't mind. I love your mother and I love you all too because you're hers. I'm not trying to be your dad. I can never be that. But I'll always be here for your mother and for you, if you need me.'

Impulsively, she hugged him. He looked pleased but pretended to push her away. 'Off with you and bring me another cuppa, will you? Then it'll be time to go and fetch your mother and new brother from the train station.'

The station was noisy with the sound of steam engines and the hubbub of hundreds of voices as crowds moved around the concourse. The air was thick with the smells of coal smoke, cigarettes and perfume. Most of the young men and women were in uniform, moving to and from the train platforms. An older woman, dressed in furs with a tall feathered hat stalked across in front of them, dragging a small dog on a lead. Harry winked at Jeannie and she grinned back. It was mayhem.

'Which platform does the Perth train get in at?' She raised her voice to be heard.

'I'll ask one of the guards.' Harry strode off and she watched him stop a man in railway uniform.

He beckoned her over and she ran to catch him up, apologising as she bumped into people. A soldier's duffel bag hit her head and she rubbed it ruefully. She caught up with Harry just as the next train arrived at the platform in a great hiss of steam and puffs of grey-blue smoke. A stream of people alighted and she bobbed up and down eagerly, looking for Mammy. And there she was, coming from almost the last carriage. Someone was helping her down with a pram and her suitcase.

Harry surged on to help while Jeannie followed against the flow of movement.

'Sorry, sorry,' she called to the people going past, her gaze fixed on her mother.

Harry had his arm around Mary as she reached them. Jeannie hugged her too and then peered into the pram. She gently pulled the blanket down from the baby's chin to admire him.

'Oh, he's lovely, so he is,' she breathed. 'Hello, my wee man. I'm your auntie. Oops… your big sister, at any rate.'

'Shhh,' Mary said. 'Be careful. We've got to keep to our story, all of us. Forever.'

'Aren't we going to tell Dennis later when he's grown a bit?' Jeannie asked. 'He's got a right to know.'

'That's for Kathy to decide,' Mary said. 'Let's go home, my feet are killing me. Here, Jeannie, you take your wee brother for a bit.'

Jeannie was so wrapped up in pushing Dennis in his pram that she ran over someone's toe. The man yelped and jumped aside.

'I'm so sorry,' Jeannie said, appalled. 'I didn't see you there.'

'Jeannie? Is that you?'

She looked up to see Bill's astonished face. He glanced from her to the baby and his jaw dropped.

'Oh no, he's not…' she stuttered.

Mary gently took the pram and wheeled it expertly out of the way of Bill's feet. 'Harry and I are taking Dennis home. Why don't you stay and chat to Bill? How are you, Bill? You won't mind if I get my wee son home where it's warm, will you?'

Mary didn't wait for an answer. Jeannie stared at Mammy's and Harry's receding backs as they vanished into the throng. She noticed Mammy didn't mind using Dennis's pram as a kind of battering ram to make a way to the station exit.

'Jeannie, will you come to a café with me so we can talk?' Bill asked.

Chapter Twenty-One

'So, you've got a new little brother?'

Bill's lovely, familiar yet exotic accent flowed over her and it was a moment before Jeannie could answer.

They had ended up in a small café a street away from the busy station. The waitress had brought them a pot of coffee, two cups and a small plate of grey-looking scones with a scrape of margarine in them.

'Yes. Mammy got re-married to Harry.' Let him figure out the dates, she thought.

'Congratulations to them.' His gaze flicked to her bare finger. 'Your mother seemed keen for us to chat.'

'You mean, she's changed her tune since she practically threw you out of the house?'

Bill laughed easily. She liked that about him. His laugh was rich and infectious and made her smile. She liked his brown hair too and his warm, hazel eyes that crinkled up when he was happy.

'You're not wearing your engagement ring. Does that mean something?' he said.

'I'm not engaged to Arthur any more.'

'I'm sorry to hear that. Can I ask why?' He broke a scone in two but didn't eat it.

'We had a... disagreement and couldn't find a way forward.' Jeannie paused. 'Actually, Bill, there's something I have to tell you. And if you don't want to be near me after that, I will quite understand. You see, Dennis isn't my wee brother…'

The whole sorry story came tumbling out. Jeannie was determined to tell Bill everything so that she knew exactly where she stood with him. If he, like Arthur, wanted to take a swipe at her, then so be it. She wasn't embarrassed any more. She loved Dennis and she'd defend Kathy with all her breath.

'So, you see, it's been difficult for all of us,' she finished, and waited for his reaction.

Bill nodded. He took his time, eating half a scone and following it down with a gulp of coffee before he spoke.

'Poor Kathy,' he said.

'That's it? Poor Kathy? You don't think she deserved everything she got? You don't think she's awful and that you'll be infected with the shame of it if you sit here with me? You don't think Dennis is a—' She couldn't bring herself to use the horrid word.

'Jeannie…' Bill laid his big, strong hand over hers. 'The same thing happened to my cousin and our family – my aunt and uncle – came up with the same solution. Her little girl is happy and stable. I'm sure Dennis will thrive too.'

All the tension left her and Jeannie felt as if her body was boneless.

'Here, eat a scone,' Bill suggested with a grin. 'You look like you need one. They don't taste of much but hey, there's some flour in there, I think. I'll fill up your coffee too. It's chicory coffee so doesn't taste of coffee, just like the scones don't taste of scone. Worst thing about the war.'

He's chatting to give me time to sort myself, she thought gratefully. I love him for that. Well, actually, I just love him. I'm in love with him. But how does he feel about me when I've given him the brush-off so many times?

'If I asked you to the cinema, would you come this time?' Bill said.

'Why do you want me to?' She had to know what he felt.

'You know why, Jeannie Dougal. You know I love you and that I've loved you since I first set eyes on you.'

'You don't think I'm sweet and shy?' Jeannie asked. Arthur's words still rankled.

'You're certainly sweet and you're loyal and kind but you get kinda angry if you think someone's taking advantage.'

'Angry? I'm not angry,' she protested.

'Hey, you're forgetting the night we met. You were annoyed with me right from the get-go even though I don't know why. And when you thought I'd followed you home, you were practically spitting nails,' he grinned.

'I thought you got landed with me because your friend Jonny liked Eileen. I didn't want you to feel you had to stay and buy me a drink or dance with me.'

'You didn't think to ask if I wanted to stay. When I'd just met the loveliest girl with dark hair and sea-grey eyes and a strawberry kiss on her cheek.'

Jeannie blushed.

Bill took both her hands. 'You're missing the main point.'

'I am?'

'I said I loved you. I want to know if you feel the same way.'

'I do love you,' Jeannie said. 'I fell in love with you when you kissed me.'

Bill's eyes crinkled. 'Yeah, that was a smasher of a kiss for me too. I feel I'd like to repeat that experience.'

'Not here,' she murmured, her heart beat quickening.

'I hear the back seats of the cinema are great for kissing. But first, I want to take you back to Kiltie Street and tell them the good news.'

'The good news?' Jeannie wasn't concentrating properly on his words, distracted as she was by the movement of his mobile mouth and the thought of promised kisses.

'Will you marry me, Jeannie?'

'Oh, yes, I will.'

'And now, perhaps that kiss is appropriate.' He leaned over and kissed her full on the lips.

There was a slight stir in the small café as several older women whispered in outrage and a small boy giggled.

Bill smiled and looked at them all. 'She's just agreed to marry me, folks. Isn't that wonderful?'

–

Eileen woke with a smile on her face and a lingering sense that Jimmy was with her. In her dream, they were walking together, swinging their arms and discussing their wedding. They had agreed on the guest list and the dishes to be served and the kind of music to be played for the dancing afterwards. The dream had moved on quickly to the wedding itself in a private function room of a posh hotel in the city centre. She and Jimmy were dancing. She kept glancing at the simple gold ring on her fourth finger as her hand rested on his arm. He leaned in to kiss her and the sunshine on her eyelids wakened her gently.

She opened the window onto a sunny June day and breathed in deeply. It was Saturday which meant a day off work. She was due at Jeannie's that afternoon to help with her wedding plans. She splayed her bare fingers in front of her. The light streamed between them. She had no engagement ring and no wedding ring. Her dream had been so vivid. But Jimmy hadn't returned to Glasgow since he'd asked her to marry him by letter. His latest letters described the searing heat and the ever-present black flies that swarmed around them. She guessed he was in North Africa even if he couldn't say for fear of the censor blacking it out. She'd hoped for a summer wedding but it wasn't to be.

'Stop being so bloody selfish, Eileen Boyle!' she said to her reflection. 'It's Jeannie and Bill's big day next week so concentrate on your best friend and forget your troubles.'

Besides, the only thing that mattered was that Jimmy was still alive. After the awful gap when she didn't receive any letters for months, they were coming regular as clock-work. No doubt they'd stutter and stop soon but Eileen was now convinced that Jimmy would make it home.

'Maybe not for a while, a long while, but eventually he'll be here,' she told herself while she washed from the jug in her bedroom and dressed in a pretty, white summer dress. 'And I'll be waiting.'

She was late arriving in Kiltie Street because her mother needed shopping done. She'd queued for a good half hour to get some fish which smelt as if it was going off. Agnes kissed her.

'You're a good girl. I'll bread these and fry them up and your father won't notice if they taste a bit odd. Look, I've picked some of my sweet peas, so give this bunch to Jeannie and this one to Mary, will you?'

'Thanks, Mum, they're lovely. They smell much nicer than the fish. Jeannie and her mum will love them. That's very thoughtful.'

Agnes flushed and fussed with putting the fish into the small pantry on the cold slab.

'Tell Jeannie that Mr Boyle and myself are looking forward to the wedding,' she called over her shoulder.

Eileen smiled. Her mum was a changed person but still found it difficult to talk openly about emotions. She didn't care though, as home was a much happier place where she'd get a hug and a kiss from her mum and asked how her day had been. Her father seemed more relaxed too, now that Ronnie's picture had been framed and set in centre place on the mantelpiece above the living room fireplace.

They didn't talk about him yet but Eileen promised herself that one day soon, they'd have that conversation. She wanted to know more about her brother. Life would've been so very different if he hadn't died.

Kathy answered the door at Eileen's first knock. She was carrying her little brother on her hip.

'You're late,' she said with a roll of her eyes. 'Jeannie's going crazy back there asking for you.'

'Oh dear, I'd better get through there fast. But first, how's this wee boy doing? He's gorgeous. His hair's the same colour as yours.'

A fleeting frown knitted Kathy's eyebrows but then she brightened with a smile.

'Mammy's brother had red hair so I guess Dennis gets it from him. You'd better go help the bride before she loses it altogether.'

She jiggled the baby on her hip until he gurgled with laughter. 'Come on, wee man, let's see what your mammy has for you to eat.'

'Give these to your mum, will you please?' Eileen handed over the sweet-scented posies.

She went into the parlour. There were clothes and materials all over the furniture. Jeannie stood in the centre of the small room, dressed in a beautiful white silk wedding dress while Miss McGrory knelt in front of her with a mouthful of pins.

'Hello Jeannie, hello Miss... Hannah.' Eileen couldn't get used to calling Miss McGrory by her Christian name even though she had asked them to do so outside of factory hours. It turned out that Hannah McGrory was an excellent seamstress. When she overheard Jeannie telling Eileen and Annie that she wanted a proper wedding dress but had no money for one and not enough coupons, she had sat in the canteen and offered a solution.

Hannah's sister had a friend who sold clothes at a street market in the city. She often got good quality clothes and materials including recently a nearly new wedding dress. It was too large for Jeannie but if she didn't mind second-hand, then Hannah would alter it for her.

'Oh, there you are,' Jeannie cried. 'I thought you'd forgotten. Did you bring your dress so I can see it?'

Eileen waved her bag at her. 'Yes, I've brought it. It's not new but it's in good condition so I hope I'll make the grade as your bridesmaid.'

'I'm a bridesmaid too,' Annie said, coming in the door with a tray of teacups.

'Of course you are,' Eileen grinned. 'It wouldn't be the same without you.'

Annie was still prickly at times, although Eileen thought she'd improved greatly since she'd shared her secret with them. The burden of keeping it all to herself had made her into a sour sort of girl but it was understandable.

'Always the bridesmaid and never the bride,' Annie sighed.

'What's that all about?' Eileen teased her gently. 'Have you been a bridesmaid before?'

'Once, when my cousin got married.' Annie poured the tea and handed Eileen a cup.

Jeannie waved the cups away with a muted scream. One drop of tea would stain her gown. Hannah's mouth was free of pins now and she was instructing Jeannie to turn around and put her arms up, as she continued to alter the dress to Jeannie's slim shape.

They weren't listening to Eileen and Annie's conversation, immersed as they were in the dress.

'I want to get married but Paul hasn't asked me,' Annie said, chewing on her lip.

'You haven't been together very long,' Eileen said.

'Longer than you and Jimmy when he asked you. And look at Jeannie! She's had two engagements.'

'It's not a competition, Annie. Paul will ask you when he's ready.'

'I don't think he'll ever be ready. He's already said he's not the marrying kind.'

There wasn't much Eileen could say to that. She hoped Annie wouldn't get hurt by Paul. Being so happy herself, she wanted her friends to be equally happy in their love lives.

'Come on, let's get changed and show Jeannie what we're going to wear,' she said, hooking her arm into Annie's and pulling her towards Jeannie's bedroom.

–

Jeannie and Bill got married the following week on a gloriously sunny Saturday. The bride left from Kiltie Street. There was a short delay when Harry's chickens escaped their coop and ran out onto the street. He had recently bought five hens and made them a run in the back yard. He was also threatening to buy another pig and re-form the Kiltie Street Pig Club. When the chickens were caught and safely back in their run, it was time to walk up the road to the church.

Jeannie felt the delicious, cool caress of her long silk dress on her legs as she walked up the road, surrounded by family and friends. She wasn't nervous. Instead, she felt a rush of excitement and anticipation. Bill would be in the church already, waiting for her. She was eager to get to him and eager to start their married life together.

'I'm so glad you're getting married, because it means Franny gave me the whole day off,' Kathy said, walking beside her, looking pretty in her green dress, her hair glossy from brushing. 'And me and Judith are going to see Dorothy Lamour in *Moon over Burma* this evening at the Crystal Palace after you leave on your honeymoon. Mammy says I can.'

'That sounds fun,' Jeannie said sarcastically. 'I'll be sure to get married again so you can have another holiday at some point.'

'Och, don't be like that,' her sister said, nudging her. 'I know it's your big day and you know how much I like Bill. But it can't hurt if I get a day's holiday, can it?'

Jeannie bit her lip on a reply. She and Kathy were back to arguing and telling each other what to do just as they always had. In a funny way, Jeannie was glad of it. It meant things hadn't changed as much as she'd feared they would once Dennis was born. Kathy seemed content to be his big sister and let Mammy be his mother.

She glanced back to where Harry was pushing the pram, while Mary walked with him looking proud and happy as mother of the bride. She had a new hat with summer flowers in the headband and Jeannie thought her mother had never looked so fine. There was a healthy flush to her cheeks and when she saw Jeannie gazing, her smile was warm and loving. Her gaze said more than words could convey about what the day meant to them all.

Kathy ran on ahead and Jeannie saw that Miss Main and Helen Dunn were waiting at the churchyard gate. Helen had kindly offered Miss Main a bed at her home so that the older woman could attend the wedding. Kathy flung her arms around Miss Main who looked momentarily surprised but returned the hug with equal fervour.

They all went into the cool interior of the church. Jeannie looked up to see Bill, looking handsome in his army uniform at the altar waiting for her. His face lit up at the sight of her. His friend, Jonny, was best man. He shuffled awkwardly when Eileen and Annie followed Jeannie. Jeannie noticed Eileen was calm, as if she'd never met him. She offered a cool nod and that was that. He wasn't important.

Bill took her hand in his and she felt a tingling shoot up her arm. She heard the guests taking their places in the pews behind them and the muted murmuring as they greeted each other and made whispered conversation. There were no guests on the groom's side but Jeannie's family and friends spread out on both sides of the aisle to make up for that.

After the war, we'll go to Canada and make our home there, she thought, planning ahead. I'll meet Bill's parents and we'll start our own family.

The special ceremony began and her thoughts focussed in to the man standing beside her holding her hand so lovingly. The war wasn't over but she had everything she wanted right here and she knew they'd make it through together.

A letter from Carol

Dear Reader

I hope you are well. Thank you so much for taking the time to read my novel. This is my debut novel with Hera Books and the first full-length novel I've ever written so it's been an exciting and special journey for me. I'm very grateful that you have chosen to read it and I hope very much that you have enjoyed it.

If you enjoyed *Jeannie's War*, I would be incredibly grateful to hear your thoughts via a review, which I hope will then encourage other readers to read it. Reader reviews are very rewarding and very much appreciated and give me the spur to keep on writing in the hope of producing more books to bring pleasure to my readers.

I started to write this book in 2020 during lockdown when I was recovering from an operation and couldn't walk very far and, because of Covid, couldn't go very far anyway! I was feeling a bit sorry for myself and then began to think of other people in far worse situations and how they drew on their inner reserves of toughness and resolve to get them through.

That took me on to thinking about how people managed during the Second World War and I decided to write about an ordinary family and their experiences, starting from the very moment that war was declared.

I set my story in Glasgow because it's my home city, very familiar, and a place that I love. I also wanted to find out about the history of Glasgow during the war because I knew only bits and pieces such as having seen gaps in the tenements where buildings were destroyed by bombs, and the plaque commemorating the Barracks where so many soldiers were stationed (now a housing estate next to a Tesco Extra!).

I find the lingering traces of history in a place fascinating and it makes me wonder about the men and women and everyday families who had to struggle daily and keep cheerful and carry on either in the forces or especially on the home front – finding food, looking after children, worrying about their kids being evacuated and being ever so exhausted from the war work. I can't even begin to imagine how painful it was to let your children go to strangers for perhaps four or five years. And I wonder if I'd have had the strength and energy to do long shifts in a munitions factory followed by queuing for tiny amounts of rationed food and then keeping the house clean and making sure my loved ones were happy.

All this I've tried to convey through Jeannie and her loving family and friends via their different characters and personalities and the life events they experience. It's a hard road for all of them but deepening friendships and love get them through although there are, of course, many obstacles to be overcome along the way.

I've told the story using different viewpoints to really get under the skin of the characters so that you as a reader feel what they are going through and laugh and cry along with them. I hope that this makes the book more engaging for you. I certainly found it a satisfying way to write it.

Thank you for your support for my book and I hope very much that you will continue to follow me as I continue to work on my novels – my second book with Hera will be a sequel to *Jeannie's War* (due out in 2023).

You can get in touch on my social media pages on Twitter and Facebook.

Best wishes and happy reading,

Carol x

Facebook link www.facebook.com/carolcmaclean
Twitter link www.twitter.com/carolcmaclean

Acknowledgments

Thank you to my wonderful editor Keshini Naidoo, whose suggestions have helped to make this a much better book and to the rest of the Hera team. I'm grateful to Maggie Swinburne for her encouragement over the years and for accepting my first pocket novel and then many subsequent stories. Special thanks to Gwen Kirkwood for her invaluable information on rearing pigs (any mistakes are my own of course). Thank you also to the fabulous Romantic Novelists' Association for its wealth of information, support and friendships. Finally, thanks to my lovely family for encouraging me and telling me never to give up.